ASIN: B09W22J622 (eBook Edition)

ISBN: 9798843059040 (Paperback)

Characters and events in this book are fictitious. Any similarity to real persons, living or dead, is coincidental and not intended by author.

Printed and bound in the United States of America

First printing September 2022

Published by Alienhead Press

Miami, Florida, U.S.A.

Literally Dead: Tales of Halloween Hauntings

MAUREEN MANCINI AMATURO   CATHERINE CAVENDISH

SCOTT COLE   DENNIS K. CROSBY   DANA HAMMER

HENRY HERZ   GWENDOLYN KISTE   ALETHEA KONTIS

JONATHAN MABERRY   CATHERINE MCCARTHY

JEREMY MEGARGEE   LISA MORTON   LEE MURRAY

EVA ROSLIN   JEFF STRAND   DAVID SURFACE

SARA TANTLINGER   STEVE RASNIC TEM

TIM WAGGONER

EDITED BY

GABY TRIANA

WITH

JOHN PALISANO

ALIENHEAD
PRESS

Literally Dead: Tales of Halloween Hauntings

For those who enjoy ghost stories—
we are "horror enough"

"We need ghost stories, because we are, in fact, the ghosts."

- Stephen King, DANSE MACABRE

Table of Contents

Introduction

At my house, every day is Halloween. As a horror artist who specializes in book covers, I wake up each morning only to discover that yes, this is real. I get a whole new day to read amazing stories and then create creepy art to help the right readers find the fantastic books I fall in love with. I couldn't imagine a better job in the world.

The art for the cover of *Literally Dead: Tales of Halloween Hauntings* started out its life as a special project for a Halloween event. I had been invited by the West Virginia chapter of the Horror Writers Association to be a guest at their group signing at the Haunted Majestic, a World War II hospital ship turned floating haunted house.

Each weekend the Haunted Majestic chose a new charity to donate part of their proceeds to, and Halloween weekend was reserved for Little Victories, the only no-kill animal shelter in the tri-state area. I decided to make a special piece of art for the event, and donate all the proceeds from the sales of the print that Saturday to Little Victories. But what to create?

Well, I knew I wanted to include pets in the art. And I knew I wanted to evoke a feeling of nostalgia for Halloween.

But I needed something more. Something clever and memorable.

With every piece of art I create, I always aim for that "lean in" factor, especially when I'm creating a book cover. Potential readers often first discover a book online, when it's a tiny two-inch rectangle. That's their first impression. Very surface-level. When it's that small, readers need to know it's the *kind* of book they enjoy, even before they know they'll like *your* book. But when that reader clicks to learn more and it's a three-inch rectangle, their response can't just be, "Oh, look. Now it's bigger." There needs to be something new to discover, something that piques the reader's curiosity and makes them "lean in" and want to read the book description and fall in love with the book and want to take it home. Even though the art for the Haunted Majestic wasn't initially going to be a book cover, I still wanted to incorporate that "lean in" factor. How could I make this *special*?

Growing up, every year my family vacationed at the Wisconsin Dells, a touristy Midwest mecca of carnival rides, water parks, and world-famous fudge. One of my favorite places to visit was the magic shop. They always had a rack of what they called "invisible dogs." Of course, the only thing you could see was the collar and leash (made of nylon cord braided around a wire frame that let you pose the leash.) I never got to take one home, but I dreamed of walking my invisible dog, because even at the tender age of eight, in my mind, it wasn't an invisible dog. It was a ghost dog.

So I knew that in this piece of art, I could finally have my ghost dog. But who would be taking this little guy for a stroll on Halloween night?

When I turned 13, I realized I had reached my last year of trick-or-treating. The next October I would be a high-schooler and way too grown up to take my plastic pumpkin door to door for candy. I felt I needed to make my last year special.

After we'd poured our candy out on the shag carpet and traded each other for our favorites, my best friend Lisa and I went out into the yard, still dressed in our ghost costumes. In our cozy suburban neighborhood, the porch lights had long been turned out, and the little witches and gremlins had been tucked in bed with tummy aches.

We stood on the corner of my yard beneath a small stand of maple trees. The moonlight teased us with skeletal shadows from the branches above. Once in a while, a car would round the bend, and Lisa and I would flail our sheets and moan in the most ghostly of manners. We'd race out across the yard kicking up dried leaves, determined to make the passersby think they had seen a pair of real ghosts.

So the piece became about a pair of sheet-clad trick-or-treaters with their dogs, one of which was a ghost. And then it came to me. If you owned a ghost dog, weren't you likely to be a ghost yourself?

I remembered seeing a vintage photo of two little trick-or-treaters on a doorstep with only their tennis shoes poking out from beneath their sheets. And I thought it would be great fun to create the same kind of feeling, but when your gaze drifted down, you'd realize that one of the ghost trick-or-treaters didn't have any legs–and had an invisible dog. I had figured out my "lean in" moment!

The night of the Haunted Majestic event, my prints raised over $300 for the Little Victories animal rescue. (You can donate directly to the shelter here: https://bit.ly/DonateToLittleVictories)

One of the wonderful West Virginia horror writers even got to deliver the check to the shelter and he sent me pics of some of the loving dogs and cats that would be helped. It made me so happy!

When Gaby Triana saw the art I had created for the Haunted Majestic and Little Victories, she felt it captured her Halloween sensibilities, too, and decided to curate an anthology around the style and tone of the art. I was honored. To me, there is nothing more magical than to have my art inspire *more* art. I'm so excited for you to read these stories, penned by some of the masters of the horror genre and some of the most phenomenal new voices as well.

When I look at the final art now, it speaks to me in a new way. I still see all the things I intended when I created it, but now I also see something more. It's not just the sum of my inspirations and brush strokes.

Yes, the piece is about nostalgia and my love of that time of year when everyone finds joy and beauty in the darkness. I can smell the hint of full-sized chocolate bars in those orange plastic pumpkins. I can hear the crunch of newly fallen leaves. I can feel the faint chill in the air as winter creeps closer. I am so grateful that I get to visit this world each and every day when I create my art.

But most importantly, what I see now in this piece is friendship, even in the face of the unknown. No matter how hard things are, no matter what distance might separate you, the ones you love will be by your side to see you through the darkness. You only have to reach out and take their hands.

Lynne Hansen
August, 2022

The Curiosity at the Back of the Fridge

CATHERINE CAVENDISH

Welcome. Welcome.

It is indeed most gratifying to see so many of you here today. I am sure you are all eager to hear why I have invited you, aren't you? Well, your waiting is at an end. So, gather round, everyone, because the story I am about to tell you is a strange one indeed.

I was introduced to "it" by an old man who lived on the edge of our village. His name was Robert Clements, but everyone called him Bobby Clem. Of course, most of you are far too young to remember him.

Bobby Clem lived in a tumbledown cottage atop a small hill. If you passed by during the day, you would swear it was derelict and long abandoned, but at night, a candle burned in every window. I never found out why.

What's that, you said? Why didn't I ask? Ah, sometimes it is better not to ask too many questions. You might not like the answers. No, it was simply the way things were. It is a tradition I have chosen to keep alive.

I first met Bobby Clem when I was a small boy. Indeed, I was small in every way. At nine years old, I was shorter than the seven-year-olds—a shy, only, motherless child. She had died when I was a mere baby. Dad and I lived alone together, and my father would work all hours trying to keep food on the table and clothes on my back.

On school holidays and weekends, I was left to my own devices while Dad was at work and I took to wandering off on my own, exploring the many country lanes and shady pine woods.

One day I came across a man with a shock of white hair. He was bending over a trap, releasing a dead rabbit. Job done and prize retrieved, he stood and towered over me, but I was used to craning my neck. The man's unkempt beard covered his face and neck, leaving only piercing blue eyes and a kindly smile. Dirty, old corduroy trousers were tied at his waist with frayed string, while a threadbare overcoat and grimy shirt completed his appearance.

"What's your name, lad?" His voice sounded gruff but not unkind. Despite having been repeatedly instructed never to speak to strangers, maybe it was something about his eyes—an innate benevolence. Suffice it to say, I made an exception in his case.

"Brian," I said.

"Well, Brian. Do you want to come and share some rabbit stew with me?"

I had nothing else to do, and rabbit stew was one of my favorites. Like any boy of my age, anytime was dinner time.

On the short walk to his home, he questioned me about my life. I told him everything, from losing my mother to being bullied at school, taunted because of my height and poverty. All the other kids seemed to have so much more than I did. I told him everything, but all I learned about him was his name. Bobby Clem. And I kind of knew that anyway. He was spoken of in hushed whispers by grown-ups. Robert Clements who used to be a professor at the university. Now reduced to the local down and out. "Stay away from Bobby Clem," we children were told. "Or no good will come to you." But I didn't have any friends. No one wanted to play with me. Bobby Clem was the first person who had taken an interest in me, and I so wanted a friend of my own.

I had passed his cottage many times but never paid it much heed. Now, Bobby pushed open the door and it groaned, swinging wildly on broken hinges, revealing a sparsely furnished room, its rickety table sporting a leg supported by ancient, moldy books. Galvanized buckets stood like sentries awaiting the next heavy rainfall which otherwise—judging by the gaping holes in the roof of the one-story building—would cascade down, flooding the place.

Bobby Clem led me through the room into the kitchen, such as it was. My new friend slapped the rabbit down on a none-too-clean pine table. From the sink he selected two of the least dirty plates and a vicious looking knife. He then proceeded to skin and butcher the rabbit. I looked around in vain for a cooker, but only a fire burned in a small range. A cooking pot, like a witch's cauldron, hung suspended over it.

I thought there was no electricity, but a sudden, clanking buzzing told me otherwise. In the corner of the room, an ancient, massive fridge stood, plugged into a single socket. Bobby saw me looking.

"Ah, there's a story behind that fridge," he said, as he carried on preparing our meal. "One Halloween, years ago, a man knocked on my door. It was a raw night, a blizzard blew, and this stranger stood on my doorstep, dripping from head to toe and shivering. I brought him in, sat him by the fire, gave him dry clothes, a blanket and something hot to eat and drink. In the morning, the storm had blown over, and the sun was shining. The man was so grateful for my hospitality, he wanted to repay me.

"I refused to take payment, and he made to leave. He called me outside, saying he needed some help with his van. It was a big, old cranky thing, and it wouldn't start. I used to tinker a bit with cars when I was younger, so I checked his engine. Sure enough, there was a loose cable. Once I reconnected it, the engine turned over fine, and the man was away. I went back inside, and there it was." He pointed his bloodied knife at the fridge. "How he got it in here… let's put it down to one of life's mysteries, because it got here somehow, didn't it? I opened it, and it was piled high with everything you could want for a delicious Halloween feast. Turkey, all the trimmings, even pumpkin pie. I'd never eaten that before. Have you eaten that, Brian?"

I shook my head.

He smacked his lips. "Delicious. Hey, it's Halloween in a few days, maybe your father will let you come and eat pumpkin pie with me."

I doubted that, but as Halloween was on Friday, and Dad was working nights all weekend, he wouldn't have to know, would he?

Bobby chopped up the meat, added carrots, potatoes, herbs, and onion and dumped the whole lot into the cooking pot, along with fresh water he drew from a hand pump by the sink. "There, we'll let that stew for an hour or so. Are you hungry, Brian?"

My stomach gave a growl. Bobby laughed, and I liked the sound. It was tinkly and sincere.

"Now, let's have a look in that fridge. Is there anything in there, I wonder?"

He opened the door wide. I stared at the empty shelves. It was certainly the cleanest thing in that house, except… "What *is* that?" I pointed to a large black blob that looked a bit like a jellyfish, stuck to the back wall.

"Oh, that's my friend. The Curiosity, I call him. As it's so close to Halloween, I thought he might come out. But no." He slammed the door shut. "Must leave him to his privacy. He doesn't like to be disturbed."

"But—"

Bobby put a finger to his lips. "No questions, Brian. You'll meet him right enough. At the proper time. But it must be on his terms. Do you understand?"

Of course, I didn't, but I nodded and hoped that would suffice. It seemed to.

Whatever else Bobby Clem was, he cooked a delicious stew, and, a couple of hours later, stuffed to the gills, I made my way home with promises to return on Halloween.

OCTOBER 31ST. It rained. All day, torrents of it poured down. A river ran down the road at the end of our path. Small children cried as their trick-or-treat costumes were ruined or parents decided it was too wet to venture out. I didn't care. They never included me anyway, and for once, unlike them, I had plans I could keep.

I arrived at Bobby Clem's cottage where the aroma of a delicious meal set my taste buds tingling and my mouth watering even before he opened the door.

"Welcome, Brian," he said. "We're all ready for you. Look what a feast we have."

I stared. Bobby had moved the kitchen table into the living room. It was heaving with a roasted turkey—its skin golden brown—little chipolatas wrapped in bacon, dishes of roast potatoes and vegetables. There was gravy and the promised pumpkin pie. I never questioned how he managed to create all that in one cooking pot. No questions, remember? Not ever.

Bobby Clem had cleaned the room so that it shone. Even the floor revealed polished floorboards. The only evidence of the dilapidated state of his cottage was provided by the buckets into which rainwater dripped.

"Some people spring clean. I do mine on Halloween. It's my 'thank you.'"

I pondered that while I took my place at the table. "Oh, you mean a 'thank you' to the man who gave you the fridge?"

"Not entirely."

It was then I noticed a third place setting.

"Is someone joining us?" I was a little disappointed. I suppose I wanted to keep my new friend to myself.

"Our benefactor," Bobby said. "Now you can meet the Curiosity."

I blinked. There was no one there, but a slithering noise came from behind me, moving closer.

"Don't be alarmed by his appearance, young Brian. He can't help that any more than we can help being quite hideous to him."

I swallowed and dared to look down as the Curiosity slipped past me. It moved on pseudopodia—I had recently learned that word at school where we had studied the life cycle of an amoeba. It thrust out its jelly-like protrusions and made its slow way round to its place at the head of the table. A few seconds later, its head—if you could call the blob a head—emerged. Bobby sat down and proceeded to load the Curiosity's plate with pumpkin pie.

"He doesn't like turkey," Bobby said, setting the plate down in front of his friend. "He has other…tastes. But he adores pumpkin pie. Now, Brian, help yourself. Tuck in and eat. The Curiosity has provided all this fine food for us. Don't ask me how. It's enough that he does it. Every year. But only at Halloween. The rest of the year he keeps himself to himself, and I…look after him."

I tried to work it all out in my nine-year-old head. "So, the fridge is his?"

"That's right. The stranger— I never did learn his name— looked after him. For some reason, the Curiosity prefers to live in there. I suppose the temperature suits him, and he is left alone, which is what he likes. He can turn very nasty if you disturb his slumber."

Bobby Clem rubbed his hand, and I noticed a scar where his little finger should have been. Odd that I hadn't noticed it before.

"He sleeps for most of the year. And before you ask, I don't know what type of creature he is, where he came from, how old he is, or any of the usual things. I know that he exists. That he *is*. And that's all you need to know, too, Brian."

From that day on, every year at Halloween, I joined Bobby and the Curiosity for a sumptuous feast. I grew up. Dad died, and I moved into the cottage. Years passed, and the place was falling down piece by piece, so I built us this nice new home with our own generator. We took care of our friend and benefactor together until Bobby Clem passed away.

I see we have another question. You there, the little boy at the back. You remind me of… never mind. You want to know what I've learned about the Curiosity over the years? Well now, that would be telling, wouldn't it? But as you asked so politely, I'll tell you…some of it, at least.

When Bobby Clem lay dying in his bed, he seemed to shrink a little more each day. His skin took on a strange transparency that I'd never seen before. Sometimes it was as if I could see the blood pumping through his veins but becoming thicker and more sluggish with each passing day.

Meanwhile in the old fridge, the Curiosity was positively blooming. He pulsed as if infused with fresh blood. No longer black, he shone with a reddish radiance. It was like he was tapping into Bobby's impending demise, maybe helping him on his way.

Then one day, Bobby slipped into a coma. During our last conversation, he had made me promise not to seek any kind of medical help. "Not under any circumstances," he said, "and when it's your turn, you mustn't either. The Curiosity will take care of everything."

I asked him what he meant by that, and with a great effort, he said, "My time is over, so I see more clearly now. I understand more. The Curiosity is not one being. He is made up of many who have gone before, and on All Hallows' Eve, they provide for the one who is their current guardian. Hence the feast. When I'm gone, you'll see them, but only on the first Halloween after my passing, and the glimpse will be so fleeting, you'll think it was a dream."

Those were his last words, but he was right. That first Halloween, soon after I'd buried Bobby's body out there in the woods, I saw them. So many shadows, ghostly figures busying themselves cooking, baking…and there, among them, was Bobby Clem. He smiled and waved at me, as he put the final touches to the pumpkin pie.

He was right, though. I have never seen them again. As for the Curiosity and I…we carry on as before. The feast appears as if by magic once a year. To this day I don't know if I dreamed that legion of ghostly cooks, but I certainly love their pumpkin pie. As for my mysterious friend, he asks so little in return. Merely that I provide him with food for the rest of the year.

And that, my dear ones, is where you come in.

A Bookstore Made of Skulls—Salem, Mass

MAUREEN MANCINI AMATURO

There is a bookstore made of skulls on the cobblestoned street outside my hotel, and I could only think, *How appropriate. Why haven't others thought of that?* Seemed so fitting. After all, a skull houses the brain, and books house food for the brain. Whoever designed this storefront must have been on the same page. Of course, only in this eerie New England town could this design be so right. Everything in Salem had a witch or skull on it, including the police, fire, and ambulance logos. A witch skirting a moon is part of the official city emblem.

Bookstores are my favorite haunt anyway. I can't resist them, but this one had arms that reached through the storefront, across Hawthorne Boulevard, through the hotel lobby, and straight up the elevator shaft to me. I had been to Salem many Octobers in the past. I had spent many Halloweens on these streets and knew every mystical shop, witchcraft boutique, potion vendor, and tarot card reader in the city. This bookstore was new. Though I knew this particular façade was just another retailer capitalizing on the town's reputation, it worked for me. I couldn't dress fast enough.

I grabbed a quick coffee in the hotel lobby and headed straight for Essex Street. I had plenty of time for a quick look-see before I had to meet Michael at the Bewitched statue. The streets reeked of Mardi Gras that morning, as they did every weekend in October for the past forty years. I could smell the apple-cinnamon donuts from the corner vendor. I could hear the bucket drummers who set up in the middle of Essex Street, their top hats upturned on the sidewalk for tourists to fill with dollars. I could see lines forming at the trolley stop. In the heat of my excitement and because of the hot coffee I was holding, I did not feel the October chill that only a New England sea town could conjure. Squeezing through the costumed, painted, stilted, caped, and shopping-bag-laden, I zoomed through like an offensive lineman. If I ziplined to the skull-dressed bookstore, I would not have gotten there quicker.

I was just as anxious to examine the sculpted façade as I was to enter. I stood eye-to-eye with a skull to the left of the door, entranced by the dimension, the carving, the intricacy. The skull above it wore a different expression, and the one below, too. They all did. *How do you make an expression without muscles, with bones only? Brilliant.* Whoever this sculptor was had quite a skill. My hand rose involuntarily. My fingers slid over the cheekbones, into the eye cavity, across the jaw. I was compelled to touch it without reason. I couldn't help but think it would be such fun to put makeup on each of these sculpted faces. After tossing my empty coffee cup into a nearby trash can, I made my way back to the skeletal store front. The crowds pushed and punched and prodded me as they gushed by. I thought I'd better get inside.

The doorknob, too, was a skull. No surprise. Close up, I could see that what I thought were knots in the wooden door were small, painted skulls. Talk about running with a theme.

The door was heavier than I expected, and I pushed with both hands.

No one else was in the store. That was a surprise. Such quiet. The walls, ceiling, and floor were all made of the same wide-plank, dark wood. The knots in each plank, like eyes, watching me. It was freezing in there, so cold, I could see my breath. There was a scent I couldn't quite identify. Patchouli? Basil? Mildew? Densely packed, built-in bookshelves lined the walls. The wooden floor creaked as I moved from shelf to shelf. Every book had a black binding and red cover. How organized it looked, so neat. Moving around the store, I scanned the bindings. No titles. *Strange.* Maybe this was a set for a photo shoot? For a performance? When I reached the end of one wall, I heard giggling. A quick look over my shoulder, but no one was there. The clock above the entry said six. The minute hand was moving, but apparently not doing its job. When I had grabbed my coffee at the hotel, it was almost ten. That couldn't have been more than fifteen minutes ago. Where was the proprietor? Why was no one else entering the store?

"Hello. Anyone here?"

My reply was the sound of fluttering wings. The flutter sounded so close, so loud that I ducked. There was nothing in the air. Nothing perched on a tabletop or shelf. The sound of those wings suggested something big, like a hawk or an owl. But there was nothing. I stood slowly, leery something would swoop down. All quiet. Until I heard giggling again. I could see out the front window that the moving crowd was still rushing by like white-water rafters.

I felt a shadow, a presence as if someone were right behind me looking over my shoulder. Chills waltzed at the back of my neck. I debated whether to turn or not and decided to stretch my eyes left to see what I could see. Nothing. My overdeveloped imagination at play. A book to my right tilted forward begging me to reach for it. *How gimmicky,* I thought.

In case someone was in hiding, watching me, I said aloud, "So, I'm supposed to open this book and then what? Someone in costume is going to jump out from somewhere?" I reached for it and flipped through the pages. All blank. I opened another book. All blank. And another. The same. Bummer. Not a real bookstore. And no surprise scares. *Is this a spooky funhouse-type room for tourists? Will I be charged $20 when I leave?* I wondered if maybe this was a venue for card readers, speakers, actors, or some other evening event Salem offers during Haunted Happenings throughout October.

I looked around the room, top to bottom, wall to wall. *Wonder what they'll be doing in here tonight. What's this set-up for?* The intricate décor, the webs, carvings, etched glass, even the scent was proof someone went to quite a bit of trouble to create just the right look for this place. *Too bad they can't make use of all this during the day. Seems like a waste.* I heard giggling again. And I smelled a new smell, eggs–very old eggs–and fertilizer. My throat tightened. I gagged. As quickly as this stench materialized, it disappeared. The patchouli scent returned, thank God. I laughed to myself. *Would God even have anything to do with a place like this?*

I walked by every shelf running my finger along the edge. Took time to stare at the Hieronymus Bosch-type paintings on the walls, the wands and animal bones in shadowbox frames. I could taste the dust. In the far back corner, I noticed a wooden bookcase with a window-paned door filled with bottles, urns, and jars. Wow, the colors, the shapes. Had to take a closer look. They were works of art. If this was a store and there was a cash register, I'd buy one. They were that beautiful. Iridescent solids in jewel tones and swirled metallics webbing through deep, saturated, purple, sapphire, emerald. One on the lower shelf caught my eye. *Is that real silver around the rim?* It reminded me of a 1921 perfume bottle I have, green glass with art nouveau silver filigree. Some had lids with figural knobs on top—half-moons, frogs, stars, spiders, pentagrams, and of course, skulls. They were mesmerizing.

I felt something, a tickle, like a feather. I brushed against my ear and swiped at my face. Hoped it wasn't a spider. I hate spiders. I wanted out of there. I glanced at the clock. Two? Strange clock. It had said six just minutes ago. The clock seemed as confused as I was. Since I had left my hotel just before ten, I knew it could be neither six nor two. No way had I been in there more than twenty minutes. I walked back to the front of the store. When I reached for the doorknob, something reached for me. And giggled.

I jerked my leg, but something held on, gripping my ankle. Kicking, I tried to get free. I tried to leave, but whatever it was tugged at my ankle pulling me back in. The giggling became louder. The cold was colder. The red books were shifting on their shelves ever so slightly, but I could hear the scratch of their cloth-covered bindings against the wood. I managed to pull the door open a small inch, but something or someone pushed the front door closed, and I had to pull my hand away to avoid losing a finger. The giggles stopped. I heard a sing-song melody, and it wasn't pretty. I wanted to scream, "Go to hell," but thought whoever it was may already be there. I pulled at the door once more. It opened an inch or two, then slammed closed again.

The singing stopped. The books settled.

One more time, I pulled at the door with both hands. The door wouldn't budge. I dropped my arms to my side and stared at the skull-shaped doorknob. My body felt like it was made of oak. Scared stiff was no longer just a cliché. I wanted to turn, to scan the room for the prankster, to find the hidden camera. I was as angry as I was scared. *Could I trick it?* Whatever it was. Or whoever. I stood cement-like. Don't know how long. No point looking up at the clock. I knew it would lie. I slowly lifted my hand to pull at the door again. It held solid. I heard the giggling. Then the singing again.

A-Tisket, A-Tasket?

London Bridge Is Falling Down?

It had a childlike quality, but I couldn't pinpoint the melody. Then giggling. I spun around. The store was a still life. The books uniformly arranged as when I entered. Specks of dust, like a weightless ballet, moving through the ray of light slicing the storefront window. The sun's glint bouncing off the glass panes in the corner cabinet. I tried the doorknob again. I pulled hard, and the door flew open, crashing against the wall.

I forced my way into the log jam of Essex Street tourists. Rushing through the crowd, I collided with a man eating from a bag of caramelized peanuts. Unavoidable. "So sorry." On the street in the safety of the Indian-summer October sun and hundreds of people wearing coned hats and T-shirts with trite sayings, like "Not Every Witch Lives in Salem," I turned to the bookstore front. I saw a face. *Was that a little girl inside?* I squinted. The longer I stood trying to focus, the more I was run off the cobblestoned road by the families and teens anxious to reach a street performer just starting his act. I stood on my toes, peeked between bodies, stretched around strollers to stare toward the bookstore one more time, eyes fixed on the front window surrounded by skulls, and there she was behind the glass, her round face framed with auburn curls, dark circles beneath her eyes. She smiled at me. She had no teeth. And then I could tell she was laughing. She pointed at me, and I felt a grip on my ankle again. I jerked my leg and nearly kicked a passing beagle. When the toothless child in the store window stopped laughing, she waved to me. First, it was a greeting-type wave, then it was an invitation. She wanted me to come back. I reached for the cross at the end of my neck chain. The little girl's smile shrunk to a vicious, hard line. She shook her head no, then she disappeared.

My cell buzzed. A text. "Where are you? It's ten. At the Bewitched statue." I forgot I had planned to meet Michael. Wait. Ten?

Postcards From Evelyn

SCOTT COLE

Are you coming to my Hallowe'en party?

It was obviously a child's handwriting, which was puzzling enough, since Andy didn't have, or know, any children. But even stranger was the object on which the message was written.

Andy examined the postcard. It was cool to the touch, having just come through the mail slot in his front door. Finally, the weather was catching up to the calendar. It was Fall, after all, but it hadn't felt like it much yet. Summer was trying to hang on as best it could. Time for cooler temperatures, as far as Andrew was concerned.

The card itself was quite old, he could tell. The edges were worn, the frayed fibers of the aging paper soft like velvet. One corner, the sharpest of the four, had a small crease.

The image side featured a painting of a warty witch dancing with a black cat to her right and another more unusual creature—something that seemed to be a cute assemblage of squash and corn, but with bright, wide eyes and a big, gleaming, toothy smile—to her left. Beneath them sat the word "Hallowe'en" in decorative letters, apostrophe and all.

The postcard was embossed. On the reverse, the handwriting wavered over the dips and ridges of the cardstock. The ink looked like it had been black at one point but was faded to chocolate brown now, and the writing seemed to have a crude, but somewhat calligraphic quality, the lines varying in thickness depending on the direction of the stroke.

It was signed:

Your friend, Evelyn.

The most unusual thing about it all, though, was not how long ago the card had been produced, nor the fact that Andy did not recognize the name of the sender, but the postmark that sat above his name and address. If the circular inked stamp was genuine, the card had been mailed over a century earlier, in October of 1910.

Legally, Andy was Andrew Harrison IV. His great-grandfather had been the first in the family line with that name. The house had originally been his, before being passed down through the family for generations, from Andrew to Andrew.

So, maybe that was it. Andy had heard stories about mail getting lost for lengthy periods of time, only to eventually turn up and be delivered years later. Even his mother had once received a lost letter from her high school sweetheart several years into her marriage to Andrew III. Could that be the case here? Was this postcard perhaps meant for his great-grandfather, Andrew Harrison I?

Andy flipped the card back over and smiled at the depiction of the unusual vegetable monster the witch was dancing with. How odd, he thought. Then he took it into the living room and stood it upright on the mantel, over the fireplace, and stepped back to admire the strange artwork for a moment. It was October now, and the card might make for an interesting conversation piece with friends as Halloween approached.

A WEEK LATER, a second postcard arrived through Andy's mail slot. This one looked just as old as the first but was a bit more damaged from its travels, featuring numerous creases and even rounder corners. The image on the front was painted in a similar style to the previous postcard, but this one showed a group of children huddled around a giant pumpkin the size of a small car. They had knives and spoons in their hands, which they were using to carve a large face into the flesh of the oversized squash.

On the other side was the same childlike handwriting, once again addressed to Andrew Harrison. There was a new, longer message:

Dear Andrew,
Why haven't you written me back? I wonder if you'll be attending my Hallowe'en party. It's going to be such fun! Costumes and candy and games and such. Please let me know so we can prepare for the correct number of guests!

Your friend,
Evelyn

How strange, Andy thought. One ancient postcard resurfacing after so long was unusual enough, but two? What were the odds? And it wasn't as if the post office had delivered these cards with any sort of explanatory note. He might have expected a form letter apology, though he wasn't overwhelmingly upset not to receive one. He simply wondered how there could have been two postcards lost in the system for over a hundred years, both to turn up within a week of each other. Maybe some old-timer retired from the post office, and his successor found them stuffed in a messy desk drawer or disorganized filing cabinet. It was the only explanation Andy could come up with.

After sitting with it for a few minutes, he placed the second card beside the first on his mantel and suddenly found himself hoping for a third, if only to expand and round out the new holiday display.

His wish came true a week later.

The third postcard featured another witch—this one much angrier-looking—with a pointed hat, chasing a child through a field of frightened jack-o'-lanterns. And the tone of its handwritten message was much more stern than either of the first two:

I don't understand why you haven't written me back, Andrew. You're just like your father, it seems! And your grandfather, too! They never responded to my invitations and never came to any of my parties, either! Why won't you?

The card wasn't signed, but Andy knew who it was from. The handwriting matched Evelyn's previous messages perfectly, and the month and year of the postmark were the same.

A chill crashed through his body like a wave. What *was* this? Some kind of joke? Had a friend of his decided to play a prank on him using old postcards from an antique shop?

Somehow, he knew that wasn't the case. He could feel that these cards were genuine and that they were intended for him. He wondered who this Evelyn was.

His parents might have known something about her, but they had both died last year. More likely, his grandparents might have had some idea about the mysterious sender, but they were long gone. There were no family members left for him to ask, and he had no connections to any of his forbears' friends, if any of them were even still around.

Andy dropped the third postcard flat on the mantel, in front of the other two, no longer concerned about how the display looked, and went about his evening. He was unnerved, but his thoughts of Evelyn eventually dissipated as his mind wandered to other, work-related matters, such as the big meeting taking place at the office the following morning, for which he was completely unprepared. He'd better review the materials he'd brought home, he realized.

A few days later, after the frustrating and chaotic work week had ended, it dawned on Andy that his father had left a few things behind in the attic—a handful of keepsakes, as well as several boxes of paperwork he'd held onto over the years. Perhaps they contained scraps of family history, Andy thought. It was probably a long shot, but maybe there was something in those boxes that could answer the lingering question of who this Evelyn girl was.

He poured himself a Friday-night, possibly-too-tall glass of bourbon and went up the attic steps to investigate. He brought the bottle along, too, anticipating a refill.

He spent most of the night going through his family's papers. Mostly it was old insurance paperwork, the deed for the house, old bank statements, and a variety of other legal forms. He also found a number of old photos, including a few he had never seen before, such as one from his parents' wedding and another from his own first birthday. He even found a couple of himself as a child, all dressed up for Halloween. In one, he was a vampire, his face made pale with powder, his hair slicked back, with plastic fangs over his own teeth and a black cape draped over his shoulders. In another, he was a devil, his face painted red except for a black triangle on his chin to indicate a pointed beard. A pair of soft foam horns adorned his head. In one hand, he held a small plastic pitchfork.

Andy sipped bourbon all through the discovery process, and before long, the photos and text were getting blurry, causing him to slow his motions a bit, whether he realized it or not.

Finally, at the very bottom of one box, just as he was about to give up for the night, he found an old, tattered newspaper clipping, stained yellow with age. It was a brief report about a small group of children—among them a girl named Evelyn—who had been poisoned and killed at a party held on Halloween. One of the child attendees had been suspected and was being held in custody while the matter was being investigated, but as of the writing of the article, nothing had been resolved. In the corner of the cutout, "OCT 1910" was written in pencil in an unfamiliar hand.

Andy shuddered at seeing the name Evelyn in print, as an icy sting pierced through the warmth the evening's whiskey had provided. Clearly someone in his family knew about this young girl. Otherwise, why would they have saved the clipping? Given the timeframe, he guessed she must have been a school friend of his great-grandfather's.

The thought didn't linger, however, quickly turning to mist in his mind before Andy decided he ought to go to bed. He abandoned the boxes and his now-empty glass in the attic, and stumbled down the steps, sliding along the slats of the unfinished wall to his right for balance. Five minutes later, he was passed out and snoring in a heap on his still-made bed.

When he awoke the next morning, he was confused and much groggier than he could remember being in a long time. It was extremely rare for him to drink to excess at all, and when he did, it was never alone at home. What had he gotten up to last night anyway? He remembered pouring whiskey and heading into the attic for something, but the rest was a blur.

At least it was Saturday, though, and he had nowhere to be.

Until he remembered it was Halloween. Where had the month gone? He would have to run out after all, to buy candy for trick-or-treaters. He silently cursed himself for not planning ahead. But he had been distracted by problems at work these last few weeks, not to mention the mysterious mail he had been receiving.

His head throbbed. Some toast and coffee helped a little. A hot shower and a few ibuprofen helped a little more. He got dressed in jeans and a T-shirt with a flannel on top, then grabbed his keys and headed to the store.

That afternoon, shortly after returning home with several bags of sugary treats, he heard the flap of the mail slot squeak open and then slam closed with a clink. He felt a chill and wondered if it was just the cool Fall air blowing through the gap in the door, or if there was another reason.

The image of the newspaper clipping from the night before suddenly appeared in his mind. And along with it came the image of his great-grandfather as a boy, who he'd only ever seen in photographs, smiling deviously. On the heels of that, Andy flashed to a childhood memory of his grandmother and mother talking, speaking in hushed tones about someone who had been "sent away" many years before. Andy felt like the pieces of a puzzle were coming together and wished he had someone he could talk to about the murkier corners of his family's history.

When he went to collect the mail, he found only one piece waiting for him. A postcard.

This one, the fourth, was decorated with the image of a translucent white ghost, floating well above the ground, with a large, bulbous pumpkin head seated atop its billowing form. It was both comical and creepy. He was almost afraid to turn the card over.

The postmark on the back was just like the others, and the message, of course, was from Evelyn.

Fine, Andrew. If you won't respond about coming to my party, I know just what I'll do: I'll bring the party to you! All my friends will be along with me! We're going to have such fun! More fun, I suspect, than we ever had with your father, or your grandfather, or that monstrous boy you know as your great-grandfather. So, do get ready! We can hardly wait to get dressed up and play games and drink punch!

See you on Hallowe'en night!

The card slipped from Andy's fingers and dropped to the floor. Then he looked at the clock and realized how little time he had left to prepare. Other than the postcards, he hadn't put any decorations up around the house. He'd have to put together a costume for himself, too. Anything to keep his impending visitors at bay. To keep them distracted and happy. What kinds of games, he wondered, did little ghost children like to play, anyway?

The Crawlers in the Corn

DAVID SURFACE

It was half-past five when Danny got on his bike and started the long ride toward Carl's house. The sky behind the trees was a bright red glow darkening around the edges like someone slowly turning down the flame of a lamp. Dry leaves crackled and whispered under his tires as he rode through them, making them scatter and swirl.

All around, the ghosts were coming out, little gangs of them hurrying along like packs of dogs, low to the ground. He could hear their high-pitched, excited voices pierce the darkness as he pedaled past them. The first grinning jack-o'-lantern he saw flickering on someone's doorstep made him feel a rush of the old mystery and excitement, then another pack of children running through the leaves in their costumes and masks sent a small stabbing pain through his chest. Last year, that had been him. And all the years before that.

We're too old for that shit now. That was what Carl had said last year when they'd gone trick-or-treating. Carl had made it plain that this would be the last time. Thirteen was pushing it, he'd said. Fourteen was out of the fucking question.

The red glow was almost gone from the sky when Danny

turned onto Carl's street. On his right was a row of new houses with their lights just coming on. Across the street on his left was nothing but farmland, stretching for miles and miles. On the horizon, a single red light at the small airport far away slowly blinked on and off. In between was the cornfield. It had always been there, as long as Danny could remember. Probably longer than Carl's house, longer than any of the houses on this street. They'd never played in that cornfield or explored it. There was something about it that kept them on their side of the fence, something that was more of a feeling than anything they could put a name to. Until they did.

It was Danny who'd thought of it. *The crawlers in the corn.* As soon as he said the name in his mind, it was like he could see them. Dry, stick-like things moving through the stalks like long-legged insects. Taller than a man but low to the ground, keeping hidden. Coming close to the fence but not crossing over. Peering through the stalks with their hollow eyes like dark shadows between dry ragged husks.

When they were little, Danny would dare Carl to stand close to the fence. They took turns daring each other, pressing their backs against the fence until they could almost imagine the crawlers reaching through to touch them, then they'd run away screaming and laughing. Later, they made up stories. Danny said the crawlers were the spirits of a Native tribe who'd been slaughtered by settlers and were coming back to wreak vengeance on their murderers' descendants. Another time, he'd said they were the ghosts of murdered children who'd been buried in the corn by a serial killer. When there was a rash of killings in town by a local organized crime mob, Carl had said it was the victims whose bodies had been dumped there, coming back to take their revenge. And though the stories kept changing, one thing that didn't change for Danny was the *idea* of what lurked on the other side of that fence, the feeling that he got whenever he looked at those endless rows of dry stalks, especially at sunset. He could still feel a trace of that feeling, even now.

Danny rang the doorbell and waited. A minute later, he heard Carl unlock the door from the inside. Danny knew Carl's parents were out of town for the night—that's why Carl had asked him to come over. But the locked door was a surprise. Why would Carl lock the door this early, at sunset?

The door swung open, and Danny had to laugh. There was Carl, wearing his jeans, no shirt, and a fancy-looking silk bathrobe covered with red flowers that looked like it might have belonged to his mother.

"Holy shit," Danny laughed. "I thought we weren't doing trick-or-treat."

"Come in, Mister Bond, come in," Carl said in his best British accent, waving Danny in with one hand.

Danny stepped into the brightly lit foyer with its black-and-white checkerboard floor and chandelier gleaming high above and followed Carl back to the kitchen. He'd been coming to this house since he was six years old and knew every room, every twist and turn, from the basement all the way up to the attic where he and Carl had played imaginary games when they were smaller. Carl had no more patience with imaginary games; these days he was more interested in other things.

"Look what we got," Carl said, opening the refrigerator. Danny saw a six-pack of Budweiser, the white and red cans illuminated by the lightbulb inside.

"Seriously?" Danny asked. "Aren't those your dad's?"

"Who cares?" Carl said. "He won't miss 'em."

"I don't know, Carl..."

"What... you gonna chicken out again?"

Danny felt a surge of anger rise in his throat, but he choked it back. He'd tasted beer before, last summer when Carl had stolen a can from his big brother's supply. They'd brought it out to the backyard after dark and took turns passing it back and forth, taking nervous, eager sips. The sour, bitter taste had shocked Danny, and he'd almost spit it out. Carl had called him a wimp. *I didn't go to the trouble of getting this, all so you could act like a fucking wimp.*

Both of them stood there in the refrigerator glow, staring at the gleaming white and red cans. "We'll save 'em for later," Carl decided, shutting the refrigerator door.

Carl grabbed a box of Pizza Spins and brought them into the living room where he and Danny sat on the long white sofa, eating the Pizza Spins and trying not to get the red powder on the cushions so Carl's mom wouldn't kill them. After a couple of minutes, Carl got up and put a record on the turntable. The sound of a lone trumpet playing over a wash of violins filled the room. It was one of those soft jazz albums Carl liked to play these days, and Danny didn't like. He figured it was Carl's way of feeling grown-up and sophisticated.

So, Danny thought, *this is what Halloween is going to be like from now on—soft jazz and Pizza Spins.* Danny would have laughed if it hadn't felt so goddamn sad.

"It's kind of weird, isn't it?" Danny said.

"What."

"I don't know. This. Not being…out there. Tonight. You know."

Carl sniffed derisively. "What's weird about it? Why should it be weird? Tonight's just the same as any other night. Why should it be any different?"

Danny looked out the window in silence. He could see that small red light blinking far away across the cornfield, the way it had been doing for years. *But it* is *different,* he thought. *It's not the same as any other night. Or why would Carl be working so hard to prove that it's not?*

When Carl went to the kitchen, Danny got up and walked over to the turntable and turned down the soft, jazzy noise oozing from the speakers. The quiet that rose up around him to take its place was a relief.

The red light blinking outside caught his eye again. He looked through the window at the cornfield across the street. He thought again of all the stories he and Carl used to make up about the crawlers in the corn. It was a childhood game, and that was all it would have been, if Danny hadn't seen what he saw one night.

He'd been about eight or nine years old when it happened. It was Halloween, and he was spending the night at Carl's house. They'd been trick-or-treating since sundown, running from house to house under the full autumn moon. Carl was ready to call it quits and go in, but Danny didn't want to stop. It wasn't really the candy that he wanted. He never ate more than half of what he brought home anyway. What he wanted was more of this night, more running through the dark with the full moon seeming to race over their heads, the feeling in his veins that he could fly if he wanted to. He didn't want it to stop. Carl went inside, but Danny stood alone in the front yard, just breathing in the cool October air, watching low flying clouds passing over the face of the moon above, imagining he was one of them.

A cool wind rose from the far side of the field and passed over the corn, setting it into motion. A loud rustling and rattling washed over Danny like the rush of waves in the ocean. Stalks and tassels waved and nodded like rows of people bowing down and waving their hands. All except one. One dark shape stood tall and still among all the others. A cloud passed over the moon, throwing the cornfield into darkness. Danny strained his eyes to see the dark thing that was standing there, not moving. A feeling came over him that he didn't like, a feeling that the thing was watching him. Then he saw it take a step forward.

The rest of that night was a blur to him now. He remembered trying to explain to Carl what he'd seen, and then to Carl's parents. Their impatient, uncomprehending faces. He remembered waking up screaming in the middle of the night, the feeling of shame and the long drive home in the dark when his dad had to come to take him away.

Crybaby. Chicken. Had Carl really called him those things? Or had he just imagined it, like other people told him he'd imagined the whole thing?

In the years that followed, Danny tried to understand what he'd seen that night. Was it a person, someone standing out there in the corn, playing a trick on him? A Halloween joke? He might have believed that if he hadn't seen the way the thing moved—the awful, spindly motion, the impossible stick-thin legs reaching and feeling their way across the ground like a spider's.

Of course, Danny knew he couldn't have seen that. It was impossible. But the picture of it was planted deep in his brain, as real as anything ever was.

The sharp *crack* of Carl setting something down on the glass coffee table in front of him brought Danny back to the present. He looked down at the white and red Budweiser can and felt a quick rush of fear and excitement. He remembered the last time they'd done this, how he'd held his breath and choked down one swallow. Then the tingling sensation inside of him and how the world started to go loose and warm. He remembered lying on his back in the summer grass, laughing uncontrollably and shouting things at the stars.

"Well?" Carl said, raising the can he'd brought for himself from the kitchen. "Let's make a toast."

Danny picked up the can Carl had brought him. It was cold and sweaty and felt slippery in his hand. "To Halloween," Danny said, raising his can toward Carl who scowled.

"Fuck that," Carl said, then raised his can even higher. "No more Halloween!"

Danny didn't want to drink to that, but he decided he could drink to his first toast in secret, or to any damn thing he liked. The first sip was just as sour and bitter as he remembered, but he held his breath and swallowed it down. Another couple of swallows, and the hard edges of everything around him started to soften.

Danny saw Carl peering at the turntable with a suspicious look. "Did you turn the music down?"

"Yeah," Danny shrugged.

"What. You got a problem with it? You don't like jazz or something?"

"No, it's alright..."

"You think the fucking *Rolling Stones* can play like that?" Carl got up, walked over to the turntable, and turned the music up. "Don't touch it again." Carl glared at Danny. His face was flushed bright red and his green eyes looked bleary and strange.

They both sat there, not talking, listening to that awful music. Danny glanced out the window at the red light winking on the horizon.

"So," Danny said. "How about a ghost story? *It was long ago, on a night like this...*"

"No!" Carl snapped. "We are *not* telling fucking *ghost* stories tonight! What's wrong with you? You want to be a little kid forever?"

Maybe because the beer had loosened Danny's brain, the

answer was right there behind his clenched teeth. *Yes. That's what I want. I want to be a little kid forever. You got a problem with that?*

"Here..." Carl was thrusting a plastic bag toward him. "Put your can in there."

Danny had only drunk about half of his can and wasn't sure what to do.

"What's the matter?" Carl smirked. "Can't finish it?" Danny felt his face burn. "You can pour the rest out when you go outside."

"Outside?"

"Yeah. I can't throw these away in here. Just take these across the street and throw them over the fence."

Danny felt a twinge of annoyance. "Why do I have to do it?"

"I got the beer, didn't I? The least you can do is clean up."

You didn't do anything but steal it from your own refrigerator, Danny thought. He sighed and took the bag from Carl's hand. Then he walked through the dark kitchen, opened the door, and stepped outside.

The chilly October night wrapped itself around Danny's skin, making him feel a little more awake and alert. There was no moon, only the single streetlight at the far end of the street casting its weak glow, so it was hard to see. The only other light was the tiny red one blinking off and on far across the cornfield. It made Danny think of a lighthouse on the other side of a dark and dangerous ocean.

Danny walked across the street and stepped up to the long wooden fence. He could sense the tall shapes of the corn stalks rising above him against the dark sky, and he fought against the familiar feeling that they were watching him.

Moving quickly, he tossed the bag over the fence, turned around, and started walking away before he even heard the clanking sound of the cans hitting the ground. As he headed back toward Carl's house, he heard something else, a dry rustling sound like paper on paper. *The wind,* he thought, *just the wind in the corn.* He looked up at the oak trees, tall and motionless against the sky, and saw that there was no wind. The dry, scraping sound at his back wasn't fading behind him. It was getting closer.

A blind panic flooded his brain, but he somehow managed to keep walking. *Don't run,* the two words hammered in his head like a heartbeat. If he ran, it would make what he was thinking become true. The dry, scratchy sound behind him rattled and clacked. The light on Carl's porch looked far away and somehow made it feel like it wasn't getting any closer. When Danny couldn't stand it anymore, he broke into a run. Stumbling onto Carl's front porch, Danny dove inside, pushed the door shut, and turned the lock.

"What the hell happened to you?" Carl was still sitting on the big white couch, already working on his second beer and staring up at him.

"Nothing..." Danny said, trying to catch his breath. His heart pounded in his chest. He moved closer to the window and reached up with one hand to part the Venetian blinds. He didn't want to see what might be out there, but he had to look.

"Don't open that!" Carl shouted at him. "There's nothing out there!"

Danny slowly moved his hand away from the window and kept his eyes on Carl's face. There was something in his eyes and voice that Danny recognized. The longer Danny looked at him, the clearer it became.

"I know what you're trying to do," Carl said. "You're just trying to freak me out. The way you freaked out back then when you said you saw those things out there."

The words poured out of Carl in a panicked rush, but that

look of fear was still in his eyes. It all made sense now; Carl not wanting to be alone tonight, the closed blinds, the locked door. He knew. He was still trying to act like he didn't, but he knew.

"You should have seen yourself," Carl kept going. "You woke up screaming like a fucking girl, and your *daddy* had to come and get you..."

"Shut up..."

"You even wet the fucking bed. It smelled like your piss for a month after that..."

"Shut up..."

"Or what?" Carl got up from the couch and took a step toward Danny. "What are you gonna do? Are you gonna cry? Like you were gonna cry last year because we weren't gonna go trick-or-treating? I just went because you wouldn't stop bugging me about it. Jesus, do you know how embarrassing that was? How embarrassing *you* are?"

There was a heavy thud from outside. They both turned and stared at the door. At first there was nothing. Then, a brittle sound of something scraping and scratching on the other side. Danny looked over at Carl and no longer recognized him. The features of Carl's face had been wiped away and replaced by a mask of terror.

Danny saw something flicker across the window in the horizontal slits between the half-closed blinds, partial shapes moving back and forth. *Trying to look in,* Danny thought.

Danny heard the pounding sound of Carl's feet running up the stairs. Danny followed him up, and Carl pulled him into the spare room and shut the door behind them. The dry, scratching sounds seemed even louder up here somehow.

"You locked the front door..." Carl whispered. Danny nodded. He couldn't speak.

Like a wind dying, the noises outside stopped. Danny

looked at Carl, neither one of them daring to say a word. Then Carl's eyes grew wide, and he turned them on Danny.

"Did you lock the kitchen door?"

Danny's thoughts froze for an instant—then he remembered and felt the floor fall away beneath him.

"Fuck, Danny!" Carl hissed. "You..." Carl choked on the words. "*I'm* not going down there!"

"Why should *I* go down there?" Danny said.

"Because," Carl hissed at him, "This is *your* fault!" The hatred in Carl's eyes stunned him. It was true. It was his fault. He'd left the kitchen door open. But it felt like Carl was saying more than that, like it had all been Danny's fault—what had happened years ago, what was happening now, and every mistake he'd made in between. And now he had to make it right.

Cursing, Danny opened the door and ran down the stairs through the empty living room toward the kitchen, praying it wasn't too late. When he reached the entryway to the kitchen, he stopped. The door was standing wide open, and the kitchen was flooded with cold night air from outside. He could see the dim gray light coming through the kitchen window, and the thing that was standing there in the middle of the room.

Danny couldn't see all of it, only the upper parts silhouetted against the window. It was tall, taller than he'd imagined it would be, its head or the thing that must have been its head nearly scraping the ceiling. It moved the way he'd once seen a praying mantis move, with long, impossible jointed arms bending and unbending, feeling the air. It stiffly turned its head toward him—mercifully, it was too dark to see its face. Danny felt sure that not only did the thing see him, but that it *recognized* him. He felt as though the thing had known him for a long, long time, longer than he'd known Carl, longer than he'd known anyone. It shook itself, and Danny could hear the rattling and thrashing of cornstalks in the wind, like the entire field was here in this room.

Danny started to make a break for the open door—then he saw more stick-like shapes clustering in the darkness outside, long, thin arms feeling their way inside.

With a loud cry, Danny ran past the thing in the kitchen, through the dark living room and up the stairs, two at a time. When he reached the door to the spare room and twisted the handle, it wouldn't turn. Carl had locked it. Before he could shout Carl's name, the door swung open, and Carl pulled him in.

"Did you…?" Carl started to ask. Danny could only shake his head. Carl's face went pale.

There was a small white door in the back wall that led to the attic. Carl pulled it open and called to Danny, "Come on…"

The heat of the attic, even in October, hit Danny in the face as he followed Carl inside. "Hold the door!" Carl shouted. Danny took hold of the doorknob and leaned against the door just as he heard the room behind it filling with rustling, rattling shapes.

There was a creaking sound, and Danny suddenly felt cold air at his back. He twisted his head in time to see Carl raising the trap door in the roof that led outside. Danny could see the stars in a black sky and the tops of trees.

"Come on!" Carl shouted.

"No," Danny said, "It's too high…"

"You want those things…" Carl started to say, a look of rage and disbelief on his face. The door rattled. Carl turned and stepped out into the night and was gone. Danny shut his eyes, listening for the sound of Carl's body hitting the ground—when it never came, he thought of all those long, dry arms waiting for him down below.

Danny felt the pressure on the other side of the door grow greater like the pressure in his head before a thunderstorm. He didn't understand how he could be holding all of it back by himself. Then the thought came to him—maybe he wasn't doing it all by himself. Maybe they were *letting* him. But why? Why didn't they just push their way in and end it now? They were waiting for something. They were waiting for *him* to do something. Something only he could do.

This is your fault. He remembered what Carl had said. *You did this.* He didn't understand, but he knew it was true. They were here because he had called them. Since that night long ago when he'd stood at the edge of that field and looked out over it and felt something. Even before that. This was what he wanted. This was what he'd always wanted.

Danny let go of a deep breath that felt like he'd been holding it for a long time. Then he stepped back, opened the door, and let Halloween in.

When They Fall

STEVE RASNIC TEM

Is someone there? Asking the question aloud would have been unbearable.

They bought the house because of the view: perched beyond the summit of a steep hill, the Cape Cod boasted expansive windows overlooking the center of town. Towering oaks on each side protected it from the worst of winter. It was a promising home for raising two children.

The only defect in its unadorned aesthetic was a tiny gable with an oval window protruding from the steep roof several feet from the central chimney: an odd, asymmetrical detail which made Ralph think of a giant's damaged eyeball. It was the house's tiny attic, hot and dusty, which their daughter Robin claimed as her playhouse.

His wife Emma never liked the drab colors: gray shingle siding and black shutters, an ashen roof, a few strokes of white trim. She said it was like living inside an old black-and-white film. They talked often of repainting, but they never did.

It was only after living there a few seasons did they grasp the property's difficulties. The steep road iced over most winters, necessitating a detour of several miles to ensure a safe commute. The local children loved this road for sledding (they called it "suicide hill") and despite the posted warnings, serious injuries and near-misses accumulated each year. Ralph and Emma struggled to keep their small son John away from this particular danger. Mostly they succeeded.

For Ralph, however, the worst thing about the house had been those damn oak trees. Beautiful and stately as they might be, every fall they released acorns, twigs, and leaves a half foot long across the yard. The acorns sounded like small bombs hitting the roof and chipping the shingles. The fallen nuts attracted scores of squirrels and field mice who fought over them and dragged them into corners where they rotted in musty, sour-smelling piles.

As they aged, the oaks dropped limbs, some of them tree-sized. A decade ago, Ralph wanted to have the oaks cut down, but Emma refused. "You'd be begging for more trouble. Hasn't this family seen enough sorrow?"

Now he could do whatever he wanted, but Ralph didn't want to do much of anything.

IS IT HER? *Is it him?*

The afternoon of Halloween the leaves lay thick over Ralph's lawn. He'd stopped raking years back. It was too hard. He could have hired someone, but he never did. He knew letting them accumulate wasn't good for the grass, but he couldn't remember why. He supposed it wasn't healthy for any living thing to lie beneath a layer of dead matter. He rarely looked at his yard anymore, but where dull leaves had blown away, he could see a paler, sparser version of the lawn they had when Emma was still alive.

The night before, he'd roused to a succession of soft bangs, like a series of doors closing. It wasn't the first time he'd been awakened that way. He suspected it wouldn't be the last.

He carried the rake out front thinking he'd scrape the flagstone path clean. It probably wasn't necessary, but he was feeling neglectful. Emma had loved her flagstones. The leaves were firmly compacted onto the stones due to frequent deliveries. He never went out, and no one ever visited. Smaller leaves, blown from some neighbor's yard and disintegrated to transparency, ornamented the larger ones. They resembled huge, irregular flakes of skin.

Something moved through the leaves on his left. He turned his head quickly but missed it. His vision wasn't what it used to be. A swift paleness intruded on his right side, and he jerked his head around again. Still nothing. It was aggravating. It might be a floater in his eye, or something worse, his retina detaching. More than once he'd glimpsed a fragment of memory in the borders of his visual field. He didn't know if that was normal and was afraid to ask his doctor.

A squirrel boldly approached, stopping within a couple of feet. The animal wore a child's face. Not his son's, he didn't think. But the creature was so jittery it was difficult to tell.

Ralph turned away and slammed the rake's metal teeth onto a flagstone and began to scrape. Leaves slid aside exposing a layer of tarry black. Disgusted, he tried kicking the leaves over to hide it.

The last few autumns had been strange, warmer than normal, the summers refusing to let go. Then when the seasons finally changed, they did so abruptly. The strip of ground in front of the windows had always been rich with fall flowers: mums and pansies, asters, violas, black-eyed-susans. Emma curated them for years. All he did was weed now and then.

An irregular flake of black shutter peeled away, turning into a butterfly which lit from one flower to the next. Surely it was a trick of the light, and it was about time for those flowers to turn anyway, but each flower the butterfly touched appeared to fade, curl, and wither.

A nearby bird whistled itself down to silence. The sky, the air, turned silver. Ralph felt on the verge of falling. A wind came up, and the sudden breeze brought flies, a narrow cloud of them like a dagger. There was a terrible stench, something far worse than rotting acorns, and for a moment he imagined he smelled his own death.

Ralph went back inside. Trick-or-treaters rarely came to his house anyway. The first Halloween after Emma died, he bought a silly clown mask and sat by the door with a bowl of candy. Fewer than a dozen children came. The next day he devoured the leftover sweets as if his life depended on it and made himself sick. Even fewer children came the following year. He gave those that did come great handfuls of candy. Every time he made himself smile at a child he felt as if he were wearing a mask.

The house always smelled odd when he came in from outside. Today it was stale, warm sweat with hints of shampoo. Like a little boy's hair after playing.

The dim outline of a figure shimmered in the doorway to the dining room. He avoided looking too closely. He heard a wisp of sound so vague he couldn't tell if it was a voice or not. His big empty house felt too small for him.

Ralph dodged the dining room and went into the kitchen. The gunmetal counters were clean and uncluttered, the kitchen in general pristine enough for a house showing. He could tell immediately if anything had been moved.

This year he hadn't bothered purchasing candy, although he hated disappointing children, especially the smaller ones. He didn't know why the kids never came anymore. Maybe they thought the house unoccupied. The light above his front steps burned out years ago, he wasn't sure when.

He sat down at his laptop on one end of the kitchen table. There was an email from his daughter Robin, pictures of his three small grandsons costumed as superheroes. It had been a couple of years since they moved across the country, and lately she'd been sending emails instead of answering her phone. He responded with how much he loved their outfits and how he'd love to hear all their voices. Anytime. He was home all the time. He hoped she would call.

He wanted to tell her to be careful letting them cross the street. This was unnecessary advice. She was a grown woman and a good mother. But he wanted to tell her anyway. He wanted to tell her to hold their hands. Then he thought, with three kids, how could she grab all three, protect all three? He wanted to tell her to make Jack get off work early and go with them trick-or-treating. Ralph never thought Jack was the most responsible person, but he could at least hold on to a child's hand.

Ralph watched as the shadows of the leaves drifted down outside the curtained windows, a few at a time, then a sudden torrent. Maybe it would storm, and the children would stay away, and he could spend the night in peace, assured of their safety.

He closed his eyes and put his head down on the table. He could hear the hum of the house conveyed through the wood, tabletop to table legs to floor to beams to studs and whatever else was connected. He didn't know the physics involved but believed sounds travelled quite far if some sort of contact was maintained. But maintaining contact was always a challenge.

An old house generated so many noises which could not be explained. Many of those noises sounded like conversation. The refrigerator, the water pipes, the furnace, they all had a voice and those voices spoke to him because no one else was here to listen. Maybe he shouldn't have stopped drinking coffee, but it scared him the way caffeine made his heart race.

WHAT DO THEY WANT? *What do they want him to say?*

The afternoon light was waning. He needed to find a place where he could hide for the evening, so he could turn out the lights so no one would think he was at home. It felt mean, disingenuous, but if they thought no one was at home those hopeful children walking around with their empty treat bags wouldn't have their feelings hurt.

He heard a light knocking on the door, so soft he wasn't sure he'd actually heard it, then it came again, a hesitant, shy knock. He peeked through the curtains. He didn't see anything, then he heard the child's voice through the door—he couldn't tell if it was male or female—*Trick or Treat.*

It was too early. Even the parents of the smallest children in this neighborhood waited until four-thirty or five, if they went trick-or-treating at all. These days the parents of small kids took them to neighborhood parties where they could control things, where it was safer.

Ralph sat in a chair by the door—the same spot where he had waited for the children years before—waiting for this child to give up and go away. But every few minutes came the light knock, and the announcement, barely above a whisper —*Trick or Treat.* Finally, the knocking and the entreaty ceased, and Ralph got up to make himself a sandwich before retiring upstairs, when he saw the small shadow appear in the lower portion of the front window, growing larger as it leaned in closer until the head hit the windowpane once, then twice. *Trick or Treat.*

Of course, it was just a child, but none had ever been this

bold before. *He intends a trick,* Ralph thought. Well, Ralph thought he deserved one, a trick, some awful trick.

The shadow disappeared, then reappeared in the side window, the one off the dining room. Knock, knock, as the nodding head struck the glass. *Trick or Treat.*

Ralph moved toward the stairs, intending to go up to his bedroom, where he would hide and read until the night was over, but then the shadow reappeared in his kitchen window, which was too far off the ground for any child to reach, and yet there was the nodding, and the knocking head, and the louder, insistent, *Trick or Treat…Trick or Treat.*

"Go away! I'm calling the police!" he shouted, feeling foolish, because how could he call the police on a child?

The shadow suddenly ballooned, filling the window, then disappeared.

WAS *it his rage or theirs?*

He was an adult. He knew life was ephemeral. Each person was given the slimmest shard of time. But children had no idea. They dwelled in the forever now.

Ralph and Emma always shared the Halloween duties. Emma spent hours preparing treat bags. The kids helped at first, but soon lost interest, preferring to carve pumpkins or watch some scary movie before going out to trick or treat themselves. Ralph helped with the pumpkin carving, but he hated the feel of the pumpkins' guts on his hands and between his fingers.

They used to put out elaborate Halloween displays in front of the house. Now those decorations gathered dust in the basement.

Emma would take one child out to make the Halloween rounds while Ralph stayed home with the other doling out candy, then after an hour or so they'd switch. They made sure both of their competitive children received equal attention and participation.

Emma was good at this. She had a knack for giving their kids what they needed at any given time. For Ralph, Halloween was a chaotic storm of worry and distraction. There were always too many kids dressed similarly in whatever TV- or movie-inspired garb was popular at the time, crowding each other on the sidewalks, pouring over the lawns. It would be too easy to misplace a child, or God forbid lose one to some costumed predator (although Emma insisted such things almost never occurred).

Robin insisted she was too old to hold his hand. John didn't verbally object, but the holiday made him overexcited, and his sweaty, squirmy hands difficult to hold. They tried to control his consumption of candy, but every year he managed to devour enough sweets to make himself agitated, weepy, and ill.

They were running behind. It had become obvious the sheet John was wearing with its misaligned eyeholes, turning him into a small, stumbling ghost, was too long. Every few houses they had to stop and readjust, tucking some of the sheet under John's belt which he insisted spoiled the look. Ralph was trying to get John home after his last turn so Robin and Emma could go out again. He could imagine his daughter's growing annoyance even as they turned the corner. But John was distracted, needing to explore every decorated yard, wanting to greet the wearer of every unique costume, oblivious to time.

It was a struggle of push and pull all the way home, Ralph practically dragging his son, who in his upset was spilling candy from his plastic pumpkin bucket, stooping to retrieve what he spilled, yanking his hand away.

They were crossing the street just past the top of the hill, less than twenty feet from their yard, when the push and pull between them broke, and John fell back just as a car topped the road, unable to see the little boy lying there.

Emma and Robin saw it all from their front door. The sound of Emma screaming, as if she'd been broken, was something Ralph still heard. He remembered little of the funeral itself: unable to let go of his wife's and daughter's hands, the stillness around them, all those others watching from a safe distance.

ARE *we ghosts hiding within our costumes of flesh?*

Their house, Ralph's house, was now thought haunted by the neighborhood kids. Of course—that's why they stayed away. His life had become too sad and scary even for Halloween. He felt it as an insult, but he couldn't blame them. The past few years the days after Halloween were spent removing the bits of rotten pumpkin people threw into his yard.

Emma noticed the changes in their house, experienced those unexplainable events, before he did. Ralph largely checked out, but Emma went to therapy, joined grief groups, started a diary chronicling her bereavement. She never blamed him, at least not directly, but she must have thought—he didn't know what she thought. She never said anything about his part in it, and he never asked.

She used to ask him if he had moved things in the kitchen, in their bedroom. He had no idea what she was talking about. Eventually she moved out of their bedroom, but the disruptions—chairs moved, cosmetics disappearing, sheets torn from the bed—followed. He didn't hear the late-night rapping which drove her awake. Or the early morning weeping of something, or someone, lost.

They tried repurposing his room. For awhile it was her sewing room, but she was never comfortable there. They changed the wall colors several times. But whatever paint they applied discolored into muddy and unpleasant shades. John's old room became the guest room no one ever used.

Robin lost her attic space to John's toys and other select possessions neither Ralph nor Emma felt able to throw away. They asked her, and she gave them her permission, but Ralph knew it was a terrible mistake.

The days fall away quickly, and disintegration cannot be stopped. What happened to the kisses they once exchanged, all those kind words? Ralph had no idea how to preserve them.

A month after Robin left for college Emma tripped on the staircase and fell halfway down, shattering her hip. She was never the same again. After another year she went into a care home. Three more years and she, too, was gone.

WHAT WAS *he more afraid of? That these presences were real, or they were not?*

Ralph sat halfway up the staircase eating a sandwich, a glass of pale apple juice on the step beside him. It was five o'clock and he could hear children out on the sidewalk with their parents, and someone kicking through the leaves, but no one knocked, or rang the bell, or yelled *Trick or Treat!* He was fine with that.

The staircase walls were crowded with pictures, most of them Robin and her kids, and early portraits of John prominently placed. Ralph had some photos of Emma in his bedroom upstairs. The only photos of himself were tucked away in albums somewhere. He never looked at them.

Most of the older photos on these walls were ones Emma had hung of her own family—father and mother, uncles and aunts, numerous cousins, and unidentifiable extended relatives. He didn't know any of them, but it would have felt disrespectful to take them down. They were all ghosts now, or at least ghosts to him, the photos taken before they knew how they would end.

Ralph heard more kicking through the leaves, laughter and talking, distant doorbell rings, knocks on other doors. Most seemed to understand what his home's darkness implied and continued on their way. It was time for him to go upstairs.

He went up to his bedroom but couldn't bring himself to go inside. He felt rather than heard the footsteps behind him. He opened the door to the gritty old staircase and ascended into the attic, shutting the door firmly behind him. He fumbled for the light switch. The bulb was dim but burned.

He was surprised by how clearly he could hear the noises outside, the shrill voices of many children, shoes on the pavement, in the leaves, the rustlings of dozens of treat bags, cars on the road, the occasional explosive horn. Ralph went to the head-sized oval window and peered out.

He had an unobstructed view of the wide, slate-colored sky hanging over the center of town, the smoky clouds drifting in, and below, the armies of costumed children swarming the streets, the lawns and porches, everywhere Ralph looked, their impossible numbers flickering in and out of the shadows, doubling and tripling at times, anonymous, their mysteries hidden behind their masks.

Closer in, just below, his yard was full of more teeming figures, this year their outfits looking primarily homemade: pirates and princesses and ghosts, bizarre creatures in their antique Victorian clothes and rotting paper bag masks, hundreds of spirits hiding under a variety of sheets, brilliant white and softly beige, all the shades of smoke and gray, heavy and stiff, diaphanous and virtually transparent, although Ralph caught no glimpse of the children inside.

If he had known, he might have bought candy and prepared for a real Halloween this year. But he couldn't possibly have bought enough.

His son's toys lay nearby. He glanced at the boxes laden in thick layers of dust and felt ashamed.

He couldn't help feeling observed and judged. The stars were eyes in the darkness gazing down. They witnessed every bit of neglect, every careless deed.

The children continued to flood his lawn, the leaves disappearing beneath their feet. They seeped out into the street and beyond. They pushed out to the edge of the steep hill and the road leading dizzily down, and spilled over, hundreds of costumed children falling into the dark and nothing.

Ralph's eyes grew weary of staring. He heard the slippage on the roof, the groan of shifting timbers, and felt a gravity changing everything. Two dark holes appeared side by side in the night sky in front of him, depths so black no light could pass through. The vast shrouded face spread beyond the edges of the roof, obscuring the stars. It was all he could see or think about.

Always October

JEREMY MEGARGEE

His mind is a rotten apple core, but the ghost hunter cannot stop. There's a sense of time slipping through an hourglass, and it is pivotal to finish before his window closes. He trudges through night streets, heels crunching discarded candy underfoot, and on corners he sees the last few ghouls and wraiths gathering their hauls before calling it an evening. Nostrils flare, and he scents the air.

It is close. This one stinks of wrath and self-loathing.

The small blue house comes into view, looking like a colored egg with cracks in the paint, and the malice radiates outward in sickly waves. The infant wails untended in some dark room on the second floor, and even from the sagging porch, the ghost hunter can hear the young parents screaming obscenities at each other. The origin of the fight never matters, for it repeats itself, a circular argument that leaves them both in each other's faces, beet red skin, saliva spurting from competing lips, and veins standing out on clenched fists.

He lurks, hunching down near a window, and he hears them roar, the two sad souls never thinking of the effect their fighting will have on that infant later in life, both of them lost in the maelstrom of their own discontent. They're so focused on each other that they never even sense what stands in the corner behind them.

The ghost hunter watches it, and his jaw tightens. It is crooked hate, stingers that drip venomous juice, blackened teeth all painfully crowded together in mouth slits; a bulging torso that leans inward, almost like the entity is horribly self-conscious. The six arms hang limp and lifeless, and it dribbles brine from dark orifices. It twitches, seeming almost to seize eternally, lapping at the air with a dog-tongue and supping on the misery and anger and hatred that bleeds out of the two young lovers.

It notices the ghost hunter peering through the window, and the rage intensifies. A meal interrupted, and this simply will not do. It rushes, a mad hound, and it throws itself from the open window, crushing into the ghost hunter and using its torso to batter at him, swinging arms like slack clubs that beat about his head and shoulders. Hissing like a rattler, it struggles to clamp teeth down on him, but he uses his forearm to keep the entity at bay, shielding himself from the malice that splatters out in gallons. The ghost hunter successfully holds back the form, which just makes it angrier, a raw impotence that causes it to thrash its unfortunate body into something that resembles a tantrum.

It was a criminal when it was alive. It cheated and it hurt, because hurt was where it was born. It never knew anything but anger simmering in its own cookpot. The ghost hunter grits his teeth and struggles to maintain his footing, and he does what comes naturally. He embraces the entity. He tightens his arms around it, and he squeezes. It sweeps anguished, red-rimmed eyes up to the sky, and it howls ceaselessly at the moon. It is fading into the ghost hunter, its body becoming a mess of sloppy organics, ectoplasm breaking down into thick ribbons, and although it does everything to prevent it, finally the entirety of the thing is assimilated. Nothing remains of the rage demon, and the ceaseless, argumentative din from the living room stops. The ghost hunter staggers on wobbly legs, feeling the indigestion of that hateful thing in him, but he finds his gumption and steadies. He watches briefly from the window, seeing the confusion on the faces of the young parents, and the tender touches of forgiveness to come.

Although it is a beautiful thing to witness, he cannot linger. Halloween can offer only so many hours of a thin veil, and he must collect the others. It is his responsibility, and nothing will turn him from the path.

SHE WEAVES THROUGH BODIES; skin like milk, thighs crisscrossed in fishnet stockings, and eyes a cornflower blue. Ethereal, barely there at all, gliding and awakening libido as she goes. The costume party is all flashing strobe light and sloshing alcohol, so there's already a sense of reality skewed. No one suspects that she's a ghost. No one notices that her skin isn't just a canvas of pallidity, it's actually transparent.

The ruse would be perfect, but the ghost hunter watches from the multitudes, and he sees her for what she is. She flirts freely, grazing fingertips across chests of men, and whispering sweet nothings into the ears of women. They all gravitate to her. She's a people pleaser, and she learned to appease at an age she never should have, innocence stomped down into gristle in the formative years. Promiscuous when still flesh and blood, a natural charmer, but death brought out the succubus within. Now she's all wispy fingers and hungry void of a heart, locked in a limbo of lust that goes on forever. This

Halloween party is a banquet, and she'll hunt here until dawn if the ghost hunter lets her. She can tell he has no intention of doing so.

She spots him, and there's no violence in her examination. A coquettish smile tugs at the corner of her mouth, and as she approaches through the crowd, flashing lights cut through her entire form, showcasing that she's more intangible than she seems. She gets close, cutting her eyes up and down, drinking in the ghost hunter slowly, water for a parched and sensuous mouth, and he stands motionless before her. Her fingertips brush his cheekbone. He does not feel them. She nibbles at her lips, bringing the appearance of blood to them even though there is no blood left in her. She speaks of the things they can do together, all the vulgar and raunchy and delicious things that wait in the bedrooms beyond. Her voice is soft and sinful, and it's a lullaby that threatens to break the ghost hunter down until he's just putty in her unnaturally warm hands, but he knows her and looks deeper.

He sees the doe in her, the vulnerability that she buried long ago, with all the other memories that made her sick to her stomach in life. The touching and the little manipulations from grownups that were supposed to protect. How it broke her inside like a glass figurine, and her whole life was just a struggle to learn how to pick up the shards without cutting herself too badly. He sees, and she sees that he sees. Her expression droops, and all the predatory sexuality goes out of it. There stands before him a woman who never loved or learned how to be loved because of the nightmare she was birthed into.

He tries now to give her even a glimpse of affection without pressure, and she caves to him, falling into his arms, a banshee weeping out oceans of emotion that have never been allowed to flow, and there's no fight in this one, no great resistance at all once the process begins. She melts into him, a willing candle that wants to burn out, and he takes her in where she belongs, the whole of her ghostly frame vanishing into the lockbox of his chest.

The ghost hunter can feel her curling up in there, comfortable and safe, something never afforded to her in life, but now given in the afterlife. He wills her to sleep, and she does.

THE WORK ISN'T DONE. The night isn't through. The others still haunt, and if the ghost hunter hopes to be complete, he must finish what he started.

October dwindles, and the dead leaves swirl through shattered windows, the house just a remnant of what it used to be. It senses the passing of a season where it appears almost normal. Broken shutters droop, the door creaks forlorn, and the foundation falls deeper in on itself. A haunted beauty in the time of Halloween, but just a ruin the rest of the year.

It is haunted by a little ghost in an oversized white sheet. Dark eye holes and dark circles underneath. He wanders room to room, the same old explorations, but there is never anyone to talk to. His sheet drags behind him when he walks, catching the brittle leaves that blow in through the windows, and his short legs seem destined to walk and walk despite never knowing his destination.

There's a dusty piano in the foyer, and sometimes he stands on his tippy toes and plays with the keys, sending melodies jangling through the emptiness. He doesn't know where to go, and he doesn't understand what has happened to him. He hides beneath the sheet because it's warm, and since he's been here, everything has been cold.

He found a runt of a pumpkin in the root cellar, which he brought up with him to the bottom of the spiral staircase, leaning his body against an ornate banister while he carves into the pulpy surface with a butter knife.

The ghost hunter stands in the open doorframe, watching the little ghost. It hurts him inside to look at this one; just a small child bundled into a tattered sheet, wholeheartedly lost in this world of deathly stillness.

It takes a while for the little ghost to notice him, and when he does, he drops his pumpkin. It rolls across the floor, and a small, clothed hand lifts up the butter knife and brandishes it, trembling in the ghost hunter's direction.

"I'm not here to harm."

The ghost hunter approaches, and the little ghost remains unsure, but soon he lowers the knife and lets it clatter down against the stairs. The ghost hunter crouches down and tentatively reaches out and lifts up the sheet, exposing dirty cheeks, messy sandy blonde hair, and big, scared eyes that saw too much of life far too soon.

The ghost hunter holds back tears, clearing his throat, and he gazes up at the rooms above them. Bad memories. Repressed memories. Things that never should have happened.

It all comes back, a flood of dark water, and he can't afford to be swept away. There isn't time. Halloween is dying, and October never lasts. He reaches out, brushing his hand through that sandy blonde hair, and he cups the back of the child's head. The boy stiffens at the touch, immediately wary and expecting brutality.

"It was never your fault."

The ghost hunter draws the little ghost forward, pressing him up against his chest, and all form becomes liquid and malleable, the sheet and the boy within vanishing into the core of the ghost hunter, leaving nothing behind but a swirling circle of October leaves.

He stands after it's done, looking around him. He's aware of the clock running down.

He's not really a ghost hunter. He's just another ghost.

He was a man once. A man with dissociative identity disorder resulting from the terrible child abuse that he experienced in this house. When he died, his identities unfurled and split away, like handwritten letters blown to the four winds. He's been looking for them a long time, October after October, and now, in this house where it all started, he has found the last of them.

His alters flicker in front of him, born of quarreling kin and the same familial specters he watched at the window. The rage demon trembling and radiating hate. The people-pleasing seductress. The little lost boy in a sheet. Other faces too, alters he hunted in years past, always on Halloween, always when the veil is thin, because that is the way.

They wink out, just parts of him reclaimed, and as the minutes spell the end of October, a door to a different place opens, etching itself into the wall of the house. It glows, and touching the knob makes him feel integrated.

It's been a long time since he has felt complete. Not scared. Not lost. Not angry. Just serene and wondering what comes next.

He opens the door.

How To Unmake a Ghost

SARA TANTLINGER

The rumors have always been true, and it's alarming how easy you stumble across this once-guarded secret. Whispers of the thin veil, the ancient power Samhain holds, have turned out to be more than mere mythology, but you already know this.

You found me, after all.

I'm not going to be the one to congratulate you if this book makes itself visible. The pages only appear to those who have summoned a ghost on Halloween night. If you're looking for a "well done" on a successful summoning, you've come to the wrong place. Despite that, I am here to guide you on where to go next because it's not sustainable to keep a spirit forever. We aren't decorations you can contain in a glass jar. Latching onto a spirit for too long drains a human, eats away at their body from the inside out like a phantasmagoric cancer.

You aren't new to this; you've summoned before and keep coming back.

Now, you're dying.

Sage and salt drifts through the air, and I can smell how it clings to your skin, mixed with the light sheen of your sweat.

Your hair reeks of smoke, and those wax-stained fingertips tell me you've been trying to find solutions to your ghostly problem.

I know what you're thinking: "Ghosts can smell?"

Yes, we can, thank you very much. It's one of the few senses we're able to carry over into the other world. I can also see your sad face, those deep circles beneath tired eyes, and I can hear the too-fast beating of your heart as it plays an anxious rhythm.

It was sweet of you to leave sour candies and chocolate morsels on my grave. You whispered to the gravestone, told it how you plucked the candy from your neighbor's bowl that he leaves out every year on the porch for children to pilfer through. You told me how we always snuck over, even as adults, to grab a few treats when we were too poor to buy our own. I heard your story, but remember, I have no taste. I don't even have a tongue, or a mouth. Beneath black eyes and a skeleton nose, you'll only find an empty surface covered in swirls of mist. Ghosts aren't allowed to speak for themselves. I can only compose this slim book, so please forgive me if it takes awhile for each sentence to appear on the pages in your hands. It's a difficult process to will my words onto the paper, and sometimes the paper misbehaves. Everything in the after-life has its own intentions. I'd say trust nothing you see or hear, but I need you to trust me.

And of course, I can't touch you. That's the sensation you hunger for most; I can see the longing reflected in your eyes. How those pupils grow wide like inky dewdrops searching for the thing I can never give you. No matter how many times I'm summoned, no matter what night or with what power, I will never be able to press fingertips against the warmth of your body.

Don't look away. I need you to focus. The blush on your

cheeks could be from the crisp air, so put aside your embarrassment.

Does the October chill make you feel alive when you inhale it into your lungs? I hope so. I hope you breathe and live, for me.

Listen, keep these notes close to you. I know the leather binding is frayed and the pages torn, but it's important we get through this. To return your ghost back to the spirit world after the initial summoning, you have to wait for Halloween night once again, and you did. You made it a whole year with a spirit draining your life, so that's a good sign. It means you might be strong enough to survive the rest of this.

An attached ghost weighs in your heart with the heaviness of cement. They don't mean to sit like a block beneath your ribs, making each day seem grayer than the one before. They barely realize how much of your joy they're feeding off. The spirit gnaws and gnaws at you until you're left a hollow, sticky husk.

This is the price.

Your ghost is with you, always, for that year. You can curl into yourself, into the memories of who the ghost was as a human. Such vivid and bright remembrances, they become too easy to drown beneath. It feels real, like the ghost has crawled back from the grave and is holding your hand. Soft touches and earthy scents. A distortion of existence so great, I can't blame you for choosing to live there instead of in the actual world. Reality, however, always comes shattering down sooner or later. With such a force, it's inevitable the ghost begins to leave you.

And then, you have two options.

The first is to keep your ghost until you die, and with the spirit attached inside of you like a parasite, you won't live long. Every day you are alive will carry so much gloom, unless you disappear inside of your head. That's the problem. You'll construct a fantasy from favorite memories inside your mind, and then one day when you dare to try and look at the real world instead, it'll break you.

Other times, people let the ghost go, only to summon them back again and again each year.

Sadly, that's the option we see the most. But you're here, you've come back, so maybe option two is what you will declare as a victory. Option two is to simply unmake your ghost.

Well, it isn't very simple at all, but it's the only way you might find some sense of joy in your existence again. The choice is yours, really. Are you ready?

STEP ONE: Right after sunset on Halloween night, when the final blink of orange light dies in the sky, return to where your ghost was buried. If their human body has been cremated instead, you can take their ashes to any quiet location, preferably the woods. For you, go back to the cemetery down Blue Mountain Lane. You know the path by heart and could walk to that headstone with your eyes closed. No matter the weather, rain, snow, or a gathering of storm clouds, make sure you're there.

Please note, everyone will be in costume, and you'll likely pass a few teens who have snuck into the graveyard at sundown like you used to do. You need to blend in.

Take one sheet, cut out two holes for eyes, and place the sheet over your head. Make sure you can walk, and run, without tripping on the fabric. You never know when things could go wrong, and you might need to sprint back down the road and hide from whatever you purposefully, or accidentally, summon.

The ghost sheet is cliché, I know, but it's important. You must not be recognized by anyone. Otherwise, they might be tempted to follow in your footsteps, and then you'll have additional ghosts to unmake. The more ghosts, the more likely you'll be drained down into a prune of wrinkled skin, and who will unmake your ghost then?

Remember to bring the following: one bag of hard candy, a sharp knife, seven white candles, conjuring oil, a hammer, a lighter or matches, and something that belonged to your ghost when they were alive.

STEP TWO: Lay down the bag of candy on a strong surface, maybe a flat gravestone. Don't worry if it seems disrespectful. We ghosts have had worse done to us.

Pick up your hammer and smash all of the hard candy down into a fine powder inside the bag. You should be left with a colorful dust of what once was sour apple Jolly Ranchers, bright Lemonheads, and maybe even those multicolored Funny Bones Candy. Whatever you have brought, pulverize it and then spread the powdery rainbow remnants into a circle around you on the ground. Take all of your other items with you, and make sure the chosen space is empty and you aren't putting the circle atop an overgrown grave. Otherwise, you risk rousing the spirit of whomever is trying to rest in that spot, and they certainly didn't ask to be disturbed.

From within the circle, pour the conjuring oil so it mixes with the candied dust.

Set up the seven white candles inside the circle with you. The seven represent each step of unmaking your ghost.

• • •

STEP THREE: I wish these steps got easier, for your sake. I really do. Though, how could any part of making or unmaking a ghost ever be simple? You summoned your ghost from your heart, and to your heart I wish I could return.

I remember. You don't think I do, but I recall every second of you sobbing so hard that your breath barely came. You choked on those aching cries until the spirit of me was pulled straight from your grieving heart. I see the pain and how it drains you, how it shrivels your once brilliant smile into a tight frown. It's one of the few memories I've been allowed to keep.

Do it again. Cry for your ghost. We'll never get this done if you don't water the ground with your tears. Just the space within the circle, cry there.

You figured this out before, how to open the veil a little wider with the searing hunger of your grief. I need you to do it again. I know it hurts. I'm sorry. Close your eyes, search for the raw wounds you keep hidden away in the crawlspace of your mind—the moments too painful to dwell on for long. Whatever gets the job done because we don't have much time.

STEP FOUR: Dig your nails into the softened soil where you have emptied your sorrow out onto the wilting grass. Scoop away enough dirt to bury the item you've brought. The item that once belonged to your ghost when they were human.

What is it? Let me see.

A card that reads "Happy Halloween" on the outside where the curved orange letters are surrounded by dancing black cats wearing silly masks and riding broomsticks. Cute.

The inside of the card is filled with more cats, merrily sharing jack-o'-lanterns of treats, but there, between the graphics is scrawled handwriting. Someone has written

"Happy Anniversary" and a sweet love letter. You're careful to make sure your tears don't hit the card—that ink too precious to smear.

Hold the card open for as long as you like, and though you so desperately want me to remember this, I don't.

Did you write the love note? Did I? Again, I'm sorry. I don't have this memory anymore, and you know why I don't. You've been aware of the consequences all along, but it hasn't stopped you from making a ghost to latch onto.

Bury the card. Cover it completely with the tear-stained dirt. You can stop crying now, if you're able. I won't judge you if you can't.

STEP FIVE: You won't be surprised that step five is blood. The oldest ingredient in any book or ritual since many an ancient time ago. Why?

Because it's always blood. It will always be blood. Life holds such power, and blood acts as the vermillion threads connecting us, connecting all worlds and planes of existence no matter how far apart we may seem. So, if you're fucking around with life or death, why wouldn't it be blood?

Excuse my language, but you know what you did, don't you? I'm not going to pretend in your innocence. You created a curse for us both, so bleed into it. Give back to the earth and spirits you've so casually trifled with.

Pick up the sharp knife you brought. It doesn't matter where you cut, so long as you bleed. The palm is an easy trick on television shows and in movies, but the bloodletting can come from anywhere. A quick slit across the forearm is fine, too—don't go too deep. We don't need much. Just enough to prove your commitment. Now, bleed your scarlet penance into the dirt.

. . .

STEP SIX: Check the candles. Are five of them blown out? Then you've completed the first five steps successfully. Two more to go.

This step is a little unusual. I need you to give me a memory.

Choose one. It must be powerful. Once you give the memory to me, it's mine. You can never have it back.

What have you chosen? Oh, more than one...are you sure? You have to be sure. Like I said, I can't return these.

The certainty on your face leaves no room for doubt. Close your eyes. You'll feel a sense of cold, almost like a brain freeze from sucking down a milkshake too fast.

In your mind, you give me Halloween nights, and the first thing I remember is how you always did know how to bring out the nostalgia in me.

We're both eight, and I'm stuffed into a storm cloud cutout while you're wearing a lightning bolt dress. Both sets of our parents loved to get us matching costumes, as if we were sisters separated at birth rather than two lonely girls who happened to attend the same school. I never thought of you as a sister, even when we were so young. I just knew you to be a light I was drawn toward.

They'd follow behind us, chattering about nothing in the background while we filled our plastic pumpkins full of mouthwatering candy, plus the apples Mrs. Taylor always gave out. She constantly bought those ones with peels shiny as wax. We'd leave her redbrick house and make up stories about the different poisons she probably coated the apple skin in each year.

We're older in your next memory. Teens free of parental supervision, and they never knew how our friendship burned brighter by the second…an overheated bulb ready to burst into millions of glass pieces. If they knew, they would have watched the shards turn our flesh to ribbons and say we deserved what we got. Moms and dads who claimed to love us, but it was 1994 and they bought into propaganda, into all those vile words about how people like us were morally sick.

I never felt sick with you. I only felt free.

You give me the memory of your 18th birthday. I kissed you in the graveyard. In *this* graveyard down Blue Mountain Lane. Your fingers tangled in my long hair, and your lips tasted like sticky watermelon from that shiny roll-on lip gloss you carried like a safety charm.

The memories end here, these marvelous glances into who I once was when we were together, but there's terror, too. It follows us, and you try to turn off your mind as if it's a faucet before those slivers of darkness seep into the good reminiscences.

The shadows are quicker, and there, I see us running away as the people we once loved find loathsome insults to hurl at our fleeing forms. We made it, though. We made it out and carved our happiness into the world for ten short years before I…

I died. How did I die?

You refuse to show me. The sad blue of your eyes keeps the violent details of my death hidden from me, but I have carried pieces of it with me into this strange afterlife. Almost forgotten, but you are the key turning loose the lockbox of my past.

Someone hated us very much, and they made sure I never returned home one night to you.

We're not here to remember my last day as a living person, but you and I are bound intimately to such pain. If I still had a heart, it would break itself over again knowing you will never remember our first kiss, the way your electricity shot through me that night. And every night after. This sweet memory you've gifted me, but the knowledge of my brutal demise, of everything stolen from us, is too powerful to be taken away from either one of our minds. Pain is cruel like that.

All of these things I remember. Does it mean it's working, the ritual? To unmake a ghost, it requires so much more sacrifice than to make one. You should have left me alone after I died, but we never could stay away from each other.

I'm sorry, I got distracted. You completed this step, and I thank you for the memories.

Do you see the iridescent shimmer around the candy circle? You've opened the veil wide enough for us to complete this.

STEP SEVEN: The final step.

I miss you. And of course, you miss me, too, but pulling me back to you hurts. I am unraveling, but not unmade. Please, unmake me entirely. Let me go. That's the final step, you see—you have to let me go.

Every Halloween, you call to me, and I come back because this tether binding us has always been stronger than steel. The pain of it, though, every year it damages me more. Every year, I am less and less of a spirit, and more of a spectral bruise on your chest, stuck between worlds. Your love will fade me into nothing.

The longer I stay attached to you, the more inclined you are to live inside your head with faint memories. There is a world out there, full of things we never got to do. If I beg you to go see all of salty beaches and snow-capped mountains and painted deserts we never experienced, will you listen?

You've made your ghost and summoned me to you so many times. Any more will reduce me to something unable to continue on even in the spirit world. The last candle burns outside of our candy circle, and the blood has stopped flowing from your self-inflicted cut. You've buried the card, and you've poured your grief into the soil and clovers where we used to sit together.

Struggling each day with a ghost latched onto your heart is no way to live. Promise on Samhain that you understand this. You're always welcome in the cemetery down Blue Mountain Lane, always welcome to come whisper "Happy Anniversary" to my headstone on Halloween Night, but never summon me or any other ghost to you again. You won't survive another unmaking.

Blow out the remaining candle.

Find another lightning bolt dress, will you? Remember you have always been electric. I will forever be the storm cloud following you every night, but when the veil closes, let this be the final time.

A Halloween Visit

DANA HAMMER

Gabriella Morrison glared at the selection of candies remaining in the bowl — a few errant candy corns and a leftover candy cane from last year's Christmas. It figured that the children all helped themselves to the good candy, leaving her with the dregs. That's the way children were these days. Selfish.

She set the bowl down on the brightly painted hutch that greeted guests upon entering her home. She pulled her pink silk robe tighter around herself and turned off the porch light. It was past nine o'clock, and the trick-or-treaters would all be heading home now. She slipped off her high-heeled, feathered house slippers and sighed with relief as her feet flattened into the plush, white carpet.

According to her podiatrist, a woman of eighty-seven had no business walking around in high heels. But her podiatrist was a grim, dour woman with a gray-streaked ponytail, despite the fact that she couldn't have been more than forty. The woman wore dowdy, sensible shoes, with plain white sports socks peeking out, and she never, ever wore lipstick.

Overall, it was a look that said, "I dislike sex," and Gabriella did not take fashion advice from such people.

The night was still young enough for a drink before bed. Gabriella put an album on her record player — one of her own. People said it was vain for her to listen to her own music, but Gabriella thought that was nonsense. She had been a gifted jazz singer, and if you don't enjoy your own art, you shouldn't be making any. She poured herself a gin and sipped it as she sank onto her purple chaise lounge, closed her eyes, and hummed along with the song. The lyrics were vapid nonsense about being in love — the usual drivel that ladies sang about in the 1950s — but her voice! The voice was powerful, heavy, and strong. She had been so proud of it. She was still.

Nowadays, her voice was trembly with age. She could still carry a tune, but her singing had none of the command that it once had. It was the great tragedy of her life — that her one great skill had abandoned her.

Of course, her heavy drinking and chain smoking might have been part of the problem, but she preferred to attribute her loss to the cruelties of fate, rather than the pleasures of the flesh. She took a long drink and savored the burn on her useless throat. Happy Halloween to Gabriella Morrison.

The doorbell rang. She sighed, looking at the bowl on the hutch. Should she offer the old, sticky candy cane? It was all she had left, unless the child was partial to gin or cigarettes. She considered ignoring the bell, but then she remembered what had happened the last time she ignored the door on Halloween. The eggs, sticky and tacky, all over her house. What a nightmare it had been to scrub! Or, anyway, she imagined it had been a nightmare for the neighbor girl, who she hired to scrub it.

She got up, smoothing her hair, and putting her slippers on

again. The bell rang one more time, loud and pushy. Gabriella hated doorbells, hated being summoned like a servant, or like a pig to the feeding trough.

She turned on the porch light and opened the door, holding out the bowl. Standing on her porch was a tall child, dressed as the Grim Reaper. His black robe fell all the way to the ground, and his hood was well-crafted, made of high-quality leather, trimmed in…was that fox fur? It was! Gabriella was a woman who knew her furs, and she blinked in surprise to see such a luxurious material used in the construction of a child's Halloween costume.

"I'm sorry, but I don't have much left," she explained, shaking the bowl.

"I'm not here for candy," the child replied. But it was a distinctly un-childlike voice. In fact, it was the voice of a grown woman. And not just any woman – it was the voice of a battle-hardened, commanding woman, like a trauma nurse, or her eighth-grade math teacher.

Confused, Gabriella pulled the bowl back.

"Then I'm afraid I can't help you. It's late, and I'm old, and I've no patience for Halloween pranks."

"Ah. Halloween. Right," said the Grim Reaper. "I see the confusion. You think this is a costume."

"Well, isn't it?"

"No. You see, I am the Grim Reaper. Or, one of them, anyway."

Gabriella rolled her eyes. "I see. Well, good night."

She shut the door, annoyed at the intrusion. She was about to take her slippers off again, when the voice came again, loud and clear, despite the closed door.

"You murdered a woman in 1958."

Gabriella gasped. Images flashed in front of her eyes — the dull blue bus in the pouring rain, dark hair spilling on the pavement, a set of false teeth flying across the street, Marla. Marla Howard. She hadn't allowed herself to think of that name in decades.

She opened the door.

The Grim Reaper stood there, unmoving.

"Do you believe me now?"

"No," replied Gabriella. "But it seems we have things to discuss. Come in."

THE GRIM REAPER took a seat on Gabriella's chaise lounge, sitting straight and pious.

"Excuse me. That's my seat."

"Oh, pardon me."

The Grim Reaper hurriedly got up and moved to the sofa, while Gabriella watched with narrowed eyes. When the Reaper was firmly planted on a floral cushion, Gabriella took her spot, resuming her gin.

"Let's get one thing straight," she told the Reaper. "I didn't murder anyone, and I have no idea what you're talking about."

"You know exactly what I'm talking about," the Reaper replied. "It was 1958. Her name was Marla Howard. You were fucking her husband at the time, and she found out, and was threatening to tell the whole world how you'd slept your way into a record deal."

Gabriella gaped a moment, before regaining her composure.

"Listen to me, Grim Reaper. I don't know who you really are, and I don't know why you're here, but I'm not wealthy. I can't pay you off in any serious way. So, you can make wild accusations all you like, but it won't amount to anything."

"Please, call me Emma."

"What?"

"Emma," said the Grim Reaper, ever so politely. "It's the name I prefer. Grim Reaper sounds so…I don't know. Grim."

"Fine. Emma. Whatever. You've come into my house and told your ridiculous tale. I hope you've amused yourself on this otherwise very dull Halloween night, because amusement is all that you'll get out of this little scheme of yours."

"Why did you invite me in?"

"Morbid curiosity, I suppose."

Emma shook her head, slowly. Gabriella imagined her smirking under her hood.

"No. You invited me in, because you wanted to hear what I had to say. You wanted to know if I had any evidence and what I was planning to do with that evidence. Well, you can rest easy. I have no evidence. Only an eyewitness account."

"Eyewitness. Are you trying to say you were there when this person was murdered?"

"That's exactly what I'm saying. I was the one who took her."

"Took her?"

"Took her soul, I mean. I sent her into the hereafter."

Gabriella gave a mean-spirited laugh. "Oh, this is too much. You're really committed to this character, aren't you?"

"It's not a character."

"Will you take off that stupid mask? Show your face."

"I would, but you wouldn't like what you saw, if I did."

"Why? Is it all worms and scarab beetles under there?"

"You've watched too many horror movies."

"I'm not the one pretending to be the Grim Reaper."

"Emma, if you please. I don't like 'Grim Reaper.'"

"Jesus."

"Emma."

"Oh, for crying out loud."

Gabriella was at her wits' end. Grim Emma had admitted that she had no evidence, which meant she was no threat, which meant that Gabriella wanted her out of her house. Now.

"You want me to leave," said Emma. It was not a question.

"Of course, I want you to leave," snapped Gabriella.

"I can't. Not until I've collected your soul."

"My..."

Suddenly, Gabriella was afraid — the kind of fear that pierced through her gin-soaked bravado. Had she really invited this stranger into her home? She was an eighty-seven-year-old woman. What had she been thinking? This woman was obviously insane, and she was dressed as THE GRIM REAPER.

She got to her feet and headed for the phone.

"I'm calling the police."

But just as she was beginning to take a step, an unseen force shoved her back onto the chaise. Gabriella screamed.

"Quiet," said Emma.

Gabriella quieted but falling back onto chaises was a young woman's game, and her breath came fast, short, and sharp.

"It's normal to be afraid when your time comes. I completely understand. But before I take you, there are some things we need to discuss."

Gabriella's heart was thumping hard in her chest. Was it a heart attack? She wasn't ready!

"You're not having a heart attack," reassured Emma. "You're just panicking. It happens."

Gabriella picked up her gin glass, needed another drink, but the glass was, sadly, empty.

"Now. We need to discuss Marla Howard."

"No!"

"Yes. You see, when a murder occurs, we Reapers have to take the soul, even if it's not the person's time. It wasn't Marla Howard's time yet. There were still many things she needed to accomplish in her life, but you cut it short."

"I didn't—"

"You did, and you might as well stop denying it. I was there, remember? You pushed her in front of that bus."

"Holy shit. Are you really the Grim Reaper?"

"I'm a REAPER, and my name is EMMA."

Emma's shout reverberated through Gabriella's bones, made them vibrate, even though it wasn't particularly loud, as far as shouts go.

"A Reaper. Not The Reaper," Gabriella muttered. "I suppose there are many of you. Or are you 'a' Reaper in the same way that a mall Santa is 'a' Santa? Like, you're one of the Grim Reaper's helpers?"

"Funny. You're a funny lady, Gabriella. But your humor won't save you. Not tonight."

Emma was perfectly, maddeningly still on the couch.

"Will you take off that ridiculous costume?" Gabriella shouted.

"No. First we need to talk."

"It would be easier to talk if I could see your face."

"That is very, very untrue. Trust me."

Gabriella sighed, shaking her head.

"I'm too old for this. I'm too old for these games."

"Yes, you're an old, old lady," mused Emma. "You're lucky. Not everyone gets to be an old, old lady. For instance, Marla Howard never got to be an old, old lady."

All of a sudden, a scepter appeared in her hand. It was long and made of gnarled wood with rubies encrusted on the handle. Gabriella was terrified, but not so terrified that she couldn't appreciate the craftsmanship that went into the creation of such a beautiful piece.

Emma waved the scepter in the air and conjured up an image of Marla. It was made of smoke, or a smoke-like substance, and it swirled in front of Gabriella, mocking her.

Marla had been a plain woman, but stylish, with piercing green eyes, and a boisterous laugh. She'd worn dentures, even though she was only thirty. Rumors said that she kept a pet tiger on their estate and fed it a steady supply of squirrels that she caught in traps. They said she'd tricked her husband, Rex, into marrying her by claiming to be the heiress to a fortune, when she was really just poor white trash with little taste.

When Gabriella had met Rex and Marla, it was clear from the get-go that they were all wrong for each other. Rex was a true gentleman. He worked for a living, running one of the biggest and most successful recording studios in the country. He was all wrong for a trollop like Marla, with her loud voice and wildly gesticulating hands.

Gabriella knew better. She would solve the problem and help her career in the process.

"Do you know how Marla got those dentures?" Emma asked, swirling her scepter to bring Marla's teeth in to focus.

"Bad hygiene, one presumes," said Gabriella.

"No."

Emma swirled the scepter again, and an image of a much younger Marla swirled about. She was maybe fifteen, dressed in shabby, ragged clothing. She stood in front of an even younger girl, who was maybe ten. A large, angry man grabbed at the ten-year-old, and Marla blocked him. With a vicious, huge fist, he punched Marla straight in the mouth, sending her teeth flying.

The image disappeared.

"Why are you showing me this?" Gabriella demanded, angry at being forced to watch something so horrible.

"I'm showing you what kind of person Marla was," Emma explained. "I'm showing you the light that you snuffed from the world."

"She was…"

But Gabriella couldn't finish the sentence. The truth was, she hadn't known Marla all that well. She only knew that she was in the way of the things that Gabriella wanted, and that she threatened to ruin her. Gabriella had been forced to stop her. She'd had no choice.

"Let me show you something."

Again, Emma waved the scepter, and again, an image flickered and swirled in front of Gabriella. This time, it was an older, more mature Marla. She was perhaps fifty years old, and she was standing on a large expanse of grassy plain, looking through a pair of binoculars.

"Marla had a special place in her heart for tigers. Did you know that tigers are endangered?" Emma asked.

"So?"

"So. If you hadn't killed Marla, she would have gone on to create a tiger sanctuary and research center that would not only save endangered tigers, but would promote new understandings of the natural world and inspire a new generation of conservationists. She would have done great things, given enough time."

Gabriella did not care about endangered tigers at all, but she supposed it wouldn't do to express that right then.

"You don't care," sighed Emma, sounding terribly disappointed.

Gabriella did not confirm or deny this statement.

"Fine. You don't care. The point remains. You took her life too early, and so I was called upon to escort her soul. Now it's your time. You've been allowed to live your full lifespan, which is a gift. But because of what you've done, you have to pay the penalty."

"The penalty. At last, we come to the point," grumbled Gabriella. "I told you, I'm not wealthy."."

"I don't want money, you insolent twat!"

Gabriella smirked. "Are Grim Reapers allowed to call people twats?"

"Shut up," snapped Emma. "We need to discuss your penalty."

"What do you want from me?"

"I want you to take over."

There was a long moment of silence while Gabriella processed this.

"I beg your pardon?"

"I want to retire," Emma stated.

"Can Grim Reapers retire?"

"Emma," Emma insisted.

"Okay, can Grim Emmas retire?"

"Fuck you, Gabriella. I'm a Reaper, and I'm here for your soul, and you're being shockingly cavalier about it."

"Forgive me. I find it hard to take you seriously in that ridiculous costume."

"It's not ridiculous, you're ridiculous. And you have to pay the penalty. And the penalty is, you're the next Reaper. I get to go on to the next world, you get to pay off the debt you've incurred with your murdering."

"I'm sorry. This is all just…" Gabriella broke off. She was a cascade of turbulent emotions. Amused, frightened, anxious, angry, and drunk, all at once, shifting like a kaleidoscope.

"This is too much for me. I need another drink and a good night's sleep."

"You're not listening to me, Gabriella. You don't get to sleep anymore. That part's over for you now."

"Because you plan to kill me."

"It's your time," Emma said, simply.

"Well, why can't I just go on to the afterlife, like everyone else? Why do I need to take over your job?"

"Someone has to do it," Emma shrugged, "so it might as well be you. And if you were to go to the afterlife right now, without atoning for your sins, you'd go straight to Hell."

"Hell? Is that a real place? I always assumed it was…I don't know. Metaphorical."

"No, I'm afraid it's quite real, and literal."

Gabriella digested this. "I can't believe this is really happening. Am I in shock? Am I hallucinating? I really don't know how to feel about any of this."

"You don't have to feel any way about this, because it's happening, regardless. You can either go to Hell or become the next Reaper. Your choice."

Gabriella thought for a few moments.

"As a Reaper, would I have to wear that hideous outfit? With the mask and everything?"

"Yes."

Gabriella frowned.

"It's not so bad when you get used to it. Breathy and comfortable. Good in all kinds of weather."

"Fox fur is not for any kind of weather," Gabriella snapped.

"Okay, not that part. Still, you get used to it."

"Well, as a Grim Reaper, where would I live? How would I decide who to kill?"

"You don't kill anyone, you idiot! You just escort their souls."

"Okay, fine, I escort their souls. Where? How do I know

where to take them? How do I travel from place to place? How does any of this work?"

"It'll all be explained during your training."

"There's training?"

"Of course. How else would Reapers learn how to do their jobs?"

"Well, until now, I didn't think Reapers were real, so I guess I haven't given the matter much thought."

"Touché. Anyhow, once you accept, you'll be trained by Exclonicus, the head trainer. You'll be put in a cohort with other Reaper recruits."

"This is insanity."

"It's not. It's just new to you."

Gabriella looked the Grim Reaper over from head to toe. She took in the black garb, the rigid posture, the fancy scepter.

"How long have you been a Reaper?" Gabriella asked.

"Too long," replied Emma.

"But how long?"

"Long enough to be tired of it."

"How did you get to be a Reaper? Were you like me? Did you...hurt someone?"

Gabriella hesitated to admit to her guilt, but she supposed it was past the point of secrecy. Emma clearly knew everything. Now they were just hammering out the details.

"I don't care to speak of it. Maybe some other time."

Gabriella didn't like being put off. She didn't like this woman who burst into her home, made accusations, threatened to kill her, and tried to force her to be the Grim Reaper. Gabriella didn't like one single thing about any of this.

"You know what, Grim Reaper?"

"Emma."

"Get out of my house."

"We've had this discussion, Gabriella."

"We have. And you know what I've decided?"

"What?"

"Fuck you. That's what I've decided."

"Classy," snarked Emma.

"I'll show you classy," snapped Gabriella. And with that, she hurled herself at Grim Reaper, with all the strength that her frail, old, skinny, drunk body could muster.

Emma, taken by surprise, failed to block Gabriella's hand, as it reached up and pulled off her mask.

Gabriella looked straight into the naked, unprotected face of Death. She saw it in all its shining, twisting, maddening glory. She took it all in for one bleak, soul-shattering moment.

And immediately fell down dead.

EMMA STARED down at the corpse, dejected. She had already delivered the soul to Hell, and now had some time to kill before her next job. She played the record that Gabriella had been playing when Emma had interrupted her. It really was a remarkably good album.

Gabriella had been a talented woman, once. She could have succeeded all on her own, with nothing more than her talent. It was a shame she'd felt the need to be so vicious and cruel in her machinations to reach the top.

Emma was tired. She'd been in the Reaper business since 1740, which was longer than most Reapers lasted. The only Reaper she knew who'd been doing this longer was Reginald, whose big claim to fame was that he escorted the soul of William Shakespeare. He talked about it. Often.

Emma had really thought that Gabriella was it, that she would take the offer, and allow Emma to finally retire. Stupid old woman. What a waste.

There was a knock on the door. A voice yelled "TRICK OR TREAT!"

Ah. Halloween. Right.

Emma spied the candy bowl on the table and noted its sad, disgusting contents. She waved her scepter and added a few things; candy bars, chocolate truffles, toffees. She put on her hood again and answered the door.

Standing there was a young man, far too old for trick-or-treating, but it wasn't her business to tell children how to spend their holidays. However, there was something unnerving in this boy's eyes, something cold and glinting and blade-like.

All at once, she understood who she was looking at. Images flashed in her mind. Cemeteries, corpses, crematories, tombstones, formaldehyde. Curious, she tilted her head, watching as he rifled around in the candy bowl, looking for the best treat.

"You're interested in death," she said to the young man. It was not a question.

He stopped his searching hand and looked at her quizzically.

"You look up information about it. You want to be a funeral director when you grow up. A rather unusual choice of profession for a young man."

He looked at her with alarm.

"How do you—"

"It's not important how I know. The important thing is that I do know. And if you come inside, I have an interesting proposition for you."

The man-child looked at her with suspicion.

"I'm perfectly harmless," she said, shrugging. "But I understand your hesitation. Perhaps we can meet another time and place? A restaurant maybe?"

The boy took a moment to consider this, then made up his mind. "No, it's okay. We can talk now."

Emma smiled beneath her hood and opened the door, allowing the boy to enter. She was delighted to have made his acquaintance — so young, so full of enthusiasm for the art of caring for the dead. She would have the deal sealed by morning.

She hoped he wouldn't be frightened by the corpse on the floor.

Bootsy's House

DENNIS K. CROSBY

"I can't believe you got me up in this damned house, man," said Justus.

"Bruh, chill. It's just a house…with a small fortune hidden in it," said Damon with a grin.

"Last dude that came up in here ain't right no mo'."

"Who? Miles? Mannnn, please. He was a two-bit hustler who got in over his head and got himself caught. We too good for all that nonsense. We got this."

In the kitchen of one of the most beautiful and notorious homes in Hyde Park, an affluent neighborhood just south of downtown Chicago, Justus stood next to Damon. They'd taken four steps in, after a suspiciously easy break-in, stopped, and stared. The kitchen was large, old, yet still seemed functional. For the briefest moment, Justus wondered how many people it took to staff the place.

"Yeah, he got caught. Got caught and been mumblin' Boo-boo-Bootsy's comin' ever since. He's in the psych unit at Cook County, man. They're gonna send him to Elgin soon," said Justus.

"He wasn't right *before* he went in there either," said Damon.

"C'mon, man. He was fine, and you know it."

"So, what? You think the place is haunted, too?" Damon waved his hand in front of his nose after opening the refrigerator.

"Look, all I know is, he was cool, he came in this house, and now he ain't."

"Well, I also know there's a bunch of money in here that nobody's found. So, you wanna go get it? Or you wanna run and hide cuz you think Old Man Bootsy is up in here hauntin' the place and driving people crazy wit' some stupid ghostly revenge plot?"

A beat passed before Damon continued.

"Dude, just imagine what's in here? You know the stash Charlie Mack had. Everybody knows. And it's here, sittin' by itself, with noooooobody around. Brotha, this is the easiest score we'll ever have. You can't be seriously afraid of some stupid silly ghost stories, man. C'mon wit' cho' Run-DMC-shirt-wearing ass."

Justus walked through the kitchen, absently touching surfaces as if he expected the house to respond in some way. He'd already gone further than he'd planned with this partnership. He thought maybe he'd do this stuff once, twice at the most, out of loyalty. But Damon had a way of just talking him into things. It wasn't that he was weak or skittish. It wasn't that Damon was powerful or overbearing. Justus simply wasn't an alpha. Damon, though? Damon could sell ice cream in Antarctica during a snowstorm and come away with a small fortune. Everything that came out of that guy's mouth slid through the ears like soft butter on a hot tortilla.

Justus was content with their current arrangement. Scope out a house in the suburbs, hit it while the family was out, and go home. Not like a Cicero home, or Berwyn. Not even Oak Park or River Forest. Those were too close to the city. They'd scoped out homes in Barrington Hills and Highland Park, even spots in Schaumburg brought in good hauls. Distance didn't matter. They'd more than cover their gas money with the stash. They'd been doing it for almost a year, and it was working just fine. This arrangement, though, came with one hard and fast rule.

Stay away from the hood.

Especially Bootsy's house.

Damon was hard to turn down, though. Everyone in the neighborhood knew that if Damon actually applied himself to something good, something legal, he'd be unstoppable. He could turn heads and sway minds. Instead, he opted to focus his strengths on burglaries. And now, Damon was in a haunted house on Halloween.

And as usual, Justus was about to say yes.

"Fine," said Justus. "Let's go get this paper."

"Ha! My man!"

After a break-in that required nothing more than a pair of bolt cutters, Justus and Damon left the kitchen and stepped into the hallway that would lead them further into the three-story mansion that was once the home of Bootsy Robinson. Businessman. Philanthropist. Family man.

And the most notorious serial killer no one ever knew about.

WITH EACH STEP, the history of Bootsy's house ran through Justus' mind. He tried to block it out, but it wouldn't go away. Bootsy's house was every bit a Chicago legend as Mrs. O'Leary's cow, the Curse of the Billy Goat, or the devil child living in Jane Addams' Hull House. Now, he was inside it. Inside the haunted Hyde Park mansion. How could its history not creep around in his head?

"Dude, this place is almost one hundred years old," said Justus. "It was built in the 1920s for the Elstons."

"You giving me a history lesson? Now?" Damon turned to give Justus a side eye and sneer.

"I'm just sayin'," said Justus, shrugging.

"You ain't sayin' nothing I don't know. It was a family of nine from London. I know this. Forrest Elston was a physician, and his wife was the daughter of some king or junk like that."

"He was an earl," corrected Justus.

"Yeah, well, Earl's playin' by himself, man." Damon snickered.

The reference wasn't lost on Justus. It just wasn't the time. He didn't want to be here. But he was torn between common sense and loyalty. He liked the thrill. He liked the money, a lot. The son of a single mom who worked three jobs to care for him, Justus had grown up struggling, so cash was a big pull for him.

As they walked through the main hall, Justus caught a glimpse of a portrait—Lady Jane Elston. She seemed *grand*, as old people called her. Looked a little stuffy, but then again, she was royalty. Well-removed from the line of succession to the British throne, but she was, nonetheless, on the list. As he stared at the portrait, the face transitioned momentarily. One moment, it was Lady Jane, and the next, a flaming skull.

The skull exploded from the portrait, came directly at Justus, and in an instant, he jumped back and yelped.

"Dude! What is wrong with you?" Damon helped Justus regain his balance.

Justus was pressed up against the wall, chest heaving, tongue dry, staring at the portrait of Lady Jane, which now seemed fine. It was unchanged, though he could have sworn she hadn't been smiling when he'd first laid eyes on it.

"I, uh...thought I saw a spider," said Justus.

"A spider? Bruh?"

"Naw, man, like one of them big ones, with hair and all the eyes and stuff. It was…it was…big. And hairy."

He wasn't looking at Damon, but Justus could sense his friend's disapproving head shake. He gathered himself, turned, and walked down the hallway with Damon in search of riches. A part of him marveled at the home. Bootsy's house sat on the corner of Lake Shore Drive and a street that had changed names so many times, the street marker was simply gone. With an unobstructed view of Lake Michigan, the Elstons, and later Bootsy himself, likely spent a great deal of family time near the window. When the Elstons owned the place, Bootsy, then a child, was the maid's son, so they may have even allowed him to enjoy the view as a boy.

Until he became old enough to work for them, of course.

The story of Theodore "Bootsy" Robinson, shared later in life, was that he loved that house. He loved the Elstons, too, until they reminded him that he was not, in fact, family, or even a friend. He'd gone on record saying the disdain the Elstons had shown once he came of age fueled him to excel in everything he did. He'd left his mother to attend school. He'd graduated at the top of his class, got a great job working in real estate development, and only returned to Chicago to attend his mother's funeral. In his book, Bootsy said that he was in attendance along with his wife, Elouise, and their three children. Bootsy's father had never been around, and all the family from his mother's side was either dead, too poor to travel, or simply uninterested in visiting the Windy City in winter. And the Elstons, the family that had employed his mother for over forty-five years, were nowhere to be found.

That hadn't sat well with him.

People who'd heard that story thought many parts of it were sad and strange. Some details stuck out more than others. Like the fact that, despite being grown, most of the children of the Elston family had remained in the home well into adulthood. Stranger still was the fact that they'd all seemed to simply move out overnight. Of course, the real kicker was Bootsy's decision to buy the home and move his family in at the alleged written request of Forrest Elston.

It was all so very strange.

Until they'd found the Elston family buried beneath the home.

After that, it was no longer strange and more a tale of vengeance. A week later they'd found Bootsy's journal where he described, in detail, how he psychologically tortured the Elstons. He wanted them weakened. He wanted them afraid. He wanted them helpless. He wanted them feeling everything he and his mother had felt when they'd lived and worked in the house. Only when he was satisfied with their pain did he put them out of their misery.

Many believed his ghost continued that legacy.

DAMON WASN'T foolish or ignorant. The story of Bootsy's house ran through his mind, too. But he'd had this plan in mind for a while. Charlie Mack had robbed a bank in Oak Park five years ago and gotten away with over six hundred thousand dollars in cash. He'd crossed over into Chicago before the bank got wind. Once he had some distance, he hid. He hid in Bootsy's house. The place was massive, and there had to be plenty of places to stash himself and the money. It was a three-story wonder made of gray stone. The largest window on the lower level faced Lake Michigan. The side of the home that faced a now unnamed street had a large window overlooking the gated front yard. The top of the home was flat, not steepled, and seemed to have an attic. But the place had been abandoned for years.

Ever since Bootsy's long-lost great-grandson, Theodore the Fourth, made the horrific discovery in the basement.

While the courts held the fate of the house in limbo, it sat empty with the echo of blood and terror reverberating off the homes and vehicles on the block. It was the perfect place for Charlie Mack to hide. Or so he'd thought. When they found him a few days later, he was catatonic, murmuring Bootsy's name. Just like Miles.

And no one ever found the money.

So, while outside the neighborhood kids were just starting to go door-to-door in a trick-or-treat frenzy with their parents, he and Justus searched for cash. They ignored the crystal vase that sat upon the mantle in the foyer, the Picasso and Monet, the glass case near the entryway to the family room containing a colonial pistol set. Etched in the brass plate on the wood box the pistols were set in were the words, "Property of Aaron Burr." There were riches in Bootsy's House that Damon never imagined.

But he was determined to find the cash.

Fortunately, they wouldn't be bothered. It was Halloween, for one. People were very busy. Also, the entire property was gated. A six-foot fence of wrought iron surrounded the home, with ornate gates on the front and back. Both gates were chained and padlocked by order of the court until final disposition of the home had been decided. It was both a crime scene and a landmark. The courts were tasked with trying to determine which moniker was more important. If it were the latter, it would stand a testament to Chicago architecture, though with a seriously tainted reputation. If it were the former, it would fall, and the property would go up for auction to whomever decided to take a chance on the location.

Damon could understand why the city wanted to keep it. What he couldn't understand was why they did so little to secure it. When they'd arrived, Damon and Justus used simple bolt cutters to take off the chain to the back gate and had quietly slipped inside the property. They were stunned to find that the back door effortlessly swung open as they approached it. Damon chalked that up as wind, too.

That should have been his first clue to leave.

JUSTUS.

Come here.

"What the hell was that?" Justus whirled around.

"Dude. Chill. It was just wind. This house is old. Lots of cracks in the walls and windows," Damon lied.

"Bruh, that wasn't no wind. Somebody said my name."

Damon shook his head in an attempt to brush it off and move on. On one hand, he started to wish he'd come in alone. Justus was a good friend and a good partner and lookout. They'd done some solid jobs together over the last year. But it was clear to Damon that Justus would never be the brains of the operation. It wasn't that he was stupid. It really had to do with the fact that he lacked imagination and guts. Justus would always play it safe, hit the houses that had little reward and because of that, he'd never get the big bucks. Damon had the imagination to think big and go big. And there was nothing bigger than Booty's house.

Damon also had ears.

He heard the voice.

But there was no way he'd tell Justus that. He was not

going to jeopardize this score by admitting that the place might actually be haunted.

"Ain't nobody here but us, man. Now chill out. The faster we get this money, the faster we get out," said Damon, continuing on.

Damon believed that statement. And given what he'd just heard, he leaned into that statement a little harder. He didn't believe in ghosts and haunted houses and such. But a part of him was afraid that maybe, just maybe, they believed in him.

"Do you even know where we should be lookin'?" asked Justus.

"I told you, man—in the upstairs study."

"Yeah, but do you know where that is?"

"It's upstairs, fool!"

He knew what Justus meant, but he was annoyed, and maybe a little scared by the voice he'd heard. Everyone knew the stories about this place. He couldn't let that deter—

CRASH!

Damon froze in place, his heart stopping then beating again. His lungs were desperate for air after holding his breath for minutes on end. He crouched a bit, trying to stay undercover. Nobody else was there except Justus.

Justus.

Why was he so quiet?

"Bruh, before you even say it, I'm sure it's just something that fell. This place is old, man. Walls are weak."

Damon's words were met with silence and another crash in the distance. It seemed to come from upstairs toward the back of the house. The same place they needed to go to reach the study.

"Dude? Justus?"

Damon turned to regard his friend. The frightened naysayer was abnormally quiet. He wasn't quite sure of what to make of what he saw. Justus, felonious partner and reluctant ally in their latest endeavor, was gone.

"Bro? Dude, where you at?"

Damon backtracked down the hallway looking for any spot Justus may have wandered into. The old wooden floor gave way to his weight and let out an exhausted squeal, causing Damon to stop, regroup, and travel slower. For all his talk about them being the only two people in Bootsy's house, events of the last few minutes left him wondering.

Even now, back near the entryway, there was no sign of Justus. Had he just left? How could he just disappear? The guy was literally right behind him. With the way the floors creaked, Damon would have heard him taking off. He craned his neck, listening for the slightest sound. He heard nothing. But what he felt was a different story altogether.

Along his arm, something moved, crawled, slowly, deliberately. He swatted at it. The feeling returned, and when he looked down, there was nothing, yet the sensation was there. It moved up his arm to the back of his neck and lingered. He brushed his hand over it, swatted, and still it lingered, as if someone were deliberately teasing him with a feather, but there was no one.

"Gah!" shouted Damon, as he twirled and spun, arms flailing, desperate to get the invisible bugs off. "Justus?" he whispered breathlessly, suddenly feeling that maybe they weren't alone after all.

Damon turned and jumped back with a loud scream. Justus had finally reappeared. His partner stood there, staring, silent, almost lifeless. And he was…blinking. Not with his eyes, but his entire body. Justus's whole shape was blinking in and out like a television desperate to find a signal on a channel that had not been paid for. Damon swayed, as his legs lost strength. Clouds of vapor escaped his mouth, as he breathed, rapidly, in sync with his heartbeat. Hairs on his arms stood at attention and he felt warm liquid sliding down his inner thigh. As Justus blinked in and out, lights flickered from the vintage fixtures, and another crash came from elsewhere. This time, in the large family room to his left, followed by a low, lingering wail.

Get awaaaaaaay!

"B-b-bruh! Stop playin'!" pleaded Damon. "Come on man, stop. You got me, all right."

Damon watched his partner's head spin around completely. Then Justus smiled. A wide, toothless grin, with black sludge slipping past his lips to his chin.

"Oh, hell no!" Damon screamed.

Sprinting past his ghostly friend, away from the crash in the family room, Damon ran down the long hallway until he found the staircase leading up to the second level. He paused long enough to look back to see if anything was behind him. Surprisingly, there was nothing. Nothing. Not even Justus. Turning to look ahead, he found Justus again, down the hallway, toward the rear of the house, gesturing him to come forward.

Still blinking in and out of sync.

"What the..." He stared at the illusion, his knees weakening.

Time seemed to stand still as Damon weighed his options. Follow the gesturing apparition that resembled his friend, or turn back, rush out of the house, and hope to avoid whatever made the noise in the front room? As he quickly ran through the possibilities, his name floated in the air from down the hall in a voice that seemed old, strained, and pained. It was angry, evil, and carried a malevolence in its tone that was unmistakable.

Damon!

Come here!

"Option three, it is!"

Damon sprinted up the stairs.

At the top of the stairs, Damon stopped to look back. It was the one thing you were not supposed to do in horror movies, but you also weren't supposed to run up the stairs of a house that was disproving your assertion that it was not haunted. He saw nothing coming up after him. Peering around, he saw nothing real, imagined, or otherworldly that would keep him from moving on. From what he recalled of the plans of the house, Bootsy's study was down the hall on the left. He wanted out, but the money was right there, it had to be. Six hundred thousand dollars. And he'd be the one person that scored from Bootsy's house. After all this, he couldn't come away with nothing. Scared, yet stubborn and determined, he moved in the direction of the study.

More portraits hung on the wall, framed black-and-white photos of Bootsy and his wife, Elouise. Curiosity had led Damon down the life of crime, and recent activities did not seem to cure that personality trait. He stopped to look closer. Damon recognized them from the pictures in the paper and the back of Bootsy's autobiography, a book he'd written while still respectable…and alive.

The photo showed the Robinsons standing in front of the mansion with their young children. They seemed happy. They seemed…righteous, for lack of a better word. Damon stepped closer to the photo, as something in the background caught his eye. Something in the window on the second level. Seemed to be someone looking out. No, it was a someone screaming. The person was…moving. The person was alive.

The person was him.

"What the…?"

Damon watched himself bang on the glass and scream in a

decades-old photo, as a shadow descended upon him in the background. He watched his face grow slack, press against the glass, and slide down. The shadow behind him descended on him, as it took shape. The form was familiar. It had turned into a tall, slender, Black man with short hair and a light beard. He was wearing a black Run-DMC T-shirt.

"Justus?"

"Yeah, bro."

Damon spun around and found his partner, his friend, standing behind him. He was solid now, not blinking like the old rabbit-eared thirteen-inch TV in the kitchen of his grandma's house on the west side of the city. It was Justus. But at the same time, it wasn't. Something was off.

"Dude. Wh-wh-what happened? Where did you go?"

"I've been here the whole time. Bro," said Justus.

"Why you say it like that, man?"

"Like what? Bro."

What Damon saw next made him regret every decision he'd ever made in his felonious life. It was no longer Justus' entire body blinking in and out. Now, it was just his head. One minute, he wore his normal face, and in the next, it was the darkened, sinister face of Theodore "Bootsy" Robinson. Bootsy smiled and snarled, then Justus returned with a similar look. Bootsy's mouth opened wide, like a snake unhinging its jaws, then transformed back into Justus. As the faces alternated, Justus' body suddenly lunged at Damon, who'd backed up against the wall of portraits, which all began to rattle against the sturdy structure. The lights flickered, and wind howled through the halls.

Damon ducked under Justus' lunge, shifted his weight, and took off down the hall. He ran into the first open room he could find and slammed the door shut. There was a lock on the door, and he fumbled with it before finally getting it secured.

"Damon!" Justus screamed in a hideous, otherworldly voice.

The door rattled. The walls continued to shake, and the lights came to life only to die, repeatedly. Damon spun in a circle trying to figure out what his next move should be. He had to get out, he knew it, he wanted it, with or without the cash. But then, he spotted it—a bag on the desk in the corner caught his eye.

It was a brown leather mail bag. He moved toward it as if called to it. Standing over it, he reached out, hesitant at first, then excited as he caught a glimpse of greenish white paper sticking out of the edge. Flipping back the top, he stared inside at the treasure he'd been seeking. On the other side of the desk were four more bags.

"Holy—"

Damon's dread turned to a huge smile then back again, as the door burst open. In the doorway stood Justus—at least, it was his body. Every fiber of Damon's being knew the truth. It was the eyes that gave it away. The same eyes he saw in the black-and-white photo. Justus was gone.

That was Bootsy Robinson standing there.

Damon ran to the window and tried to open it, hoping to crawl to the roof and jump to safety. But it was locked. Outside he saw dozens of kids with their parents, trick-or-treating. He banged on the glass and screamed, hoping to break it. He prayed that, at the very least, the sound might carry to the street. But in a city like Chicago, in a neighborhood like this, a block from Lake Shore Drive, on a cool Halloween night…no one could hear his screams as the dark shadow came at him from behind.

. . .

"YOU HEARD what happened in that house last year on Halloween night? And the one before that? Dude, you could not pay me enough to go in there," said Justus.

"Dude, stop. Damon Stuckey was good, but not good enough to not get caught. And don't get me started on Miles Jenkins. He was way out of his league trying to hit that house."

"Maaaan, that's Bootsy's house. Both of them got caught and came out of there mumbling something 'bout Bootsy comin'. That's not a coincidence, man. That's a warning."

I'm tellin' you, we got nothing to worry about. The place is empty. And it's Halloween night, the best time to go. The neighborhood is too busy, and they're gonna avoid this spooky house like the plague. We pop in, find the cash Charlie Mack left in there years ago, pop out, and we'll be at the Zanzibar with the ladies in no time."

Ricky Timms crossed the street and walked toward Bootsy's house, as neighborhood kids began to trick-or-treat. Justus watched him then looked up at the top window of the old three-story city mansion. The figure behind the glass looked down, watching Ricky walk toward the rear of the home. He then turned his attention to Justus and smiled.

Once again, Justus had already gone further than he'd planned. After his initial discovery, he thought maybe he'd do this stuff once, twice at the most, out of loyalty. Now, though, he was starting to enjoy it. Maybe it was genetic.

Justus smiled back.

"See you soon, Great-Granddad," he whispered to himself.

Theodore Robinson the Fourth, known to all only as Justus, crossed the street after Ricky Timms and headed for Bootsy's house.

Soul Cakes

CATHERINE MCCARTHY

"I remember the very first time we made soul cakes, Nan," I say.

Nan dons an apron printed with a charm of miniature bees. Her kitchen is a hive of activity and the heart of the home. Always has been. She wears a wistful expression, wanting to hear more.

"I was around the age of five," I go on, "and me and Granddad had spent the morning planting crocus bulbs in the back garden."

At the mention of his name, she pulls out a lace handkerchief and blows her nose. She loves to reminisce but doing so always makes her tearful. I study her face. Skin like parchment. Gossamer, as if it might tear at any moment. Her pale blue eyes are rheumy and clouded by cataracts, but her mind's still sharp as a pin.

I lean against the kitchen sink, watching her wipe down the table, as she waits for me to continue. "My nails were caked with dirt, and you stood me on a stool in front of this sink and scrubbed them clean with a little yellow nail brush shaped like a duck."

I tilt my head back and sniff the air—Imperial Leather, the brand of soap with a little paper label stuck to its middle. Nan's favourite. A glance at the soap dish tells me she still uses it. What remains of the soap bar is cracked, just like her skin. She won't replace it, though, not until it's a tiny sliver of a thing. Thrifty, is Nan.

"'A good baker always starts with spotless hands and nails,' you said to me."

She smiles and hobbles over to the store cupboard. No recipe. Nan instinctively knows which ingredients she needs to make the cakes. Her back is turned to me, and I note the stoop in her shoulders, see how her spine has shortened and twisted with arthritis.

"Caster sugar, flour, raisins." Her voice is as fragile as eggshell but sweet as honey. One at a time, she takes down the jars and carries them over to the farmhouse table in both hands like a child. The fingers on her left hand curl towards the wrist, gnarled knuckles and skin speckled with liver spots. I would offer to help, but she's fiercely independent.

Butter and milk from the fridge, plus two eggs from a chicken-shaped receptacle that sits on the worktop. It clucks as she removes the lid, and we chuckle like a pair of old hens. A favourite item of mine as a child, I'm surprised it still works after all these years.

From the spice rack, she selects a little jar of allspice and another containing strands of saffron. "My own special ingredient," she whispers. "A peace offering to a dying sun god." It amuses me no end, Nan's devout Catholicism, sprinkled with a hint of pagan.

"When I was a little girl, I wouldn't touch saffron," I say. "It reminded me of sinew, like corned beef." I shudder. "But you explained how saffron was made from the stigma of crocus flowers, not flesh. You know me, Nan, I've always been a picky eater."

She focuses on lining the baking tray with parchment and says nothing.

For many years, until I went away to university, Nan and I would make soul cakes on Halloween, or Nos Calan Gaeaf – Night Before Winter – as it's known here in Wales. Nan has her own word for it, though – Ysbrydnos – Night of the Spirits. Ysbrydnos—the one night of the year when the barrier between the living and the dead is rice-paper thin.

When I was a little girl, she would tell me stories of Ysbrydnos, such as the naming of the stones. She spoke of how all the villagers would write their names on a stone before throwing it onto the bonfire. Of how the following morning the ashes would be inspected, and if your stone was missing, your death was imminent.

And then, of course, there were the stories of ghosts, far too many to remember, though none of them fazed me. In fact, I found them comforting. The thought of a lost loved one being close again warmed my heart. If Granddad's spirit is able to visit, it will do so tonight. It does not frighten me in the least. In fact, I'd love to see him one more time, especially as I didn't get to say goodbye. I don't think Nan could bear to part with him again, though. Perhaps she'd go with him this time. My throat constricts, and a tear threatens at the thought. I'm feeling nostalgic today. Here in Nan's kitchen, nothing changes —it simply ages. Gets a little more worn around the edges with each passing year.

I watch her sprinkle a dusting of flour on the table. Late afternoon sun sits low in the sky, streaming in at the window and highlighting the tiny white particles in the air. She watches them float downwards, and I know she, too, is thinking of

Granddad, hoping his spirit is with us. Ashes to ashes, dust to dust. Then she rolls up her sleeves and begins.

Butter cubed, golden sugar weighed, she creams them together with a wooden spoon until the mixture is light and fluffy. No fancy food processor for Nan. She's old-school. Skinny forearms, veined and bruised, struggle with the effort, but the frown on her face proves she won't let it beat her. She pauses every few minutes to dab at the sweat on her brow. She seems anxious today, troubled. Perhaps she'll open up later, once we're sitting with tea and cake.

"I wonder if we'll have many callers tonight, Nan? Kids these days expect shop-bought candy, not homemade cakes."

She's concentrating on separating the eggs, so doesn't answer. The tip of her tongue pokes between her lips. Focused. It's a habit I've inherited.

Once all the ingredients are combined, she rolls the dough and cuts a dozen little rounds with a cookie cutter, marking each with a cross before placing them on a baking tray. As she opens the oven door, the warmth from the old Rayburn envelops us in a warm blanket. She stoops and places the baking tray inside, then straightens and makes the sign of the cross—forehead, chest, left shoulder, right shoulder, uttering the words, "Father, Son and Holy Spirit," in the hope that the Lord will prevail and the cakes will come out of the oven crisp and evenly baked. I can't help but smile; minutes earlier she offered peace to a dying sun god.

I step aside for her to get to the sink. Needless to say, she has no dishwasher. The kitchen window overlooks the back garden, and while she washes up, she glances now and then in the direction of Granddad's greenhouse and sighs. I picture him, too—Wellington boots, straw hat, and a smile as wide as the ocean.

"You coming out the garden with Grampy, Bethan?" he'd

say, and I'd jump at the chance. He taught me how to sow vegetable seeds, how best to help pollinate tomatoes, but it was the story of the Robin's pincushion I liked best. A prickly gall, caused by the larvae of a tiny wasp on the stems of his dog roses.

"Why's it called that?" I remember asking him.

"What? Robin's pincushion?" He'd squatted over the rose, pretending the pin-like prickles had stung his bottom. "Now, imagine I'm a robin," he'd said, laughing. "Robin's pincushion —get it?"

I didn't like the thought of a robin getting stung, so I'd imagined squeezing the gall between my fingers and watching the wriggly grubs oozing from within before squishing them. I didn't tell him, though. Granddad would not have approved of such violence.

Nan opens the oven door, and the smell of freshly-baked cakes wafts towards me. A buttery, cinnamon scent promises sweetness, and my mouth waters. "Put the kettle on, Nan," I say, and she does. From the dresser, she retrieves two bone china cups, saucers, and matching plates and adds milk to both cups. I've drunk mine black since Uni, but she's forgotten. Tempted though I am, I know for a fact that if I were to lean over and steal a cake off the cooling rack, she'd flip me on the hand. "You'll burn your mouth, Bethan," she'd say, so I shove my hands into the pockets of my jeans and wait.

As the kettle whistles, there's a gentle tap on the back door.

"Gwen? It's only me." Nan's old friend, Dilys, pops her head round and enters without waiting for an invite. My heart sinks. I didn't know she was expecting visitors. Once Dilys starts talking, there's no stopping her, and I had hoped to have Nan to myself today.

"Come in, come in," Nan says. "It's lovely to see you." Dilys wraps her arms around her. I watch, dumbstruck, as

Nan's chin quivers and her shoulders heave. Whatever is the matter? I take two steps towards her, but what she says next stops me in my tracks.

"I still can't accept she's gone, Dilys. Twenty-five years old, her whole life ahead of her." She collapses onto a chair, and I find myself falling down a dark tunnel, a bottomless one, it seems. Arms flailing, feet desperate to find purchase, the tunnel walls are black as coal. Down and down I go, my cry of despair echoing in the void. Snow-white words tumble with me, appearing out of nowhere and disappearing before I have time to digest them. Words like *fatally injured, lorry collision, student dead.* I try to grab them as I fall, wishing to crush the lies they speak, just as I would have crushed the prickly gall for hurting the robin, but they slip through my fingers like a knife through butter.

I hit the bottom, and the impact severs the junction between my spine and brain stem in one fell swoop. The world as I know it turns black.

THE WITCHING HOUR is upon us, and the boundary between my new existence and my grandmother's is as transparent as a tulle mourning veil.

The comforting scent of sugar and spice still lingers in the air, and the realization that I never got to taste my last soul cake fills me with sadness. Ridiculous, I know. The house is pitch-black. Silent, too, apart from the ticking of the grandfather clock in the hall. *Tick-tock, tick-tock,* the rhythm of a heart that no longer beats.

I require no light to guide me to her room. In death, such things are mere fripperies. I stand at the foot of her bed, watching her sleep. A blanketed bundle and a tuft of silver hair, as innocent as a newborn lamb. My death has broken her heart, of that there is no doubt.

I wander over to her side, leaving no imprint on the deep-pile carpet. On the cabinet sits a lamp with a tasseled shade, her spectacles, and a funereal order of service with my photo on the front. I'm wearing a bridesmaid dress, and my hair is coiffed in an elaborate updo. It feels like yesterday, my cousin Sian's wedding. Such happy memories. I close my eyes and think back, finding myself immersed in a swirling bowl of peaches and cream. A champagne fizz of excitement.

I pick up the pamphlet, curious to read the details. The inscription beneath the photo reads:

In Loving Memory of
Bethan Williams
1st April 1996 to 10th October 2021

Three weeks spent in purgatory, according to my Catholic upbringing, though I never did believe a word of it. I know in my heart that it took me three weeks to accept what has happened, that's all. And it was Nan and her soul cakes that triggered the acceptance.

I look down at her face. Even in sleep she frowns. Her old soul is troubled, and I would give anything to free it from torment. I kneel beside the bed, her dandelion breath cool against my cheek, and plant the lightest of kisses on her forehead.

"Thank you for everything, Nan," I whisper, though there is no need to lower my voice.

She issues a little moan, and for a moment I fear I've disturbed her, then her frown disappears and her face relaxes. Her right arm is free of the blankets, fingers curled in tension. Gently, I lift her hand and hold it in mine.

"See you soon, Nan," I whisper. "But not too soon, I hope. You have a few more years of soul cakes to bake yet."

Sensing a gentle hand on my shoulder, I turn. "Ready to come to the garden with Grampy?" he says. His hair is the colour of frost on a windowpane, his smile still as wide as the ocean.

I get to my feet, take hold of his outstretched hand, and together we step into the light.

Ghosts of Candies Past

JEFF STRAND

My kids were old enough to go trick-or-treating by themselves, but I still went through their bag of candy before they were allowed to eat any of it. This was partly to make sure none of it appeared to have been tampered with, and partly because as the person who provided my pre-teen children with food and shelter, I got first dibs on the really good stuff.

Moni and Tim emptied their plastic jack-o'-lanterns onto the kitchen counter, being careful to keep their stashes separate. They'd managed to acquire a tremendous amount of candy in just a couple of hours—I admired their ambition.

One very large piece in Moni's pile caught my attention. "Oh, wow, did they bring those back?" I asked, picking up the Marathon Bar. The red and yellow packaging had a ruler on the side, showing that it was eight inches long. I called out to my wife: "Hey, do you remember Marathon Bars?"

"What?" Becky called back from the living room.

"Marathon Bars."

"What's a Marathon Bar?"

"Never mind." I looked at Moni. "They had these when I

was a kid. It's chocolate-covered caramel in the shape of braids. The whole idea was that it took a really long time to eat one, so you were getting your money's worth."

My dear children looked at me as if I were much, *much* older than them.

Speaking of the getting your money's worth, it said "15 cents" right there on the wrapper. I wondered if this was some sort of nostalgic pricing promotion. Maybe that was why a household was giving away full-sized candy like they were millionaires.

Then I noticed the 3 Musketeers bar, which had old-timey packaging and was *huge*. A great big slab of a candy bar. "And that's a vintage 3 Musketeers," I told my unimpressed offspring. "This is how they used to do it. Three candy bars in one. Three different flavors. That's why it was called 3 Musketeers."

"How do you know this stuff?" Moni asked.

"I'm not sure. Read it somewhere."

"*Why* do you know this stuff?" Tim asked.

"There's nothing wrong with acquiring information." I picked up another candy bar, called Chicken Dinner. Five cents. "This one hasn't been around since the 1960s, I think. There's no actual chicken in it."

I frowned as I looked through the rest of their stash. This was all old candy. Not just the stuff that wasn't made anymore, like Bonkers! and Sugar Mamas. Candies like Hershey's bars and M&M's had old-style wrappers.

"How many houses did you go to?" I asked.

Moni and Tim shrugged.

"Give it your best guess."

"I don't know," said Moni. "A hundred?"

"You trick-or-treated at a hundred different houses, and every single one of them gave you old-time candy?"

Becky finally walked into the kitchen. "What's going on?"

"Look at their stash," I said. "They're saying that a hundred different homes gave out candy with vintage packaging. How is that possible?"

"Dad's acting weird," Moni informed Becky.

"I'm not acting weird. I'm pointing out a weird occurrence. I get that I'm the only one in this house geriatric enough to have ever heard of a Marathon Bar, but I can't believe I'm the only one who's a little freaked out by this. Are we the only house in the neighborhood that didn't give out retro candy?"

"Are you kids pranking your father?" asked Becky.

Tim shook his head. "If I was going to play a joke, it would be funnier."

I wasn't sure how much this should be messing with my mind. It was, after all, just candy. Maybe everybody else knew that it was the Halloween of nostalgic candy, and I simply hadn't been paying attention.

"Are you done yet?" asked Moni. "You're just supposed to be checking it for razor blades."

"Hold on a second," I said. I wanted to verify something. I hurried into the living room and peered into the mostly empty bowl of candy we'd been handing out to trick-or-treaters. Om-Nom-Noms. Miniature chocolate-covered cookies. I grabbed one and returned to my family, feeling sick to my stomach. I tossed it onto the counter.

"What's this?" Becky asked.

"The candy we gave out."

"And...?"

"I bought Nommers. Light brown package. No mascot. These are Om-Nom-Noms, with a white package and a blue mascot who looked too much like Cookie Monster for the copyright attorneys."

"What are you saying?" Becky asked, looking at me as if her darling husband had gone just a wee bit insane.

"What do you *think* I'm saying? The candy changed! The candy I bought to hand out to neighborhood kids transformed into the version of it from about thirty years ago!"

"Do you know how that—"

"Yes, I know how it sounds! It sounds nutty! It sounds like I'm a lunatic! But either this is part of an elaborate plan to drive me bonkers—and Bonkers were discontinued in the '90s, by the way—or something supernatural is happening."

"Or," said Becky, "you're very tired. You've been working hard lately."

"Nobody else thinks this is bizarre?" I picked up the Om-Nom-Noms and shook the package. "Are you saying that I'm literally the only person in the household who doesn't find this just a teeny tiny wee little smidgen peculiar?"

The package shook back.

I yelped and dropped it.

"What's wrong?" asked Becky.

"The candy moved!"

The package of Om-Nom-Noms trembled on the floor. Then it split open, with a gout of chocolate and cookie crumbs spraying into the air.

All of the candy on the table began to quiver. We all gaped in shock as the candies violently tore open, spewing their melted contents all over. Though I felt vindicated, I was far too transfixed by what was happening to gloat.

The candy, mostly chocolate, swirled around. It began to form arms...legs...a chest. Finally it stood up, perhaps three feet tall, a thin, twisted, chocolate creature. Its eyes were Starburst. Its teeth were candy corn. Various other colorful candies were embedded in its chocolate form.

"I live..."

"Kill it!" Tim shouted. "Send it back to hell!" He grabbed the plastic jack-o'-lantern and began hitting the creature with it. Chocolate splashed with each blow, but was immediately drawn back into the beast.

The creature tilted back its head and let out a phlegmy-sounding laugh.

Tim, realizing that his efforts to kill it were useless, settled for dropping into the fetal position and crying.

"What are you?" I asked. I knew the answer was "a monster made out of candy," but I was hoping he'd elaborate.

"I am the ghost of a better time," said the creature. *"Candy used to be so very much better. So much bigger. You saw that 3 Musketeers, right? You—your apathy—allowed candy to shrink through the years, creating the puny specimens you know today. 'Fun Size'—bah! But I'm back to restore balance to the sugary universe."*

"Fair enough, fair enough," I said. "We won't stand in your way."

"You could have applied economic pressure. You could have simply refused to purchase these diminished morsels. But you just... didn't...care! You let candy turn into a laughable hollow shell of its former glory!"

"Do you mean me, specifically?" I asked. "I don't think one family refusing to buy smaller candies would have any real impact. It would have to be a letter-writing campaign or something."

"Then you should have written the letters!"

"I would argue that in some ways candy is better than ever. Jelly Belly jelly beans are smaller than normal jelly beans, but they taste like the actual flavors they're supposed to be! Like, if you eat a buttered popcorn Jelly Belly, it tastes like buttered popcorn! Juicy pear tastes like a pear. It's uncanny. When I was a kid, no candy ever tasted like the fruit it was supposed to mimic. Grape candy doesn't taste like grapes. They called it cherry, but it was just red."

"Maybe don't debate the chocolate monster," said Becky.

"I respect his opinion. I'm just saying that he's zeroing in on one small part of the overall picture. Look at how many different flavors we have now. We used to only have regular M&M's and peanut M&M's, and now we have tons of varieties. Who would've ever thought we'd get Snickers variants? That's crazy!"

The chocolate creature frowned. It pointed a sharp dripping finger at me. *"You know not of what you speak."*

"Candy bars are smaller now. Everybody knows it. The manufacturers say it's to help combat obesity, but c'mon. All I'm saying is that if we went back in time, we'd get bigger candy bars but lose out on a lot of advantages. What about soda? Do you really want to return to a time when we only had one flavor of Mountain Dew?"

"You're getting off-topic," the chocolate creature informed me.

"Look, I enjoy nostalgia as much as anyone. But a lot of those television shows I loved as a kid are absolute dogshit. When I went to the video store, none of the new releases I wanted to rent were ever in. Yes, Snickers are smaller now, but have you tried the kind with almonds?"

"No."

"You really should."

"I'm bringing back old candy," said the creature.

"Okay."

"All of it."

"All right."

"Now."

"Like I said earlier, I'm not trying to stop you. I made my counter-argument but I'm not looking for a fight."

"All of the candy you've eaten is returning."

"Got it." I thought about what he'd just said. "What exactly do you mean by that?"

The chocolate creature pointed to Tim, who was still in the fetal position on the floor. He winced in pain and rolled onto his back. His stomach was expanding...

"No!" I screamed as Tim's stomach exploded, spraying chocolate, nougat, taffy, hard candy, bone, blood, and internal organs everywhere.

The candy just kept spewing out of him like a volcano, until my son was covered in a mix of colorful and brown gook that reached up to the ceiling.

The chocolate creature pointed at Moni. She cried out in pain, doubled over, and then began to regurgitate what I assume was all of the candy she'd ever eaten in her life. There was a lot of it. It started to come out faster than her mouth could accommodate, so her cheeks split open to make more room. Then her entire head came off, and the rest of her body stumbled around as a fountain of candy gore covered the kitchen.

My reaction lacked dignity.

Becky hadn't stopped shrieking since Tim's stomach popped open.

The chocolate creature turned toward her.

My wife didn't like sweets. Never had, even as a little kid. I couldn't remember the last time I'd seen her eat a candy bar. Maybe she'd be okay!

Thick white paste began to ooze from her mouth, then her ears, then her nostrils. I realized to my horror that while she didn't like sweets, she did have breath mints on a regular basis.

"Breath mints don't count!" I screamed at the creature. "They aren't candy!"

"They exist in that middle ground, like Flintstones Chewable Vitamins."

Becky's body exploded, sending refreshing globs flying everywhere.

"Why?" I wailed. "Why would you do this?"

"I thought I explained myself pretty clearly," said the monster.

"No! You said you were pissed about modern candy!" I gestured to the remains of my family, which didn't require much gesturing, because they pretty much filled the entire kitchen. "You didn't explain this! How does this help your cause?"

"It starts a conversation."

I wanted to kill the chocolate creature. Wanted to hear it scream in pain. Wanted it to suffer. But how could I defeat a demon made entirely out of...?

I leaned forward and bit down on its neck.

"Ow! What the hell?"

I took bite after bite out of it, trying to eat as much chocolate as I possibly could. With each bite, more chocolate would slither in to replace what I'd eaten, but I was confident that if I ate quickly enough, it would eventually succumb.

"Stop it! I was going to let you go! I need somebody to tell my story!"

I refused to stop. I was already feeling queasy. I had to push past it and just eat, eat, eat.

"Wait!"

I kept eating.

"Seriously, wait! If you kill me, how will you explain this mess? If you're going to tell the police that a living candy monster murdered your family, wouldn't it be easier if the monster was still there, for verification?"

It did have a point, but no, it needed to die. I kept eating and eating.

"*Curse you!*" the creature shouted. Apparently I'd eaten a crucial part of it, because it suddenly turned completely liquid and splashed onto the floor.

"Go to hell," I whispered. I wasn't even going to bother passing its message along to the candy manufacturers.

As it turned out, the police did believe me. This is because the same thing pretty much happened to everybody in our neighborhood, and most of the creatures were still around when the authorities arrived. It was quite a night.

You'll be happy to know that after a period of mourning I did find love again, got remarried, and even had another kid. But I never ate another piece of candy. And on Halloween, I was that asshole who gave out apples. I hope that now you understand why.

Halloween at the Babylon

LISA MORTON

My name is…I don't know.

I don't know why I don't know.

I'm in a theater, a deluxe one, sitting in a back row beneath the balcony. I don't remember why I'm here, or…

It's dark but I don't mind. Light filters in from somewhere. Dust thickens the air, turning silvery in the faint rays. I feel like I should be on the stage, not back here in a seat with a creaking wooden back and cracked leather upholstery.

I don't know how long I've been here but I think it's been… I don't know.

I wasn't always alone. There was a child in the balcony above, a little boy. He bounced a ball up and down, up and down, *thunk thunk thunk* above me. He giggled sometimes, and he cried. I tried to console him but couldn't find him. One day…I realized he wasn't there anymore. I miss him.

People come and go, in small groups. They're never here long. I don't know what they're doing.

And then there's the *other*. It's the reason I won't go to the stage. It's there, squatting in the wing at stage left where there's no light, no dancing motes, only an impermeable blackness. I can sense it back there, waiting. I sense its hate, its terrible fury. It wants to destroy.

That *other* is why I wait away here, in the back row, away from the stage…I wait…and wait…

Something has changed, though, not just in the air but in the atmosphere, the *soul* of this place. My mind is gathering itself, coming together, revealing memories…

My name is Kay…Katie. My name is Katie.

I was born in 1890. I…

Lights, moving along a side aisle. A group of four entering the theater.

They pass the rows of empty, tilting seats and pause just before the stage. They hold electric torches in their hands. They're talking but I don't understand.

Two men, two women. All dressed roughly in jackets and pants. All carrying large cases.

They set their burdens down, look about, talk. They're young, the oldest no more than thirty-five.

How old am I?

I begin to make sense of their chatter. I hear "the theater" and "haunted" and "Halloween."

Today is Halloween. That matters, somehow, to them and to me.

One of the women, maybe twenty-seven, long blonde hair, a kind face, turns – and looks at me. She shivers. The other woman, shorter and darker, notices and asks her something.

I hear the answer clearly: "I thought I saw a woman sitting in the back row."

They all look. One of the men shakes his head.

The woman who spoke turns away, says, "It's gone now."

But I'm still here, and that moment, when she *saw* me, has awakened more of me, like switches being flipped.

My name is Katie MacPherson, and I am a performer. My

partner, Sadie Thurman, and I used to tour the circuit as "Katie and Sadie." We weren't stars, but we were successful enough to make a living. Our act was a combination of comedy sketches and singing and dancing. We loved what we did.

What we did…

How long ago?

I watch as the new arrivals unpack their cases. They arrange things I can't identify. Some of the things glow; some sit on three legs like a camera, but they're small, not like suit-case-sized movie cameras. It doesn't take them long; they've done this before.

The smaller of the two men, who has a half-shaved head and a tattoo of a flower-covered skull on one cheek, sets foot on the stairs leading up to the stage, draws his foot back sharply when the wood creaks ominously. "Wonder how safe this all is?"

The taller man answers, "Probably not very. This place is scheduled to be razed the beginning of next year."

The blonde woman looks around, taking in the ornate art deco trim that can just barely be glimpsed in the gloom. "Too bad it can't be renovated – it's gorgeous."

"It is." That's the tall man, who now looks right at his blonde companion. "Britt, are you sensing anything?"

The woman – Britt – closes her eyes, takes deep breaths. She's smiling when she looks at them again. "Oh, yes," she says, "we definitely have company."

"We better," says the smaller woman, "I gave up the best Halloween party ever for this."

The man on the stage grins. "Hey, Rosa, you can show me your costume later on in private."

Rosa frowns and makes an obscene gesture.

"All right," says the tall man, who I think must be the leader. "Let's get started."

They check the things they've set up again. Some glow, silent, poised; others hum slightly. One produces a continuous mechanical wash of sound, like the spaces between stations on a radio.

When they're satisfied, they nod to Britt. She closes her eyes, calls out to no one, only the vast theater, "Hello. We're a group of friends who would like to talk to anyone who is here. We respect you, we welcome you, we mean no harm. It's Halloween, when the veil between worlds is at its thinnest, and we hope this will make it easier for you to come forward to talk with us."

Her voice sinks into me like an electrical current, unleashing more memories: performing here, the theater is called the Babylon, it's in Los Angeles, it was just built two years ago and it's beautiful, but has already acquired a bad reputation. Word's got around the vaudeville circuit that something is wrong with this place, that people died building it and more have died since. Sadie and I debated booking at the place, but in the end it was the only venue we could get into in Los Angeles, and we wanted to perform here. Sadie has some dream of us being discovered by Hollywood and put into the movies; she's pretty enough to be in the motion pictures but I know it's probably just a fantasy. That doesn't matter, though; I go along with it, like always with Sadie.

I remember being on the stage. Sadie had said we needed a song for the locals, so we'd added a sprightly version of Mr. Berlin's "An Orange Grove in California." We were halfway through it, I'd stepped forward for my tap solo, I heard something snap, and I...

The other woman with the group cries out sharply. She's on the stage, holding a small box that she's pointing toward the left wing...where *it* is. "Uhhh, the K-2 meter is going nuts over here."

The others climb the steps cautiously to join her. The man with the dangerous-looking tattoo is holding out a similar box. "Mine, too."

"Is it just me," says the taller man, "or is it *too* dark back there?"

Britt stands behind the others, her arms wrapped tightly around herself, staring into the blackness. When the tall man pulls forth his torch and takes a step in that direction, she calls out, "Josh, don't."

Josh stops, looks back at her. "What are you getting?"

"Something old. Something…*bad*."

Josh considers, glances at his three friends, steps back. "Okay, let's put that area aside for now." He nods towards the back of theater…towards *me*.

"What about that back row? You saw something there, right?"

Britt nods.

Josh turns to the other woman. "Rosa, there was some history about that, wasn't there?"

Rosa nods, does something with one of the glowing devices, reads from what she finds. "There are a lot of reports of seeing a woman sitting in the back row. She's described as being about thirty, pretty, wearing an old-fashioned dress. One medium called her Lizzy and said she was a faithful patron who got so scared watching *Frankenstein* in 1931 that she had a heart attack and died in her seat."

No, I want to say, *that's not right*. But I don't know how to say it, how to make them hear me.

"A heart attack at thirty?" Josh asks. Good – he's smart enough to know that's nonsense. "Sounds like movie hype."

Rosa shrugs. "It does, but...but there were a *lot* of people who died here before they closed it down in 2006."

"Her name's not Lizzy." That's Britt, who is walking slowly toward me. "It's..."

Katie, I think angrily, and I hear my name repeated in a burst of static from that box that sounds like radio static.

All four of the visitors hesitate, surprised. The other man asks, "Did the spirit box just say 'Katie'?"

Josh is grinning. "Yeah, Ramón, it did. We're recording, right?"

"Sí, boss," he says, "we got it."

Britt is close now, looking near me but not at me.

She doesn't see me. Because I'm...

"When did you die?" she asks.

I'm dead.

Thoughts crash into my head now; everything falls into place, a well-ordered avalanche. I remember:

October 31st, 1923. Halloween. We were in our second night at the Babylon; the first night had gone well. Sadie was convinced there'd been a Hollywood producer in the audience, and when Jack, an usher at the theater, had invited us to a Halloween party after the show tonight, Sadie said, "Yes," without hesitation, because she thought a party in Hollywood was a sure path to stardom.

"Is it a costume affair, Jack?" I asked.

"It is, but what you're wearing now would be aces!"

We both looked down, realized we were garbed as giant babies, in jumpers and oversized bonnets, for our first number. Jack handed us the address for the party on a piece of paper; as he walked away, I turned to Sadie and said, "We are *not* going to a Hollywood party dressed as babies."

Sadie gave me a playful little push. "Oh, hush, Katie. I'll find us something else."

An hour later, we were in the middle of the Irving Berlin number, the audience was already half-drunk and enthusiastic.

I'd stepped to the front for my solo when I felt a rush of *rage* from nowhere and everywhere, from something I couldn't identify, lashing out, chilling the air, snapping something overheard. I heard a scream that might have been Sadie and then...

I died, crushed beneath a huge light that had fallen from the overhead grid.

I remember now: finding myself outside my body, watching stage hands and audience members rush forward, Sadie shaking and crying as she saw the blood, saw them pulling me away from the wreckage of the light, checking me, finding no pulse, exclaiming that there was no reason for that light to fall...

But they're wrong: there was a reason. It was done by the thing that lives in that dark corner of the stage.

Britt closes her eyes, sightlessly walks to within a few feet of me. "Katie, it was 1923, wasn't it? And you weren't just some audience member – you performed here."

Yes, I think, grateful at being *seen* in this unseen way.

Britt smiles, opens her eyes, looks at and through me. I realize what she is: a medium, a creature I wasn't sure I'd ever believed in until now. And something about her has done more than just find me, it's *opened* me, arranged me, put me back together.

She laughs, a sweet, gentle sound, and adds, "It's the night, too, you know. Halloween makes it much easier for us to talk."

I understand, then: the long history of a night when the world eases into chill darkness and barriers weaken. A night for spirits...like me.

"Wait a minute," Rosa says, an urgency in her voice. "Katie...yeah..." She thumbs through the small device in her hand, eyes scanning until she blurts out excitedly, "Here it is: Kathryn 'Katie' MacPherson was part of a vaudeville team that performed at the Babylon in 1923. There was a terrible accident onstage during a show and Katie was killed." She reads something else, looks up with shadowed eyes. "It happened on Halloween night, exactly a hundred years ago."

A hundred years? I've been here that long?

What about –

"Sadie," blurts out the thing called a spirit box.

"Sadie," Britt echoes, "I think she wants to know what happened to Sadie."

"Sadie was her performing partner." Rosa draws a finger across the glowing screen, after a few seconds says, "Oh, wow – Sadie's got a Wikipedia entry. She actually became a silent movie star, under the name Sada Zola. She made about fifty silents but had a hard time fitting in when the talkies took over. She ended up buying a restaurant in Echo Park that she ran until her death in 1975. She never married."

Sadie became a movie star; it wasn't a fantasy after all. The thought fills me with such joy that I think I might detonate from it. Would they feel it if I did?

And she lived to the age of 84.

And she never married.

The spirit box mirrors me, blurting out, "Never."

The four young people look at each other. "'Never'…never *what*?" asks Josh.

My mind roils with new information, forming what-ifs: What if we'd never played the Babylon on Halloween night? What if I'd never died?

What if…the thing at the back of the stage hadn't taken its unending fury out on me?

I realize now how old, and how hungry it is. It took the boy in the balcony, the one who used to bounce his ball, *thunk thunk thunk*…it consumed him, as it has so many others. As it wants to with me, and with these four beautiful ones.

A night for spirits...like the thing in the black corner of the stage.

I need to warn her, to warn all of them.

"Stage," blurts out the spirit box, now held by Rosa, who jumps.

She looks up, locks eyes with the others. "It said 'stage.'" She calls out, oddly pointing her face up to the ceiling, "Do you want us to investigate the stage?"

NOOO!

Britt frowns, turns to her friends. "I think she's afraid of the stage."

Ramón asks, "Katie, do you want us to stay away from the stage?"

"Yes," the box blurts out.

Their faces go pale. "Yes," Josh says to the others. They're all silent for a few seconds before turning their gazes to *that* corner.

I sense it, lurking there now. Its story coalesces in my mind: It was here long before this theater, or the people who were on this land before. It is *of* the land, never human, but forced out of its place in the natural order *by* humans, and so it seeks revenge. It killed the people who first occupied this place, who lived in thatched huts and ground acorns for food; it killed the ones who came from the south and conquered; it killed the ones who built the theater, and it killed those who've been through here over the last century. Some, like the boy, it killed *twice*, first body then soul.

"Guys," Ramón says, now crouching on the front of the stage, and I want to scream at him to *get away from there*, but of course I'm silent. "We've got an EVP."

He jumps down from the stage, holding one of the small boxes he'd placed there earlier. He thumbs some switches, sound rushes out: at first it's a wash of noise, the four human voices interspersed, but then there's something that growls and then bellows in a timbre no human throat has ever produced.

Their eyes turn to that void at the back of the stage.

"Leave," says the spirit box.

Britt says, "Guys, I think we've got an elemental."

The others look unsure. Josh asks, "So, if it's an elemental… is it masquerading as Katie?"

"No," Britt answers quickly, "she's here, too, but…she's afraid of it."

This young woman is stronger than she knows. She reminds me of Sadie, outer beauty meshed with inner strength, all guided by unerring intuition.

If Sadie were here…

But she's not. She's not, but I am, trapped here by this thing.

No, that's not true. I'm lying to myself, as I lied for so long.

Sadie.

She's why I'm trapped here…or rather, what I never said to her is my trap.

That I loved her.

I was afraid, of course. We had our modest success, and Sadie was pretty enough to become the movie star she did… after I was gone. That night before, after our first performance at the Babylon on October 30th, we'd left the stage to the loudest applause we'd ever heard. We tumbled back into the wings, the dark, where I'd impulsively leaned in and kissed her, and she'd returned it – at first. Then we pulled apart, excited but anxious, wondering if we'd been seen –

And *it* was awakened by that. We both felt a rush of terror replacing the joy. We hadn't spoken about it after; in fact, we hadn't said anything to each other the rest of that night beyond the most basic mundanities. That night we slept in our hotel room twin beds, turned away from each other, neither sleeping much, wondering what we'd just unleashed…

I return to the present and see Britt crying. "I'm so sorry," she murmurs. "You were robbed of everything. She really loved you, too."

The others remain quiet, watching, waiting.

After a few seconds, Britt says, "She's waiting for you. You can move on now."

I feel how right she is. Something I can't name pulls at me now, something that is pure and light and the opposite of the thing – what did she call it, an "elemental"? The thing that crouches in the shadows.

But I won't go, not yet. I need to do something.

I need to stop *it* from harming these people, or anyone ever again. It must destroy no more souls, as it's tried to with mine.

I've spent a century hiding in the back row, but now I move towards the stage. As I pass the medium, her expression shows surprise. "What…" she trails off, following me, the others parting to make way for her.

At first I want to stop her, but then I realize: I need her. She possesses a gift that may have been granted to her for *exactly* this night, this reason.

She's with me as we approach the blackness. The thing back there rears up in expectation of feeding on more death, but it stops as we stop, mere feet from it. I direct my thoughts at it:

You need to go back to the earth from which you came.

One of the boxes behind us explodes, causing the three other people to cry out.

But not Britt. She knows her own strength now and has focused it to join me.

Your hunger can never be fulfilled. Return to find peace.

It attacks.

We are surrounded by the black. In that instant I realize that if it wins, I will vanish forever, I won't see what comes next...

It can't win. I reach out and feel Britt's human hand warm in my cold one. Together we are powerful, light pours from us, light that can banish shadows forever, drive them back...I feel it shrinking, I know Britt feels it, too...

It is gone. In an infinite second it has fled back into the depths of the earth, where it belongs.

"What just happened?" asks Rosa.

Britt turns to look at her friends, her eyes shining, unable to form words.

Then she turns and looks at me. *At me*. She sees me, even if the rest don't.

I hear her voice within me: *Thank you.*

I release her hand, and she stares at it, wondering.

It's time for me to go.

I feel something in the light, distant but not as far as before.

Sadie's waiting.

Ghosts of Enerhodar

HENRY HERZ

Zaporizhzhia Nuclear Power Plant, Enerhodar, Ukraine – February 27, 2022

RUSSIAN *SPETSNAZ KAPITÁN* NIKITIN peered through swirling dust as he crouched behind concrete rubble with three of his special ops soldiers. Sweat dripped into his eyes, and the sulfurous, somewhat metallic odor from sustained gunfire stung his nostrils. Sharp reports from Ukrainian AK-47s contrasted with those of his commandos' AS Val suppressed assault rifles. He turned to his radioman. "Get me headquarters."

A minute later, the sergeant handed Nikitin the secure radio headset.

"*Drakon*, this is *Volk*, over," Nikitin began, using call signs dragon and wolf.

"What's your status?" replied a lieutenant colonel.

"Not good, *Drakon*." Nikitin scowled at having to report unwelcome news to the commander of the 70th Special

Purpose Detachment. "The Ukrainians somehow knew we were coming. Their defense of the power plant is much stiffer than Intelligence predicted. We could probably take them out with RPG-27s, but we weren't issued any anti-infantry thermobaric warheads. All we have are bunker-buster rounds, and I'm reluctant to use those given our proximity to the reactor containment buildings. Our mission was not to set off another Chernobyl. Over."

His superior swore eloquently. "The general staff will not tolerate delay. It's imperative that we seize the power plant now. I'm initiating fire mission *dobro* in fifteen minutes. Pull back immediately and put on your chemical warfare gear. Out."

Damn, thought Nikitin, running a dirty sleeve across his forehead. *This just gets worse and worse.* He and his *Spetsnaz* followed orders. They knew from experience that the worst things happen to Russian soldiers who do not.

Fifteen minutes later and twenty kilometers to the south, a battery of three 2S5 *Giatsint*-S self-propelled howitzers elevated their barrels. Each fired six times. Their gun barrels incrementally depressed between salvos, as directed by fire control computers, to achieve simultaneous arrival at the target.

Eighteen 152mm rounds detonated above Enerhodar's nuclear power plant, the largest in Europe. Rather than shrapnel, the warheads spewed a colorless, odorless aerosol. The synthetic organophosphorus compound drifted downward, an invisible hellish snowfall.

The result of Ukrainian defenders breathing in the nerve agent turned out exactly as planned. Within minutes of inhalation, the sarin interfered with the degradation of the neurotransmitter acetylcholine at the victims' neuromuscular junctions. Drooling, runny noses, tightness in the chest, and nausea preceded difficulty breathing. The continued loss of muscular control led to suffocation in a horrific series of convulsive spasms.

The sarin also produced an unintended effect. A breeze blew remnants of the nerve agent two hundred meters southwestward, asphyxiating over a hundred civilian men, women, and children caught in its murderous path.

Dneiper Gardens Apartments, Cherkasy, Ukraine – October 31, 2022

LIKE THE OTHER married women in the building, Yryna Koval had a husband in the National Guard of Ukraine. That left Yryna to care for their children – seven-year-old daughter, Halyna, and five-year-old son, Serhei.

Shallow facial scars from mortar shrapnel four months ago gave the otherwise beautiful long-haired blonde a harrowing visage.

The Dneiper Gardens apartments towered over Dakhnivs'ka Street on the western side of the Dneiper River. When Russian forces approached the eastern side of the Cherkasy Bridge, those residents not fleeing moved to the underground parking garage for greater protection from enemy artillery rounds.

To distract their children from the horrors of war, at least temporarily, the mothers arranged a modest Halloween party. Given the circumstances, the children wore simple ghost costumes made from sheets and blankets.

Yryna distributed candy while gray-haired Mr. Savchuk told terrifying tales of midnight monsters that made the toddlers cling to their mothers. He limped from a shrapnel wound he suffered while serving in the Soviet Army in

Afghanistan, and decades of cigarette smoking gave him a gravelly voice perfect for Halloween stories.

Not to be outdone, little Serhei raised his arms under his gray blanket. "I'm a scary *Shubin* ghost of the mines."

"Yes, you're very spooky," agreed Halyna, touching the blanket. "And dark from all the coal dust." She spun and leaped toward the other children. "Watch out! I'm a *Mavka*, the ghost of a young girl, and I will tickle you to death."

The younger kids stepped back, while the older ones chuckled. One pointed. "Don't be silly. Ghosts aren't real."

Everyone jerked their heads as a distant explosion echoed, faint but ominous, within the concrete garage. Yryna and Mr. Savchuk sighed and exchanged a look. The adults couldn't distract their children from the Russians' "special military operation" for long.

Ten kilometers east of Cherkasy, Ukraine – October 31, 2022

NIKITIN BRIEFED his commandos inside an abandoned farmhouse. "We control the Dneiper's eastern bank, but a reconnaissance drone spotted explosives under the central bridge span, with detonation wires strung back to the western bank. Headquarters doesn't want to send T-90 tanks over the bridge until we secure the far end and cut the detonation wires."

"A nighttime heliborne assault, sir?" asked Lieutenant Kuznetsov.

Nikitin shook his head. "No. Too risky. The Ukrainians have night vision goggles and those damn Stinger missiles. This situation requires stealth." He grinned, though the expression did not reach his eyes. "The Ukrainians celebrate

Halloween, so let's give them a real reason to fear monsters in the dark."

He slid his finger upriver along the map tacked to a wall. "Look. Six kilometers to the northwest of Cherkasy Bridge, the river narrows. It's dotted with small islands that will screen us from view as we cross the water. I've arranged for RIB boats with silent electric motors. It's a cloudy, moonless night. We can cross without being seen." He stabbed the map with his thick index finger. "Then, we enter the Cherkasy Forest here. The pine trees will hide us from Ukrainian eyes the entire way before we break cover to assault the western end of the bridge."

The lieutenant approached the map to read the small writing. "Sir, we'll have to cross Dakhnivs'ka Street here, Ukrayins'koho Frontu Street here, and Kanivska Street here."

"Don't worry, *Leytenánt*. The Ukrainians issued a civilian curfew. No one's driving or strolling at night, and both sides of the road are forested at all three crossing points." Nikitin pointed at the eastern side of the bridge. "Headquarters wants armor across the river as soon as possible, so we've got to secure the far side of Cherkasy Bridge tonight. We have thermobaric rounds for our RPGs. Any Ukrainians defending the western end of the bridge won't know what hit them. We'll board the RIB boats on the eastern shore at 2200. Dismissed."

While the rest of the soldiers shuffled out, the lieutenant remained. He'd faithfully served Nikitin in Transnistria, Chechnya, and Dagestan, earning his superior's respect and trust in his eerie ability to sense when the shit was about to hit the fan. "Sir, I've got a bad feeling about this mission."

Nikitin raised an eyebrow. "Anything specific, *Leytenánt*?"

"Not yet, sir."

"Well, then unless you want to tell the Colonel that you lack the balls, the operation will proceed as ordered."

Dneiper River, six kilometers northwest of Cherkasy Bridge, Ukraine

FOG DESCENDED as a hundred Spetsnaz pushed off from the eastern side of the river. Their boats glided almost silently, threading their way through the myriad small islands. Only their GLONASS navigation system enabled them to find their way through the watery labyrinth.

Kuznetsov sat next to Nikitin at the front of one boat, his knuckles white from gripping the gunwale. Writhing tentacles of mist, glowing faintly from starlight, seemed to reach for him as the passage of the boat roiled them up from the water's surface. The faint odor of dead fish seemed out of place in the fast-flowing river. Kuznetsov pulled his parka collar closer against the icy cold that slithered up from the depths of the river. His fingers and toes numbed. He shivered. Something splashed behind them. He turned, but the mist and moonless night obscured the source of the noise. Something scraped the boat keel. "Did you hear that, sir?"

Nikitin shrugged.

"Perhaps it was a log," he offered, knowing it was not. *If we had passed over a submerged obstacle, the scrape would have moved from fore to aft. But this progressed the other way. Something moved in the same direction as the boat, but faster.* His stomach tightened and he perspired despite the cold.

The mist parted, and the heavily wooded western shore came into view.

The *Spetsnaz* beached their RIB boats and scurried noiselessly into the nearby trees. Loaded with weapons and gear, including body armor and night vision goggles, the commandos looked like misshapen monsters lurching through the trees.

A scout crawled forward to check for Ukrainians on Dakhnivs'ka Street. At his all-clear hand gesture, the soldiers sprinted west across the deserted road into the pines on the opposite side, their footsteps echoing ominously. They headed south-southwest.

Midnight breezes stirred the trees, prompting Nikitin to check the canopy for threats. The temperature dropped precipitously, and the previously steady wind abruptly changed direction. The convulsive branch movements made them seem like grasping many-fingered claws. Hair on the back of the captain's neck bristled. The normally pleasant resinous aroma of the pines somehow carried a more menacing turpentine odor.

Kuznetsov stared at Nikitin, raising an eyebrow, discreet enough not to mention his premonition in front of the other soldiers.

Nikitin gave a brief nod. *I feel it, too,* he thought. *But our mission is critical.*

The commandos advanced a thousand meters.

With each step, Nikitin felt a building tension in his shoulders, a sense of foreboding unlike anything he'd experienced in combat. He checked his GLONASS navigation display. "We're almost at Ukrayins'koho Frontu Street," he conveyed to his men through their *Strelets* voice communication system. "*Leytenánts,* check your platoons."

Confused mumbling filled headsets.

"What is it, Kuznetsov?"

"The headcount came up seven men short, sir," Kuznetsov replied, followed by the gasps of other soldiers.

Tension showed in the faces of nearby men. "Seven men short? What the hell?" someone muttered.

Nikitin scowled. "Quiet. Check again, *Leytenánt.*"

The count came back unchanged. *Experienced* Spetsnaz *don't just get lost,* thought Nikitin. *I cannot explain it.* Fear pierced him like a bayonet.

"Sir," whispered Kuznetsov, "we should abort the mission now."

Nikitin checked his watch and swore. "We can afford to lose a few men getting lost, *Leytenánt,* but we cannot afford to lose any more time. We continue toward the objective."

Nikitin noticed the men swiveling their heads, checking their "six" more than usual. He found himself doing the same. *Why's it so damn cold?*

After the scout's all-clear, Nikitin ordered the *Spetsnaz* to cross Ukrayins'koho Frontu Street. "We'll continue south-southwest for 2,300 meters. Stay sharp. We're skirting the western edge of a residential neighborhood before we turn east. Maintain five-meter spacing."

After five minutes, the breeze shifted direction again. However, instead of pine fragrance, the wind carried the stench of rotting flesh with sickeningly sweet undertones – human corpses.

"Hold position and crouch," ordered Nikitin.

"*Kapitán*! This is *Serzhant* Baranov." The hardened soldier's voice quivered. "You need to see this, sir. I'm at the rear of the formation."

"Coming, *Serzhant.*" Nikitin weaved between crouching commandos, their rifle barrels twitching from side to side at imagined targets. Breathing hard, he pulled up short upon reaching the noncommissioned officer.

Baranov stood next to another commando. Both of their faces were pale, and they trembled. "I didn't hear a thing, sir."

Four *Spetsnaz* lay motionless, face-up with their assault rifles nearby on the ground.

Nikitin listened for breathing. Nothing. *What the hell?* He removed the soldier's night vision goggles. The dead man's sightless bulging eyes with broken blood vessels in a reddened face stared back at him. He yanked off his gloves to wipe clammy sweat from his palms. "Looks like he was choked to death."

"Same with the others, sir," Baranov reported.

Nikitin stood. "*Serzhant,* how could this have happened without you or anyone else nearby hearing a struggle?"

The man stiffened, his face pale. "I cannot explain it, sir."

The bitter irony of his own earlier admission repeated back to him was not lost on Nikitin.

The sergeant pointed to the rear. "Ukrainian *Spetsnaz* could be following us, sir. And they must be very, very good to strike soundlessly." Sweat beaded on his forehead. "We're walking into a trap. I respectfully suggest we scrub the mission."

Nikitin shook his head. "No, *Serzhant*." He glared. "Our mission's critical, and we *will* complete it, no matter the cost. Take five men and deploy here in ambush for any Ukrainians following us. I want an update every five minutes on my channel only. Understood?"

"Yes, sir." The sergeant saluted and gave the orders.

Nikitin led the remaining *Spetsnaz* to the south-southwest. Heads and rifle barrels jerked toward any sound – the snapping of a dry twig, the hooting of an owl, or the rustling of dead leaves.

Nikitin's heart pounded when Baranov reported in five minutes later.

"Nothing so far, sir. We've taken up positions in the trees, about four meters up. It's even colder up here."

"Very good, *Serzhant*."

An eerie silence descended, broken suddenly by rustling from a bush ten meters in front of Nikitin. The man to his right panicked and fired two rounds from his suppressed assault rifle.

"No firing!" ordered Nikitin. *Christ, everyone's at their limit.*

Ten minutes passed without another update from Baranov. Nikitin cursed under his breath. "*Serzhant*, report… *Serzhant*?"

Nikitin's mouth went dry. He checked his watch. *Damnit. It's like this mission's cursed.* He broadcast to the entire unit via *Strelets*. "The ambush team's not responding. They may have encountered Ukrainians. We will head back and neutralize our pursuers so we can complete our mission."

The Spetsnaz reversed direction. They approached Baranov's last known position with rifles at the ready. Someone gasped.

Nikitin pulled up short at a grim tableau.

Baranov and the other five men twisted with each gust of wind, hanging from thick branches by nooses made from their rifle straps. Their swollen corpse tongues lolled. Eyes bulged, the terror of their final moments apparent even in death.

Nikitin's gut twisted. He pointed. "You men. Cut down our comrades."

As the soldiers complied, a distant unearthly howl – a howl no wolf ever made – rooted everyone's feet to the ground. The howls seemed to come from all compass points.

Nikitin's face paled. "Riflemen, form a ten-meter radius perimeter around me and the other officers," he ordered. "Shoot anything that approaches. Those of you with RPGs, move to the center with me."

Weaving together the last tatters of his courage, Nikitin sprinted among his men, placing them behind the cover of a ring of trees to ensure an enemy approaching from any direction would take fire. He ordered the light machine guns positioned where they had maximum fields of fire.

Another spine-chilling howl echoed through the woods,

closer this time. Two soldiers dropped their weapons to cover their ears.

Breathing hard, Nikitin scowled. *The men are losing it.* "The enemy's bitten off more than they can chew if they come at us when we're ready for them," he told his commandos, the boast intended to shore up his own confidence as much as theirs.

The howls increased in frequency and pitch, coming from the north, east, and west.

Christ, how many of them are there? wondered Nikitin, *and why are they screaming?* "Steady. Choose your targets. Semi-automatic fire only."

Keeping low, Nikitin looked south along their intended march route. *Nothing*. On a whim, he removed his night vision goggles and scanned to the north. His gut twisted. *Mavkas? Mother of God!*

Pale, snarling women and girls with long flowing hair and tattered gray clothing advanced from the north toward the *Spetsnaz*. Their angry eyes glowed green as they glided centimeters *above* the ground. Gaping wounds to arms, legs, and torsos did not impede the ghosts' movement. Sharp teeth lined their gore-stained mouths, gaping portals into blackness. Their hellish screams formed a cacophonous chorus.

"NVGs off!" screamed Nikitin. The vestiges of his self-control dissipated like smoke from an extinguished candle as he stared in disbelief at the terrifying tableau. "Fire at will!"

His men gasped as they yanked off their NVGs and spotted their foes. They winced at the unnerving ghostly wails. The *Spetsnaz* let loose, all fire discipline forgotten in their terror. Gunfire rang out like a hailstorm, and an acrid cordite smell filled the men's nostrils as blood trickled out of their ears.

More ghosts appeared to the east and west, their uncanny floating advance making them even more terrifying.

A torrent of bullets from assault rifles, light machine guns, and sniper rifles passed harmlessly through the shrouded clothing wrapping the incorporeal attackers.

Realizing their guns would not save them, some men dropped their weapons and fled southward, hoping to escape the tightening ethereal noose. They pulled up short in mind-numbing terror when more ghosts materialized in front of them like fog rising from a cemetery.

The soldiers holding their ground in the circle could only watch in horror and despair as ghosts seized their fleeing comrades and tore arms from their torsos with inhuman strength. The thirsty soil soaked up the Russian blood.

"Fire RPGs!" ordered Nikitin, his eyes wild with terror.

"But, sir," warned Kuznetsov.

Ignoring the thrust of a soldier's bayonet, a ghost seized his shoulders and sank her teeth into his neck. The spurting blood seemed to energize her. Two more supernaturally strong snaps of her jaws severed the man's head. His spasming body toppled to the forest floor.

Soldiers replaced empty magazines and fired on full automatic, but the hail of bullets did nothing to stop the incoming tide of death.

"Fire RPGs now!" Nikitin screamed, his military training drowned in panic.

Three rocket-propelled grenades streaked outward, passing without effect through the ghosts, slamming into nearby tree trunks.

"Too close, sir!" said Kuznetsov.

The liquid fuel in each warhead formed an expanding cloud, mixing with the oxygen in the air. A secondary charge within each warhead ignited the fine mist, consuming all the oxygen and generating a massive blast wave.

The most fortunate of the *Spetsnaz*, those within ten meters of a blast, died from having their internal organs liquified by the overpressure shockwave. The remainder died from whichever effect worked more efficiently, incineration or asphyxiation. Either way, they perished with the stench of burned flesh in their nostrils and screams in their ears.

The *Mavkas* of Enerhodar had exacted their revenge on the murderous invaders of Ukraine. The spirits faded to peaceful oblivion as the conflagration within the Cherkasy Forest lit the Halloween night sky.

Dneiper Gardens apartments, Cherkasy, Ukraine – November 1, 2022

BREAKFAST THE NEXT MORNING WAS "ENHANCED" by leftover treats from the makeshift Halloween party – Roshan Bonny Fruit jelly candies and the more popular Alionka milk chocolates – secreted away the prior night by those children with sufficient self-discipline not to eat all their candy at once. Still, an inescapable sense of foreboding and the faint odor of car exhaust made everything taste bitter.

Someone risked a trip to the roof to check on the battle. "Our troops still hold the bridge!"

Cheers rang out, "*Slava Ukraini!*"

Serhei tugged on the dirty hem of his mother's blouse. "Are monsters real, *Maty*?"

Yryna tousled her son's hair. "No, my dear. But some humans act like monsters."

Hayna whispered to Serhei, "Maybe Ukrainian ghosts will help us fight the Russian army."

"Maybe."

. . .

AUTHOR NOTES

The Ukrainian geography mentioned is accurate. The Russians did attack and seize the Zaporizhzhia Nuclear Power Plant in Enerhodar. Although the facilities were damaged in the battle, no use of chemical weapons has been reported.

The Russian *Spetsnaz* (special forces) 70th Special Purpose Detachment is part of 2nd Special Purpose Brigade. All weapons listed are used by the Russian military. The description of the effects of sarin is accurate.

Mavkas and *Shubin* are ghosts from Ukrainian folklore. *Mavkas* are created when girls suffer unnatural premature deaths. They gather in forests and lure young men, tickling them to death. They have no reflection in water and do not cast shadows. *Shubin* is a ghost who haunts the coal mines of the Donbas region. I was fascinated to discover in my research that Ukrainians celebrate Halloween (in recent years), but Russians do not.

The Ghost Lake Mermaid

ALETHEA KONTIS

They call me the Ghost Lake Mermaid. Technically, the lake's named Cachichuma and I call myself Mer, though Jinna calls me Dahling, and the birds and fish have their own names for things. Every town like Buckle Springs has legends—Bigfoot, Chupacabra, Crossroads Demon, you've heard them all around a Halloween campfire. (Jinna personally takes credit for the local resurgence of Bloody Mary.) Similarly, every lake has its own spirits. As far as I know, I'm the only mermaid. And that's fine with me.

My job here in Ghost Lake is to maintain the order of things. I stir the water so algae doesn't grow where the kids like to play. I encourage fish onto hooks, or discourage them, depending on the season. In the spring, I draw patterns in fallen petals at the water's edge. I even return lost things to the shoreline…unless they're shiny. I have a weakness for sparkles. Like the engagement ring someone threw off the Merry Death Bridge and the silver charm bracelet Jinna gave me with the symbols on it. She says they mean "truth" in Korean, but I don't know Korean, so I have to believe her.

Believing Jinna's wild stories is part of what makes them so fun.

I also work to keep my own legend alive. An old ghost once told me that if my story faded, I would fade with it. I can't grant the wishes made on shiny coins tossed from the bridge, but I do catch them and keep them safe. I've been known to flip a fin at anyone who cries into the water, to give them a bit of magic and maybe a little hope. And every so often there are children who, if they stare into the water long enough, notice my blue eyes looking back at them.

Sheriff Lee was one of those children. He's visited this bridge his whole life, stopping by after school, or while on Army leave, or during his daily run. Now he sips coffee and watches the sunrise, his thick hair mostly gray. I know that one day these visits will stop. I'll miss him when they do.

"That man right there is my one regret."

Jinna always says this when Sheriff Lee comes to the lake. I hadn't noticed her beside me before she spoke, but once Jinna's present it's impossible not to notice her. Her lips are the same blood red shade as her voluminous evening gown and the string tied around her wrist, like there's something she forgot to remember. And she has this cloud of long, black hair that's silky enough to make a mermaid jealous.

But Jinna isn't a mermaid; she's a ghost. Jumped off the bridge a few decades back. On purpose. "I was magnificent," she told me. "If a lady has to leave a party, she should always do so while she's magnificent."

"The day he pulled my body out of this lake…mmm. We could have been sculpted by Michelangelo." Jinna fans her cheeks, as if we're surrounded by air instead of water. "In his prime, that man was a delicious specimen. Every woman in a hundred miles wanted to take a bite out of him."

"Why didn't you?" I ask even though I know the answer.

"Child, he was maybe a dozen years younger than me, and from the only other Korean family in this one-horse town. We were probably related."

"You weren't related," I say.

"No, we weren't. But my dreams of ruining that divine man are surely far more exciting than the reality would have been." She sighs. "Surely."

I sigh with her for good measure. I like imagining happy endings for the ghosts of my acquaintance. I mean, if they'd actually had happy endings, they wouldn't have become ghosts to begin with.

"What are we looking at?"

I turn to the new voice. She's young, maybe half Jinna's age or less, making her presence all the more tragic. She's wearing jeans and a short leather jacket. A broken heart at the end of a faceted gold chain rests against her flawless brown skin. Her hair, made up of what seems to be a million tiny braids, floats around her head in a goddess-like halo.

Seriously. Another ghost with hair ten times more fabulous than my wavy golden tresses, and *I'm the mermaid*.

"The injustice of the universe," Jinna replies. "That's what we're looking at."

"Isn't an officer of the law literally the definition of justice?" The new ghost raises an eyebrow at Jinna's pointed glare. "I'm just sayin'."

"It's a long story," I tell her. I don't mention how many times she'll hear it.

"Well, you'll have to—oh my gosh, you're a mermaid!"

It's such a joy to make people (alive or dead) squeal in delight, as if their wild childhood imaginings have just been verified. Jinna didn't react at all when we first met, which I both loved and hated about her.

I wave cheerfully. "You can call me Mer."

She smiles back. "I'm Am…Amm…"

Brand new ghosts don't usually remember their names right away. They can maybe get out the first syllable. Same for the memory of their death. The more tragic the event, the tougher it is to retrieve. Some spirits don't realize they're ghosts at all. There's no use forcing it; the knowledge either comes with time, or it doesn't.

"We'll call you Amy for now," I say. "It's nice to meet you."

"I'm Jinna. How did you die?"

I roll my eyes. The question is just so…Jinna.

We watch Amy's face go through several emotions. First, she's surprised. Her gaze shifts from me to Jinna, and her brow furrows. Her eyes dart this way and that as she tries to remember something…and wait…there it is. Her nostrils flare. Her voice comes back, deep and angry. "That man. *That man.* Bastard threw me off the bridge. Didn't even let me finish my sentence."

Almost unconsciously, her hand lifts to the broken heart at her throat. There's an R written there, not an A.

"Dahling." Jinna points. "Please tell me R isn't the one who killed you. You seem smarter than that."

Amy looks down at the necklace. "Renée is my girlfriend," she says wistfully. "The delusional asshole convinced I was into him was Joe…something. His number's in my back pocket."

The water will render that evidence worthless soon, if it isn't already.

"Don't worry," I say. "When they find you, they'll put him in prison where he belongs, and your soul can rest in peace."

"Or, you can haunt his ass so hard he regrets living," says Jinna. "Personally, I'd go with that one. Only…"

A look passes between Amy and Jinna. It's as if they're

having an entire conversation in a language I don't understand.

"What?" I ask.

Jinna answers. "A Black woman gone missing in a town like this? The chances of anyone finding her..."

Amy shakes her head. "I'll be lucky if there's even a formal report."

"Oh. Right." Anger boils my blood. Just like legends, each town has its flaws, too. Ours is the Buckle Family. Every last one of them is rotten to the core. Considering the quantity of tears wept into Ghost Lake over the last century, I know the depths to which the Buckles can sink. "Then how about we change this story?"

In a flash I'm off, swimming in large circles beneath the bridge, flipping my tail a few times so the sunrise on my turquoise scales catches Sheriff Lee's attention. Then I venture farther down, bit by bit, in ever-tightening circles until I find her at the bottom.

She is newly dead. Her dark brown eyes are fixed, wide and full of fear. They convey the scream that the duct tape over her mouth would have stopped. Her hands are bound with rope and chain, the skin of her fingertips already puckering. Her feet, bound in similar rope and chain, are tied to a cinder block. The broken heart necklace at her throat floats helplessly around her chin.

Poor Amy.

I look up—from this distance, the bridge is completely obscured by mud, algae, and a school of bream. I consider the placement of Amy's chains and the angle of the rising sun. If I time it right, it's possible the light might reflect enough for the chains to wink up at Sheriff Lee. If I can clear the way in time. And if he happens to be looking down at exactly that moment. And if he thinks that what he sees is more than just a fish.

It's a lot of ifs, but I'm determined to try.

I add my futile wish to the coins in the pouch at my side. Furiously sweeping my tail back and forth, I move swaths of algae toward the bank. When I spot red in the water I call to Jinna, "See what you can do about those chains."

Jinna can't move objects the way a mermaid can, but she's a mature enough ghost to be able to polish a few links of chain. She floats to the cinder block resting on the lake's bottom.

We both remember Amy's ghost too late.

"Don't look!" we shout, but Amy is already face-to-face with herself.

When ghosts meet the mortal flesh their spirit once inhabited, they typically either vanish or freak out. Amy surprises us both by opening her mouth and very calmly telling us a story.

I have only ever seen one ghost react this way. And once she'd started telling stories, she'd never stopped.

"I got too close. Investigative journalists live with that danger. But I was always two steps ahead, full of plans and exit strategies. Renée kept on me to work with a partner. She was right. Again. When brute force enters the chat, it's game over. Doesn't matter how clever you are."

The cool monotone of Amy's words gives me goosebumps, but I don't stop finning the water as I listen.

Jinna rises to the chains at Amy's wrists. "Who did this to you?"

"Joe"—it takes her a moment, but the name comes this time —"Buckle."

Jinna snorts.

"Jinna!" I scold across the water.

"Dahling, please. What did she think was going to happen? The Buckles stole everything they ever owned, right down to the land that made up this town. To them, terrorizing anyone with skin darker than limestone is a sport. Amy-doll, you could have investigated until the cows came home. No charge is ever going to stick to that family. It never does." Jinna shakes her head. "I'm sorry you wasted a perfectly good life for this."

Amy points skyward. "The sheriff is on my side!"

"The sheriff is an idiot. A beautiful idiot, I grant you, but an idiot just the same. If he had any sense, he would have left this town years ago. Just like I did."

Amy stares through Jinna. "If you left, then why are you here?"

"Because payback is hell." Jinna flips the hair already floating softly around her head. "I wanted every sad sack in this town to see my face in the headlines, above the fold. I wanted to haunt their children and their children's children for three generations, at least."

"Congratulations," Amy says flatly. "You won, I guess."

Jinna smirks. "Yeah, well…how far did you get?"

"Close enough to make somebody mad enough to kill," I point out.

Amy is not deterred. "Sheriff Lee said my best bet to nail the Buckles was if I found an old case, a cold case, one that could be solved using today's technology."

Right. The sheriff! I surface once more to check the bridge and see only blue sky and autumn leaves. Both he and his police cruiser are gone. Hopefully that's a good sign.

"No one talked, did they?" Jinna is saying when I sink back to the shadowed depth of Amy's corpse.

"Are you kidding?" Amy says. "I asked if Buckle Springs had any urban legends, and people couldn't *stop* talking. Folks love telling ghost stories, especially about their hometown. Didn't take me long to realize the answer had been staring me in the face the whole time."

"What was it?" I ask.

"The Merry Death Bridge," Amy says.

"Ooh," Jinna squeals. "The Dead Prom Queen Hitchhiker!"

"Wow. Yeah." I hadn't thought about that one in a while.

"How about I give Bloody Mary a break and haunt our merry bridge instead? Seduce strapping young drivers into taking me to the cemetery. Or just stand in the middle of the road and watch them drive straight into the lake." Jinna bats her eyelashes at me. "What do you think?"

I cross my arms. "Aren't you a little old to play prom queen?"

Jinna bends a wrist. "Dahling, don't get me started."

"That story is wrong anyway," Amy interjects before Jinna does get started. We both stare at her.

"Come again?" Jinna asks.

"The legend in Buckle Springs is that a teenage girl used her feminine wiles to lure some unsuspecting guy off the bridge to his death on prom night, right?"

"Right," I say.

Jinna grunts.

Amy's already shaking her head. "I spent ages digging for articles about that. What I unearthed instead was the record of a girl who went missing back on prom night in the 1940s. Her date wasn't the victim—he went on to live a long life. Had twelve kids and everything. But she was never heard from again. Their picture was in an old Buckle High yearbook. Her name was Meredith…something. She…"

"Oh, ha-ha," Jinna deadpans. "Meredith. 'Merry Death.' I get it."

"Is *that* why we call the bridge that?" It does make sense.

But Jinna is hungry for more of the grim story. "Then what?"

"She was…" Amy starts again, but the memories have

vanished. She looks from me to her corpse and back again. Nothing else comes. I probably should have ushered us away from the body while we were talking. I admit, I'm surprised Amy's recalled as many details as she has. It's the mark of a powerful mind. She must have been crazy genius smart when she was alive.

"Sheriff Lee left," I say, changing the subject. "Hopefully, he saw the light."

"Or he just left," says Jinna.

I scowl at her. Can't she be a little sensitive to our newly dead companion?

"But our sheriff is still magnificent." Jinna raises her sharp chin. "If one must leave, one should always do so when they are magnificent."

This is a much better response. Amy asks the obvious question, which sets Jinna up to launch into the elaborate and distracting story of when, where, how, and why she made the very important choice to end her own life.

When? A little over thirty years ago. Where? Merry Death Bridge, of course. Jinna glosses over the gruesome "how" and jumps straight into the far more romantic "why."

Simply put, Jinna had done everything. Graduated high school. Left town. Managed a degree in mathematics, but established herself on the stage. She'd had adventures, lovers, and a five-second marriage. She'd built herself from the ground up, lost it all, and then remade herself all over again. Apart from finding her One True Love or giving birth to a child, she'd checked every decent box life had to offer. And at fifty, that last one wasn't even an option.

There she was: beautiful, successful, independent, bored, tired, and alone. So she returned to Buckle Springs (a.k.a. "the scene of the crime") and with her last breath, Jinna cursed this wretched little town and the family of bullies who founded it.

"But you led such an amazing life!" Amy says, at exactly the same point I always do. "What if—?"

"*What* if?" Jinna snaps. Because this is the question that ultimately sent her over the edge. Literally. The hopeful ones always ask this question.

"Fate had *fifty years* to track me down and cross my path with something or someone epic enough to make me care about living. I was tired of making my future up on my own, so I wrote my own ending. Nothing wrong with that."

"But—"

Jinna raises a finger. "You're stuck on the 'one true love' thing, aren't you?"

Amy nods and touches the broken heart at her throat.

"Me too," I whisper in solidarity.

"Dahlings." Jinna purses her bright red lips. "If there's a disappointed soulmate somewhere out there, then they'll just have to wait for my next life. Goodness knows they missed all the best parts of my last one."

"I have a love like that," Amy says to the broken heart.

"Then your love won't rest until she finds you," I say.

Amy nods, but I can tell she has doubts.

Jinna and I often reference the height of trees for telling time, or the colors of leaves, or the gray in Sheriff Lee's hair, but none of those have changed when a suited diver enters the lake beneath the bridge.

Much to my surprise, Amy's body is not rescued. Instead, the diver pulls out the black rectangle everyone uses for a phone these days, takes pictures from multiple angles, and then leaves.

"That's it?" I cry after the diver. "You're just going to leave her here?"

"No, that's smart," says Amy. "My body needs to be removed from the water quickly, but carefully. You'd be surprised how much evidence they'll be able to get from that duct tape alone."

Jinna agrees. "Sheriff Lee learned the hard way what not to do when it comes to pulling a body out of this lake."

She means her body. He hadn't been an officer for very long then. The lake had been covered in cherry blossoms that morning. The world both above and below the water was eerily quiet. And then Jinna's spirit showed up and it was never quiet again.

Shortly after the diver's appearance, the water level of the lake starts to fall. It does that sometimes in the dead of the summer, when there isn't a lot of rain, but this seems more drastic. When I mention it to Jinna, all she does is look at Amy and say, "I guess the sheriff really was on her side."

Three divers on a flat-bottomed boat come next. The sheriff and a woman with curly hair the same amber as the autumn leaves watch from the bridge. She's small, but when she opens her mouth and screams, *"Amiya!"* it shakes the trees. Sheriff Lee holds her back from climbing over the railing and jumping in herself.

Amiya, who is Amy no longer, holds a hand to her heart. "Renée," she whispers, and I can tell that her spirit is crying even though we're surrounded by water.

The broken heart at her throat turns to a flame that the lake does not extinguish. I've seen this spirit fire before, the angry swirling red, orange, and blue that consumes those who pass through the doorway to hell. But the broken heart flame does not consume Amiya. It merely sits at her throat, flickering.

Waiting.

When the divers cut Amiya's body away from the cinderblock, it falls back through the water and lands with a hollow thud, which is not the usual sound when large rocks fall to the bottom of the lake.

Eventually, Renée's screams fade away and the sky turns dark. The lake waters continue to recede.

"Why am I still here?" Amiya asks.

"It takes time for the living to find answers," I say. "Trust them. And trust yourself. I'm sure you were clever enough to make your murderer's identity crystal clear."

"And then?"

Jinna takes this one. "White light, peace, the whole shebang. Most souls jump through that doorway the minute it opens."

"Most souls," Amiya repeats.

"Judging by your bit of bling there"—Jinna draws a tiny circle in the water with her finger—"you'll get to choose."

"Choose peace," I advise.

"Or?"

Jinna grins. "Seek vengeance upon your killer. And his children. And his children's children. Three generations, at least."

"You don't want to do that, though," I say. "You are a smart, kind soul who deserves peace."

"And revenge."

"You're not helping."

"Aren't I?"

"Okay so what if," Amiya interrupts, "I choose vengeance, but only until the day Renée dies? Can I do that?"

I say nothing, because I honestly don't know. No spirit in this lake has ever done that before. Granted, no spirit in this lake has ever been offered the option before either.

Jinna is still grinning. "Yes."

I don't know if she says it because she knows somehow, or if she just really wants the Buckle Family to be on the receiving end of Amiya's wrath for the next few decades. (Which I do agree they totally deserve.) Did the universe offer Jinna this kind of option after her body was rescued and she never mentioned it? The very idea of Jinna *not* telling a story like that is in itself fairly impossible to believe.

"They're going to stop draining the lake, though, right?" Amiya asks.

I've been wondering the same thing. The ghosts here don't need water to continue existing, but the fish are getting crowded. And I'm a mermaid. At this point, the water level is only a few feet above the cinder block. There's not a lot of room left.

I smile when I say, "I'm trying not to think about it."

The water's down to a foot above the cinder block when Amiya's white light appears. Sheriff Lee and Renée have found her justice at last. Amiya hesitates for the briefest of moments before reaching up to the swirling hellflame at her throat and making the choice I would never be brave enough to make.

"For love," she says, and the light grows and shifts, elongating into a sword of fire that ignites Amiya's dark irises. "And for all the victims of the Buckle Family. I will make sure everyone gets what they deserve."

Jinna cheers as Amiya's spirit rises from the water up into the night, bright as a fallen star returning to the heavens.

And then the trucks come.

Sheriff Lee's cruiser pulls into his regular spot beside the bridge, but two larger vehicles with long arms and winches back as close as they can the water's edge, beeping steadily all the way. Wire ropes are unspooled to great lengths. Another boat with more divers appears on the bank.

Two burly men in waders enter the water. "What's this?" Jinna asks.

I have never seen such an ordeal. "Something else to do with Amiya's murder?"

Jinna floats around the wading men's feet like a purring cat. "Or maybe something Amiya found."

The men pass their hooks to the divers, who disappear so deep into the algae that even I can't see them. It's as if they've burrowed beneath the lake itself. But they resurface, sans hooks, and give a shout. The trucks begin inching back up to the road.

And the cement block moves.

Because Amiya's body had not come to rest on the lake's bottom.

She'd landed on the roof of a car.

I can't seem to do anything but gape at the vehicle as it emerges, inching from the depths of the lake—my lake—into the sunlight. I know every inch of this water, I swear. Would have sworn. How did I have no clue that something this massive was sitting right under my fins this whole time?

But I do have a clue. Because I know that beneath that algae is a 1940 Hudson Convertible Coupe in harvest tan with sealed beam headlamps, two-tone upholstery, and automatic brakes that can stop on a dime even when the driver doesn't know the meaning of the word as he shoves his hand down the front of my dress. Mama spent every penny she'd saved on that stylish sheath covered in waves of turquoise sequins, form-fitting right down to where it flared out at the knee.

Brett Buckle, on the other hand, had worn a bad suit, half a bottle of whiskey, and a snarl when he realized how difficult it would be to yank up my hem. He chose to tear the dress off from the top for efficiency's sake. I fought back, kicking the gearshift and scuffing the dashboard. He hit me then, because how dare I mess up his daddy's precious baby. That's the last thing I remember.

Only it isn't.

I remember every ghost, every grievance that's drifted

through these waters in the last eighty years. Every story. Every sadness. Every peace light and hellfire.

I know what happens next.

My revelation should feel like more than a fuzzy dream, but I've been a mermaid so much longer than I was ever alive. I have counseled countless torments. I have kept this town's bloody history as safe as wishing coins.

With some difficulty, Sheriff Lee opens the passenger door.

Jinna's on the shore now, black hair and red dress floating about her as if she's still in the water. And for the first time since that car sank with a young girl still in it, I stand. Slow step by slow step I emerge from the lake on two bare feet, water beading upon turquoise sequins that are scales no longer.

"Don't look," Jinna whispers, but she doesn't mean it.

Not that I would've recognized the body anyway. There's barely a skeleton left, which is almost a shame. I would like to have seen that beautiful dress one last time. The dress I am still wearing. The dress Mama paid for with her blood, sweat, and tears.

I miss my mama.

Amiya comes back to the lake once more, the night Sheriff Lee finds my justice. "Brett Buckle's brother and three of his sons were on the police force," she reports, fire dancing in her eyes. "This murder wasn't the only thing they covered up. Sheriff Lee found so much evidence of corruption that almost every case handled in Buckle Springs is about to be overturned. He's handing files over to the state as we speak."

Jinna grins proudly. "Exactly the chaos this town deserves. I approve."

We stand at the edge of the low water like tourists. The lake will rise again one day, without me in it. Because swirling in the air now are two bright lights: peace and hellfire. It seems the universe's offer to Amiya wasn't as rare as I thought.

"Which will you choose?" Amiya asks.

Jinna immediately opens her blood red lips and I know what she's going to say, but what comes out is, "Choose peace."

I know this. I feel it from the ends of my wavy golden locks to the tip of what is no longer my tail. I know she is right and that it's well past my time, but…

My eyes must convey what my mouth doesn't.

Jinna laughs, deep and throaty. "I've watched you patiently shepherd every soul that's passed through this lake for the last thirty years. If anyone deserves to rest, Dahling, it's you."

No longer trusting my voice, I point to the turbulent hellfire.

Amiya closes her hand gently over my own. "I've got the vengeance covered."

"And I will make a magnificent mermaid."

I resist rolling my eyes at Jinna. Heaven only knows what sort of guidance she'll pass along to the next generation of dearly departed. With luck, there won't be too many.

But I have hope. Because her current advice is exactly what I would have said to some poor unfortunate soul, had I still been Ghost Lake's Mermaid.

"Thanks for making this easy," I tell them.

"Thank *you*," they both say in return.

But there's one more face I want to see before I take that last step into oblivion. He arrives at dawn, like he has almost every day since he was a boy and parks his cruiser in the usual spot. Instead of walking onto the bridge, he shuffles down to the edge of the low water. Gold and amber leaves fall upon his hair and uniform. His boots leave footprints in the mud.

"Thank you, Sheriff Lee," I say, even though I know he can't hear me.

The rising sunlight winks upon the small pile of shiny treasures I've left for him, including an engagement ring and a sack of coins. He crouches down and picks up a bracelet with silver charms. There is a red string tied around his wrist, as if to remind him of something he will never forget. A fin breaks the water before us. We both know who it is. I'm going to miss her, too, the best friend I never had in my last life. I hope our paths do cross again in the next.

In the meantime, if a black-haired ghost in a fancy red ballgown stares you down from the middle of the road on the Merry Death Bridge, be sure to say hi for me.

Pink Lace and Death Gods

EVA ROSLIN

Bianca spread one jittery hand over the chiffon lace on the champagne pink dress hanging from the rack. The needlework on the gold rims glittered in the dim lights of the costume shop. She marveled at how such a treasure existed in a place that smelled of day-old Chinese takeout containers, tobacco, and weed. Eve told her about this place on Decatur, past the French Market, to the left of the Po Boy shop. Guitars and drum sounds burst from the bar down the street, reverberating in her chest. The plants hanging from black wrought-iron balconies near the shop filled the air with a sense of freshness but couldn't cover up the stench of garbage bins.

The damask fabric in front of her had expert stitching. She reached under the layers of puffiness and rough tulle. Her fingers wrapped around the cold crinoline that forced the skirt to take its huge shape. Someone had gone to a lot of trouble to make this dress as authentic as possible.

"Now that's a one of a kind," the shopkeeper said from behind her, making Bianca jolt. She let go of the dress, and a gush of warmth flooded her face. The woman shuffled closer then pursed her lips, mauve lipstick glinting from the overheard lamps.

"It's incredible." Bianca didn't want to give away her desperation, but she *had* to have this dress. She made some extra ends from her Etsy shop to help with the seamstress job with Mrs. Purdue, but Mama's mortgage debt and medical bills piled up. She hadn't treated herself to anything special in years.

"One of a kind." Tendrils of gray and white hair poked out from behind the lilac headscarf the shopkeeper wore, giving way to smooth, ochre skin. Her voice, a rich timbre, made Bianca think that the lady could have been a lounge singer. She let out a hacking cough, which sent Bianca's eyes to the tobacco pipe near the cash register. Smoke snaked around the shop, spreading its aroma in vines.

Bianca cleared her throat. "One of my friends said you have some stuff. Authentic."

The shopkeeper faced Bianca. "You going to a fancy Halloween party?" She walked along the row, her fingers flitting over some of the other costumes.

"My friends invited me to a place in the Marigny. They're all gonna be dressed up as Marie Antoinettes and duchesses, so I wanted something," Bianca said.

The shopkeeper pulled out another long dress from the rack and draped some of the fabric over her. "What about this velvet number?" The dark blue sequins on the bust glinted, but it didn't pop for Bianca.

"I think I'm set on the pink one." Bianca pointed behind her.

The shopkeeper let go of the velvet dress. "That one, I can't rent. You'd have to buy it outright. I'm not sure it's in your budget."

Bianca frowned. Where did this woman get off making

assumptions about what she could or couldn't afford? What hurt more was that she was right, and that if she bought the gown, she might have to skip this week's groceries. "Could I do a layaway?"

A resigned sigh escaped the shopkeeper's lips. "You want that dress pretty bad, don't you?"

"Yes, ma'am." Even now, the dress called to Bianca from the rack. She wanted to throw herself over it to protect it. She didn't want anyone else to find this treasure.

"Let me see if I can figure something out with you. Come on."

Bianca followed the shopkeeper back to where the pink dress hung, its beadwork looking even more luminous, and wondered if it had been a wedding gown. Maybe it glinted in the chandelier light, clinging to a soprano as she sang an aria at the old French Opera House before it burned down all those years ago.

A wistful look settled over the shopkeeper's face. "I might have turned a few heads in this years ago, but those days are gone."

"I'm sorry," Bianca said. "How long have you owned this place?"

"Thirty-seven years come March." The shopkeeper took the dress from the rack and walked with it to the cash register. She placed it on the counter and swished some plastic wrappers around, a few hangers clanging to the ground.

Bianca combed a hand through her thick curls. "You got some beautiful pieces." Her eyes scanned the rest of the shop, taking in the sights of old ballerina costumes, gowns, and a small section for children's apparel with some jewelry.

The shopkeeper let out a sigh. "The pride parade is always fun. My nephew brings all his friends around. I swear, some of them are prettier than most of the women I know."

Bianca chuckled. She fidgeted with her purse straps. "Can I pay with credit card?" She reached into her purse, not wanting to know the huge sum that she guessed the woman would charge. Her nerves fluttered, fingers jittery.

The shopkeeper pointed at her necklace. "You buy that or was it a gift?"

Bianca fingered the topaz gem. "I got it from my grandma when she died." Strands of grief scraped at her throat, as she thought of all the times she'd stayed at Grandma's, the sleep-overs they'd had, then staying by her hospital bed.

"I was gonna ask if you could part with it, and I could give you a discount, but a family heirloom like that…" The shop-keeper shook her head before quirking an eyebrow. "You remind me so much of her."

"You knew my grandmother?" Bianca said.

The shopkeeper gave her a knowing glance. "*Long* time ago. You have her eyes." She paused, looking Bianca up and down. "If you straightened your hair, no one would know. You could pass."

A dull weight sank through Bianca's chest and thudded into her stomach.

The magic word.

Pass.

For white.

As in, wouldn't have to work two jobs and scrape by. As in, all the modelling scouts who had told her if she let them touch up her face, make her whiter, she could live a different life. Pretending to be something didn't suit Bianca. Other Black folks made the "pass" comment for years, like they wondered why anyone would squander it.

She didn't want the shopkeeper to sense her hurt, so she stammered. "I hear that a lot."

"Pretty girl like you, doesn't surprise me." The shopkeeper

pressed a few buttons on the cash register. "If you trade me the necklace, I can let you have it for free."

Bianca's stomach clenched, as she considered this new price. She had to have that dress. Right now, it meant something *just* for her, not a bill collector or "past due," or a price hike in the cost of AC because of the increasing heat. But Grandma…

"I don't know."

"This dress was made two hundred years ago and has been waiting for someone as special as you to wear it again." The shopkeeper held Bianca's hands. "It was meant to be."

Before she knew what came over her, Bianca took off the necklace, handed it over, and accepted the bag with the dress in it. She slid one hand through the loops of the bag. "Thank you so much."

The shopkeeper pressed her hands over Bianca's wrists. "Take a photo then come back to show me."

DUMAINE STREET VIBRATED with the buzz of drumbeats and brass instruments that blared into the night, as Bianca passed by shops on her way to Eve's. Other revelers stumbled in the streets, bottles in hands, some of them laughing, others shouting.

One of them stopped, a man with the aroma of rum and skunk. "Hey, pretty lady, you look real fancy! Where you off to?"

Bianca continued walking without a reply. This gown made her *sweat*. She'd have a hell of a time cleaning it tomorrow and regretted not stuffing more tissues under her armpits.

"Aw, come on, now! I'm fun!" the man said.

Bianca kept walking until something grabbed her arm. The

man had his hand on her elbow, so she used her purse to smack his face. "Get away from me!" she yelled.

His friends burst out into peals of laughter that echoed against the walls of the light pink and blue buildings. She straightened herself and kept walking. The sound of someone retching onto the city streets emerged.

When she crossed onto the Marigny side of Bourbon, she sighed with relief at leaving behind the loud music. The houses here, many of them with high staircases to keep above ground for floods, had a calming energy. They reminded her of Granny's shotgun house in the Tremé. Homes there were smaller. Katrina washed away so many of them, including hers. More grief strangled her at the memories of wading waist-deep in brown water and about a dozen other things she tried to forget.

Bianca wiped her face. *Put your troubles behind.* When she passed by a window to a psychic's shop, she glanced up to check her hair then looked at a face not her own.

Marcy's face. Her neighbor from 2B down the hall.

Bianca screamed.

Marcy had come over to help Bianca put on the dress and then… her memory went blank. Everything had slipped into shadows.

What in the holy hell was happening and where was her body?

None of this made any sense. How had this happened?

A bunch of people stood outside as she got to Eve's house. They cheered as someone made a toast, clinking plastic red cups together. As Bianca got closer, she spotted a woman from the back with straight hair. She stumbled a bit at the recognition of the slutty witch costume she thought she threw out three years ago. When she grabbed the woman's creamy-soft shoulder, she did a double take at the dragon tattoo covering the top half of the arm she looked at. Marcy had one just like that.

Glancing down at her much darker skin, like Marcy's, then up at this woman in the slutty costume, the boobs jacked up and squeezing tight, her own face looked back at her. A clone.

"Hey!" she yelled at her clone.

The clone-her looked up, and a slow smile spread across her lips. "I am so glad you could join us. Your friends have been telling me all about you!"

"How did you get here?" Bianca asked the clone.

"You looked peaceful in your sleep; I would never dream of disturbing you!" her clone said.

"Look, I don't know who or what you are, but you're going to give me my body back, now." Bianca grabbed for the clone's arm.

"Join the revelry!" Her clone clinked glasses with one of her other friends, Steve, who grabbed both her hands. They waltzed together inside the house, getting lost in a shuffle of the other party guests.

The music thudded so loud that her chest vibrated with each drumbeat.

When did all of this start? She was fine after the costume shop, then at the apartment trying things on, then she recalled the saleswoman's words: *"This dress was made two hundred years ago and has been waiting for someone as special as you to wear it again."* She'd also said something about "meant to be," but Bianca thought that was just more sales talk to make her buy the dress.

"I've got to get this dress off." She tore at the ends of the frilly lace on the arms, a three-quarter sleeve, but it wouldn't budge. When she fingered the material over her chest, it felt glued on.

She had to leave and find a more private place to take the

dress off. As she went through the doorway, she bumped into a tall guy with dreads who smoked something that reeked of skunks. The smell of weed always made her cough. She glimpsed his lighter. Maybe she could burn the dress off if it didn't budge.

"Can I borrow a light?" she asked him.

He handed over the lighter. "Pretty little thing like you can have just about anything if you ask."

She turned away, flicked the spark wheel, and brought it closer to the bottom of the dress. The fire skimmed around the edges of the garment before it died out.

What? She shook her head. Was this dress made from titanium or something? She handed the lighter back to the guy and made her way inside the house. *Time to find that clone bitch.* Where had she come from? And what was with that highfalutin talk?

Bianca wove past the other partygoers, drinks in their hands, some of them dancing. Her clone ground her hips against Steve's thigh.

Ugh! Steve was one of her oldest friends. They'd shared a lot of firsts together: school dance, prom, cigarette…a bad kiss. She had never seen him "that way" and didn't like her body against his, tits pushed up, ass clinging to fabric. She wasn't about that.

"What are you doing?" She shoved her clone on the shoulder.

The clone rolled her eyes before stumbling for balance.

Is she drunk?

"Have a bit of fun, dear," her clone said. "I've acquainted myself with your friend and believe you should—" A familiar look crossed her clone's face. Bianca knew it as the expression someone makes before vomiting. Her clone raced into the kitchen, heels clacking on the ground.

Damn it.

Roars of approval and cheers blasted through Bianca's ears, as someone walked in through the door. A tall, dark-skinned guy with a top hat, white face paint in the shape of a skull. A cigar dangled from the side of his mouth, ashes floating to his bare chest covered with a vest.

She couldn't stand guys who dressed up like Baron Samedi. Lord of the Dead, the Haitian vodou legend she and most of her friends heard about growing up, sort of like a boogeyman. They were a dime a dozen at Halloween and parades, and each year it got worse. She hoped he wouldn't do the horrible James Bond villain laugh.

This one raised his arms in the air and grinned. He had on a pair of antique-looking sunglasses. He lowered them and looked at Bianca. She turned behind her to see who else he might be looking at, but everyone else was focused on dancing.

The Baron imitator approached her. She wanted to get away, but a force kept her glued in place. Something magnetic pulled her toward him, and she shuddered. Heat fluttered between her thighs.

When he reached her, he took one of her hands in his and bowed.

"C-can I help you?" Shame flushed through her chest and throat, as she found herself wanting him to take her into one of the bedrooms and, despite her sharper instincts, ravish her body.

He removed his glasses. "Au contraire, darling. I need *your* help."

She squared her shoulders. "Let me guess. You want me to leave this party with you. Why don't you try something more original?" She wasn't sure if her *I'm not interested* façade would work on him but had to give it a shot. She wasn't about to just let this guy do whatever he wanted with her.

His face changed to an expression of mock horror. "Moi? I am a gentleman and never go after a lady uninvited."

"You're really putting in a lot of effort with the act," she said.

"Act?" Violet swirls illuminated in the irises of his eyes before the pattern of a skull flickered over his face.

Bianca gasped before bumping into a few people behind her.

"I'm not who you should fear," the Samedi said, whoever he was. He had a cane that he tapped on the ground in the direction of the kitchen. "I know how to get your body back."

Bianca put a hand to her forehead. Sweat dripped down her back and chest. "You do?"

"The woman who took your body, Eloise, is a malevolent spirit. She pledged her soul to me two hundred years ago, and I've been trying to collect it." He tsked. "She keeps slipping through my grasp. But this time, she isn't getting away."

"Why?" Bianca asked.

"Because *you're* going to help me," the Baron said.

Bianca cleared her throat. "H-how am I going to do that?"

He removed a chain from his neck with an assortment of bones. She didn't want to guess who or what they had belonged to, but something told her they were real. They didn't have that polished, store-bought quality so many of the fake ones did. These were covered in the dust of years.

"You are going to press this gem over her neck," he answered.

A jewel in the middle of the necklace slid into her palm and reminded her of those crystals that she'd begged Mama to buy for her on a class trip to the Children's Museum. She'd wanted all of them, the pink, blue, green. She couldn't believe there were so many, and all of them so shiny and slick. The one she held now was a flat obsidian circle.

Cheers erupted from the house like the Saints just scored a touchdown.

When she looked back to find the source of the noise, she had to deal with the image of her clone's mouth attached to a hose of a beer keg, which she chugged down.

Bianca wanted to tear the hose from her clone's mouth and punch her.

"The necklace." Samedi pointed at the gem. "It has to touch Eloise's—your—skin." Samedi blew a trail of hot air against Bianca's neck.

"Why do you keep..." Bianca struggled to finish the sentence. She wanted to say *how do you expect me to get anything done if you keep turning me on?* but kept her mouth shut.

His warm breath disappeared.

He walked back to the drink table, grabbing a bottle of booze, then took a swig.

Bianca took a deep breath, scanned the warm room, and fanned herself.

Her clone knelt near a potted plant and vomited all the beer she'd just chugged into the dirt.

A burning sensation trickled into her throat.

How do I do this?

She walked up to her clone, throat exposed, and placed the necklace over her head. The strings were long enough that she didn't have to worry about fastening it on.

Steam and smoke rose from her clone, who screamed. She clamped both hands on Bianca's shoulders. "What have you done?"

The stone grew purple veins, like some marble tiles, as the clone tried to pry it off with her fingers. Eloise glanced behind, eyes widening, as Samedi approached. He scowled at her, nostrils flared.

"You have no inkling what I have been through!" Her clone grabbed Bianca's hands and shook them.

"You stole my body!" Bianca shouted.

"It is not too late," her clone said. "You can take it back. Please!" Something in the way her own face twisted struck a twinge of regret inside Bianca.

"Your soul is past overdue," Samedi boomed. "Don't make this more difficult."

"No!" Her clone screamed as violet swirls of air escaped her nose and lips, and her head tipped back. A flood of purple light left her mouth and eyes. She fell to her knees.

Baron Samedi held his cane up.

Was anyone else seeing this?

When Bianca's gaze flitted around the room, the other partygoers were cheering someone on to "chug" and otherwise dancing or talking.

"They cannot see us," Samedi said like he could read Bianca's mind. The purple energy kept flowing into his cane until it stopped, and Eloise slumped to the floor.

"It has been a pleasure." Samedi took one of Bianca's hands in his and kissed it, heat blooming between her thighs again. She wanted to rake her fingernails down his chest.

He chuckled as if he knew her thoughts. "Save it for someone else."

She frowned at him and wanted to slap his face. Feelings like this didn't overwhelm her this much, or so intensely. *Stupid me, thinking a goddamn spirit of the dead would like me.*

His cane touched her forehead, and everything went black.

. . .

WHEN BIANCA WOKE UP, she stumbled over a pile of clothes and tripped on her way to the bathroom mirror in her apartment. Her face was her own again, hair curly. She breathed out a huge sigh. "Thank God." Or should she say Samedi?

Her throat was raw and sore from all the throwing up that her double had done the previous night, chest tight, muscles stiff. Hopefully a few days of rest would fix that.

She stared at the pink ball gown on the floor, puffed up at the skirt from the crinoline. "God, I wish I could burn you." The closer she approached, something stabbed at her temples. Images of fields of cotton filled her mind. A woman she didn't recognize ran with a baby in her arms from white men on horses who chased her with whips.

The lithe woman with the young face couldn't have been more than twenty. She fled to the banks of a swamp and hid behind a cypress tree where she said a prayer.

Baron Samedi walked beside her and placed a necklace into her hands, the same one Bianca used last night.

Stars filled Bianca's vision, crashing into the side of her head. Bianca stared at the dress and sank to her knees.

Was the woman Eloise? Did I send her back to that place? What have I done?

She thought she heard a deep, rumbling chuckle from behind her.

Another vision filtered through her mind of a huge ballroom and of Eloise, this time a tignon on her head. The elegant, pink champagne dress clung to her body as if created for her. She bowed in front of a white man before dancing a waltz, like the other couples that twirled around the room.

"Eloise…" a voice called from behind.

Samedi.

"It is time." His words boomed in Bianca's mind.

Eloise bolted outside and tripped on some grass over the hem of her dress before getting up again and continuing to run.

Bianca shook her head, the familiar sight of her unmade bed in front of her again, her radiator beside the window. What just happened?

LATER THAT AFTERNOON when she went by the costume shop to get an explanation from the owner, she found an empty space with a For Sale sign on the door. The glass windows revealed everything had been cleared out. A few hangers remained on racks here and there, cardboard on the floor.

"Damn." Unanswered questions circled in Bianca's mind, as the drumbeats from the nearby bar boomed inside her chest. She turned around to leave.

A tall man tipped his top hat to her and smiled.

"Samedi?"

He rounded a corner and by the time she ran there to catch up, he disappeared, if he had been there at all.

The Ghost Cricket

LEE MURRAY

It was the middle of summer, and I had accompanied my master, Magistrate Yun, to a tiny village in the northeast of the county. He was called to hear the case of a man who claimed to be haunted by a ghost cricket. It was not the first outlandish tale my master had heard in his illustrious career—bandits and ruffians are known to conjure the strangest excuses to avoid punishment—but in my decade of travelling with him and recording his cases, the unfortunate tale still stands out in my mind.

The man in question was dragged into the square before the magistrate. Thin-faced and dressed in stinking rags, he scrabbled in the dirt under the hot sun, his hands tied at the wrists. The man moaned softly, raising both hands to one ear, and then to the other in a manner which was both pitiful and comical.

The petitioner, a burly farmer, stepped forward. He glared at the prisoner, then turned to the Magistrate Yun, his voice full of venom. "This man, Li Wen, claims to be a prince, but in truth, he's nothing but a filthy arsonist. He razed my crop. You must have seen the field on your way into the village. All my millet, burned to the ground."

It was true: we'd seen the field as we entered the village, the magistrate pulling open the curtains of his sedan as we passed by the square of blackened, useless stalks.

The petitioner spat, a fat gob of mucus staining the ground near Li Wen. "I deserve to be compensated for my loss. If I had not put out the fire, it might have spread across the entire county."

"Quiet," my master admonished from his seat in the shade. "It's not your place to decide the truth, nor to tell me what you deserve." He turned to the accused. "A princeling, you say? Well, this man has charged you with arson. What do you have to say for yourself?"

The thin-faced Li Wen got to his feet. "Father, I can explain," he said, and I whipped my head up in surprise as I'd expected his voice to be as coarse as his clothes. "None of this would have happened if my mother were not a whore..."

In the stifling summer heat, my master fluttered his fan and settled back to listen to Li Wen's account.

...THAT'S what my beloved half-brothers—the politician, the warmonger, and the poet—called her. Never in her hearing, though; they were far too careful for that. And nor did they let our father, the emperor, hear their taunts, since he did not hold with persecuting lesser beings and certainly not his best-loved concubine.

But my father is no more. The emperor succumbed like any mortal to a fever which turned his skin and eyes a sickly yellow. Within a week, the politician had taken my father's place on the throne, aided by the warmonger, to whom he'd promised half of all the lands and riches conquered in his name. The poet, a lover of beauty despite his ugly tongue, knew better than to argue with them, retreating instead to his pavilion in the palace grounds to practice his art.

I had hoped for a role in the new order, too. While I didn't have the delicatesse of the politician, the brash bravado of the soldier, nor any skill with a brush, I could work an abacus well enough, and I was their brother, and an emperor's son, after all.

But princes are petty beings.

"She is a whore," the politician said, while fiddling absently with his silk sleeves. "Her very presence in the palace is an insult to my mother."

"And to mine," the warmonger said.

From the same litter as the warmonger, the poet did not respond, but his smile put me in mind of a well-fed cat.

The politician inspected a hem where a thread of silk had worked loose. "You'll accompany her from the palace, of course."

"You can't do this," I wailed. "I'm your brother."

"I can do whatever I choose; you are merely an insect," the politician said.

"But our father—"

"Our father thought so, too," the warmonger cut in. "He left you this." He threw a lacquered box at my feet. It landed with a heavy thud on the silk rug.

I picked it up. I knew it immediately; it had been my father's, home to his pet cricket. Soothed by the insect's song, my father was rarely without it. I turned the hollow box in my hands, running my fingertips over the familiar carvings: a willow bough, a lake, the etched cliffs of a mountain. Inside, the pampered cricket chirruped its displeasure.

"Get out," the politician said.

The warmonger grinned. Walked his fingers in the air. "Off to the fields with you."

I looked to the poet, still hopeful he might utter a word in my favour, but he was too preoccupied studying the clouds.

Clutching the box, I turned away.

My mother and I left before noon, departing the palace where I had lived all my life without even the courtesy of a carriage. I carried my mother on my back, since she could not walk more than a few steps on her tiny lotus feet. She's petite, weighing barely more than a child, yet by the time I had carried her the four li to the village, my legs were shaking with fatigue.

There had been no point in going any further. In our disgrace, my mother's family would not want us, and, even had I known where to find them, my slippers would not survive another step. So I left my mother on the side of the road with the chirruping cricket, while I ventured into the village. There, I bartered with my accuser, exchanging my embroidered silk garments and a promise of labour for a sack of rice, these rags you see on my back, and humble lodgings near the fields for the length of the harvest. It was all I could do to carry my mother to the tiny hut. I collapsed on the dusty kang.

I should have slept deeply—I ached to the marrow with exhaustion—but the cricket's incessant chirruping would not allow it. It warbled all night, on and on and on. Every discordant chirp was like a pike to my brain. My mother, sweet soul, wasn't bothered. Perhaps she found its song a comfort, a reminder of our former life. For myself, it was a relief to rise at dawn.

Born to palace life, I am the first to admit that I am not cut out for hardship. By the end of my first day in the millet, my back was screaming, my skin blistered, and my feet oozed with blood. Reeking with sweat, and too exhausted even to bathe, I devoured a bowl of my mother's congee and slumped on the kang, desperate for sleep. But that infernal insect refused to quieten. It cheeped and chirped and trilled all night. I covered the box with a sack to muffle the noise, still it would not cease. I carried the box outside, but, lonely for my mother, the insect only shrieked even louder. By morning, my eyes were surely redder than the sunrise. My head pounded with fatigue. I fled into the fields to escape the cacophony.

It didn't help. To endure their daily drudgery, the peasants chatter endlessly. Father, surely with your learning, you will understand; they're like a horde of crickets themselves, with their constant babbling about millet and *mah jong*. But their prattle gave me an idea. That night, I didn't collapse on the kang after eating my congee. Instead, I collected the cricket in its box and limped into the village.

It didn't take long to find the dusty back alley where the local cricket fights take place. I arranged to pitch my father's coddled pet against a cricket captured in the fields that very day—one that had not endured even a single snowy season. The two males were of equal weight, both black and ugly, with heavy jaws and serrated legs, but I was confident of success. My cricket was of noble stock; I was persuaded my father had left it to me for this very purpose—to assure the future of an unjustly maligned son. I wagered my mother's ivory hair comb on the match, the villagers clamouring to place their own bets, then I lowered my father's cricket into the bowl. It merely looked at its opponent. I prodded it with a blade of grass. The stupid cricket sidled away to the edge of the bowl.

"Come on! Fight!" I screamed.

The cricket just chirruped plaintively.

My accuser crowed gleefully as his charge rammed mine, attacking my father's pet with its vicious spiny limbs. It crunched down hard with its powerful mandibles, biting the legs off my father's cricket. The outcome was inevitable. Before the match was over, I handed over the precious comb, grabbed the crippled cricket, and limped home, my head pounding with the villagers' raucous laughter.

You'd think that with the cricket missing most of its legs, I'd be guaranteed a night's sleep. No such luck. The miserable creature must have rubbed its remaining leg raw with its pitiful wailing. Thin and gut-wrenching, the sound penetrated my skull, each grating chord like a needle jabbed through the back of my eye. I couldn't bear it any longer. I rose from the kang and tipped up the lacquered box, spilling the insect onto the dirt. I ground the crackly carapace under my foot, choking the cricket into silence. Then I shovelled its carcass back into the box and went to sleep.

I awoke at dawn to blissful stillness. It was quiet when I made my way into the fields, and quiet when I returned in the late afternoon. My back still ached, and the broken blisters on my arms seeped with straw-coloured fluid, but the thrumming in my head had finally dissipated. I was almost joyful.

"Your brother, the cricket, died," my mother said sadly that evening when I returned from the fields. She was preparing an offering of rice, which she left on a leaf-altar near the lacquered box. It rankled me that she would waste our food on the useless insect, but I said nothing.

That night, I awoke to a noise so loud it made my teeth ache. The hut trembled with it, a pitiful keening that reverberated in the darkness. I glanced at my sleeping mother beside me on the kang, and my back trickled with cold sweat. How was it possible for her to sleep through a noise so loud? I knew then that something unnatural was afoot.

I shuffled away from the source of the din, pressing my back against the wall, my heart jumping at every stridulation, and squinted into the corners of the hut. When I could barely breathe for the noise, the mangled cricket staggered from the lacquered box, pulling itself along the dirt floor with its remaining leg. Father, I was terrified. The ominous shuffle of that macabre limb made my bones rattle in anguish. I watched, paralysed with fright, while the ghost cricket climbed atop the box. It perched on the mountain etched in the box's surface and glared at me with its black eyes. It waved its solitary limb angrily and shrieked some more. It did nothing else. Just screeched and screeched. Slowly, my fear turned to rage. That ghost cricket was determined to rob me of my sleep.

I approached the dead insect, kicking aside my mother's rice offering as I picked it up in my palm. I left the hut, carrying it through the gloom to the river. Inside my fist, the insect shrieked and wailed. For the first time, I wondered if it was trying to tell me something. My father had understood the nuances of the cricket's song. One of his trusted counsellors claimed that, as emperor, my father even spoke their language, that he'd actually heard him converse with the insect, but if it were possible, I never bothered to learn. What could an insect say that would be of interest to me? The dead insect might have begged me to spare it from an eternity of despair, I wouldn't have known. I plunged it into the river, burying it in the mud. Then I wiped my hands dry on my trousers, walked back to the hut, and fell asleep.

The next night, the blasted ghost cricket returned. How had it escaped being gobbled up by the eels and toads? How had it shuffled its crippled carcass through the fields without being eaten by birds? I had no idea. It was back and louder than ever. I covered my ears with my hands. There was no blocking out the noise. The little hut shuddered with its caterwauling.

I shook my mother awake. "Do you hear that noise?"

"What noise?" she replied.

"My father's cricket," I said. "It's haunting me."

My mother caressed my cheek with her palm. "It's just a silly nightmare," she said. "Go back to sleep." She turned over and went to sleep herself.

But there would be no rest with that racket going on. I had to get rid of it. I picked up the cricket, stomped on the leaf-altar, and left the hut, trudging ten li, beyond the village and into the fields, and then even further to the chiseled foothills of the mountains. Finally, I saw what I needed—a large boulder, which had broken away from the cliffs. I put the cricket down on the ground, ignoring its grumbling as I scooped out a small hollow beside the boulder with my fingernails. Then I laid the miserable insect in the hole and pushed the boulder over it. Father, it wasn't a trivial task. I had to push a log into a gap at the base of the boulder and lean in, using all my weight to lever the stone over the insect. Working like a peasant in the fields and surviving on thin congee, I had barely enough strength to move it, but inch by blessed inch, the stone moved, smothering the ghost cricket and drowning out the noise.

The night was calm. I reveled in the quiet as I traipsed the ten li back to the hut. It was dawn when I arrived, and too late to return to the kang. I had no choice but to harvest the millet without a wink of sleep.

When I returned to the hut that evening, my mother had restored the leaf-altar, and was preparing a fresh offering of rice for the ghost cricket.

"Stupid woman! No wonder the ghost keeps coming back." I struck her across her face, hard, then swatted the food out of her hand. A welt rose on her cheek. She deserved it. My brothers were right. She was a whore and a burden.

While she wept bitterly, I ate my congee. Then I settled down on the kang. Still sobbing, my mother bent to scrape the grains of rice off the floor. I sat up and barked at her to be quiet. She whimpered a while longer, but I threatened to hit her again and that put an end to it. She joined me on the kang and turned her back to me.

No sooner had she dropped off to sleep, the cricket was back, shaking the hut with its chirping. I knew it was dead, but still I couldn't believe it had escaped from under the boulder. Before it could climb up onto the mountain carving, I snatched up the box and stormed out of the hut.

I strode into the field and set the box down in the millet. Then I took up two stones, striking them together to create a spark. This time, I would rid myself of the miserable creature forever. The cricket shrieked. I didn't care. I set the millet alight. The summer had been long and hot. It took only minutes before flames shot into the air. The cricket screamed even louder. Calling for mercy, I expect. Soon enough, its cries weakened as the crop crackled and roared about it. I howled, too. Let its ghost burn in hell.

I stayed there all night, watching the box glow red with the heat…

"SEE? HE ADMITS IT!" the petitioner shouted. "I found him there, with the box, asleep beside my smouldering field."

"It was the cricket's fault," Li Wen said bitterly. "They're supposed to be good luck. Much good it did me. The wretched ghost can starve forever for all I care."

"Enough," said my master. "Bring me the cricket."

Casting a gleeful look at Li Wen, the farmer stalked over to hand the scorched box to the magistrate.

Master Yun spooled cool air over the box with his fan.

Slow moments passed.

Then I felt my eyes widen as the dead cricket crawled from the box, dragging itself up the carved mountain with its single spindly limb. When it was perched clumsily astride the box, my master bent his ear to the tiny creature. He listened carefully as the ghostly insect set up a mournful song, the wistful notes as pure and sharp as a mountain stream.

Li Wen tried again to put his hands to his ears, but bound together as they were, one ear was always uncovered. The farmer shifted his feet uneasily.

When the cricket had finished its tale, Magistrate Yun lifted his head and spoke. "Li Wen will be released. You! Farmer! You will receive fifty strikes to the face with the sole of a shoe."

"What? You're punishing me?" the farmer railed. "Because he claims he is a prince? I did nothing wrong. What about my millet?"

"You sold the man's garments, did you not? And his mother's expensive comb? And you still have the field. Go away, or I will add another fifty strikes."

While the villagers moved to the edge of the square, waiting for the punishment be meted out, the magistrate and I went into the shade of a nearby house, where he would take tea, and I would write up my report, before continuing our journey. Outside, the shrieks of the farmer could be heard over the shouts of the crowd. I didn't need to see his split lips, bruised eyes, and broken cheekbones, to know that the villagers were carrying out the magistrate's instructions.

"What of Li Wen?" I asked.

"Oh, he'll be punished for his disrespect," my master replied. "There is nowhere beyond the reach of a ghost cricket's song. Prince or no, without sleep, he'll be dead before the summer ends."

Later, when we were heading out of the village, my master pulled aside the curtains and called to the men bearing the sedan, telling them to stop at the hut nearest the burned field.

On the road outside the shabby hut, Magistrate Yun

climbed down from the sedan. "Mother," he called. Several moments passed before the old woman tottered from the hut on her dainty lotus feet. "I believe this is yours." As he handed her the box, I saw where his curved nail had scratched the lacquered surface. Underneath the scorched paint, beneath the carved mountain, the box glinted and gleamed. It was made of gold.

Tears welled in her old eyes, and she smiled, covering her mouth with her hand like any well-born gentlewoman. Then, clutching the golden box, she turned and shuffled inside the hut.

"How did you know?" I asked the magistrate as I helped him back into the litter.

"The cricket told me. He'd been trying to tell Li Wen all along."

No One Sings in the City of the Dead

TIM WAGGONER

"I honestly didn't think I'd see you again. I *hoped*, sure, but I didn't *believe*, not deep down."

Keith doesn't respond. He looks at me with eyes that don't blink, and his mouth – wet with blood – remains closed. Crimson stains mar his hospital gown, and while a cold, strong wind is blowing, the thin fabric doesn't stir. Neither does his hair. It's dusk, so there's still some sun left, but the cemetery is surrounded by tall oaks, and their reddish-brown leaves block much of the light, paint shadows on the ground, drape old, crumbling gravestones in darkness.

I step forward, but I immediately stop. I want to go to Keith, touch him, prove that he's real, but I'm afraid. What if his form is tenuous? What if I touch him and he pops like a soap bubble, here one instant, gone the next? I can't take losing him a second time. So, I stand here, motionless, just like him, fifteen feet between us, maybe less, the wind tearing leaves from the trees, causing them to dance in the air around us before falling to the ground.

A woman's voice comes from close behind me.

"What's wrong? Not what you were expecting?"

Her tone is both amused and cruel. She's enjoying this.

The Clown Lady.

I don't take my eyes off Keith, fearing he'll vanish the instant I stop looking at him.

"Is . . . *this* all he is now?"

"Not good enough for you? I can always send him back if –"

"No!"

I hesitate another moment, then I start walking toward him. Behind me, cloth rustles on the ground, and something whimpers, unhappy in the cold. I ignore it and keep moving, leaves crunching beneath my feet. Keith shows no sign he's aware of my approach, but I feel something change in the atmosphere between us. At first, I don't know what is it, but as I draw closer, I feel it more strongly, and now I can name it.

Anticipation.

His stink hits me then, a rank combination of spoiled meat, blood, shit, and piss. I don't mind it, though. It's evidence he's really here.

When I reach him, I put my arms around his cold, stiff neck, stand on the tips of my toes, lean forward, and press my lips to his mouth. His lips don't yield right away, so I push my mouth harder against his. Eventually, his lips grow warmer, and – if they're not exactly soft – they become more pliable.

I pull my face away, my mouth smeared with his blood. It's foul, diseased, and I've never tasted anything sweeter.

I look into his empty eyes and smile, my teeth streaked red with what used to run in my husband's veins.

"Happy Halloween, my love."

HE LIES on his hospital bed, eyes closed, chest barely moving when he breathes. I rise from my chair and step to the side of the bed, wanting to get a closer look, to make sure he's still alive. Without opening his yes, Keith smiles weakly.

"I'm not dead yet," he says.

His voice is thin and tired, but I'm glad he can still joke. I take his left hand, careful not to squeeze too tight. His skin is dry as paper, the bones beneath fragile as balsa wood, and I fear if I tighten my grip, these bones will snap like desiccated twigs.

"How long have you been here?" he asks.

"Not long," I lie. I didn't leave his room after he fell asleep last night. I spent the night here, sleeping in the chair.

His eyes open slowly, as if this takes a great effort.

"What time is it?" he asks.

The bed controls are attached to the inside of railing, and his hand fumbles for them. I want to work the controls for him, but he's a proud man, determined to do as much for himself as he can, while he can. So, I stand by and wait while his fingers search for the right button. They finally find it, he presses it, and the head of his bed raises him into a sitting position. When he's satisfied with the angle, he takes his finger off the button, and his hand falls limply onto the mattress. His breathing picks up speed. The small exertion has exhausted him. He's connected to various types of medical equipment – an IV drip of isotonic solution, blood oxygen monitor, heart monitor, blood pressure cuff, and more. It's all about the blood right now.

Speaking of blood, he coughs once, and a dark line of the stuff rolls down the side of his mouth. If he's aware of it, he gives no sign.

"Do you need to go to the restroom?" I ask, eyeing the blood nervously.

I think about the last time this happened, when I didn't get him to the toilet in time and he vomited a gush of dark red blood all over the room's tiled floor. It took forever for the staff to clean up the mess. I should've kept a pan by the bed for him.

He shakes his head. "I'm good." A pause. "For now, anyway."

I hope he's right.

Keith was diagnosed with liver disease in his twenties, and doctors told him he'd need a transplant by the time he hit middle age, if not sooner. He made it to thirty-six before his liver started giving out, and it was almost a year after that until a donor organ became available. The transplant procedure went smoothly, and all signs pointed to Keith being fine. And for a few weeks, he was. But then he started throwing up blood. Not a lot at first, but then more began coming up, and we returned to the transplant doctor. Tests were run, results were inconclusive, and Keith ended up back in the hospital. After yet more tests, the doctors determined the cause of Keith's problem was that there'd been an "incident" during surgery – perhaps an artery was nicked, and the transplant team didn't see it and closed him up. The leaking blood was backing into his stomach, and when the amount became too much, Keith's body ejected it the only way it could.

Three months in the hospital and six surgeries later, the problem still wasn't fixed, and this morning, one of the doctors took me aside and told me Keith's body couldn't take anymore. His new liver was dying, and he'd developed an infection that the docs couldn't get rid of. She told me Keith had a week left, maybe less.

I went out to my car and cried for the better part of an hour. Then I came back to Keith's room to wait for him to wake up. Being here was hard before, but knowing what I know now, it's unbearable. But I won't leave him. He's my husband, and I want to spend every moment with him that I can before he dies. Thank god we never had children. I can't imagine trying to deal with their grief while I'm grieving, too.

"Has the doc been by this morning?" Keith asks. "Did I miss her because I was sleeping?"

"I haven't seen her yet." This is a lie. If I tell him the truth, he'll ask what she said to me, and I don't want to tell him. I *can't* tell him.

He settles his head back against the pillow, eyes now half-lidded.

"I'm so sick of this place. I can't wait for them to fix me up so I can go home."

"Me, too."

There's a catch in my voice, but Keith doesn't register it.

"I'm *so* sleepy. Why am I so sleepy? I just woke up."

I squeeze his hand a bit tighter, but he grimaces in pain and I quickly loosen my grip.

"It's all the meds they have you on. Why don't you go ahead and take a nap? I'll be right here."

"Okay, but only a short one."

He closes his eyes, and a moment later his breathing deepens.

I think he's asleep, but then he mumbles, "Sing something for me."

I work in phone sales, but singing is my hobby, and, if I do say so myself, I'm not too shabby at it. I'm okay singing in front of an audience, but I'm uncomfortable singing for only one person. I'm too aware of them looking at me, listening, judging . . . But this is Keith. I've sang solo to him before. Of course, none of those times did I know he was dying.

"Sure, sweetie."

I'm not sure what to sing, so I pick a song at random – a slow ballad about two lovers saying goodbye for the last time. Tears stream down my cheeks as I sing softly. Keith doesn't open his eyes, and I'm glad. I don't want him to see me upset like this.

I manage to make it to the end of the song, and I wipe tears off my face. It looks like Keith is asleep, so I'll go into the restroom and get some toilet paper to blow my nose. But before I stand, I look at his chest again to check his breathing, and I see his chest isn't rising anymore.

"No," I whisper, then louder, "*No!*"

Keith doesn't stir at the sound of my voice. In fact, he'll never stir at anything ever again.

NOW THAT THE dark miracle has occurred—now that Keith's back—I don't know what to do.

I turn to the Clown Lady. "Can I take him away from here? Or is he stuck in this place?"

"Do you *want* to take him home the way he is? It would be more than a little difficult to explain him to friends and family, don't you think?"

She has a point. Even if he was completely restored to normal, how could I explain that he's returned from the dead?

The pillowcase at the Clown Lady's feet moves as the thing inside it wriggles. We both notice, but neither of us says anything.

"We could go somewhere, a place no one knows us."

"And do what?" the Clown Lady asks. "His physical and cognitive functions will improve somewhat over time, but he'll never be the Keith you knew. You won't be able to take him out in public. People will know instantly that something's wrong with him. They won't know what it is, not on a conscious level, but instinctively they'll sense that he's *wrong*. More, that he's a *violation*. Some may even attack him. The living are compelled to destroy the Returned to maintain the balance between this world and the next." Her too-red lips stretch into a poor simulation of a smile. "That's why you tend not to see many dead people walking around."

My eyes narrow with suspicion. "It sounds like you're trying to talk me out of this."

"Not at all. But I insist my clients be fully informed before any deal is finalized. Customer satisfaction is extremely important to me. Say the word, and I'll send him back, and you can take your payment and leave."

She nudges the pillowcase with her foot, and the thing inside wails, cold and scared. I do my best to shut out the sound. I turn back to Keith, reach up, stroke his cheek, find it hard as marble.

"No. We'll find a way to make it work . . . somehow."

"If you're sure . . ."

I stare into Keith's glassy eyes as I answer.

"I am."

"Very well."

I keep my gaze on Keith, but I can hear the Clown Lady pick up the pillow case, remove its contents, and then begin to greedily eat. For a moment, the baby's screams drown out the wet sounds of tearing meat and enthusiastic chewing, but then the child's voice is cut off, likely because the Clown Lady has torn out its throat.

I feel sick, and I quickly look away, the baby's screams echoing in my mind. I place my hand on Keith's chest, feel no heartbeat.

"Everything's going to be okay, sweetie. Now that we're together again."

The wind continues swirling leaves around us as the Clown Lady eats, slurping and swallowing, moaning in pleasure.

. . .

ANOTHER HALLOWEEN, almost thirty years ago.

I'm seven, it's trick-or-treat, and I'm dressed as the pink Power Ranger. My friend Lindsey is Wednesday Addams, and Lindsey's older brother Marcus is one of the Teenage Mutant Ninja Turtles. I can't remember which one. I can never keep them straight. Our parents came along to "keep an eye" on us, which I hate because I'm not a baby, but the four of them hang back and stay on the sidewalk when we go up to people's houses, talking about whatever grownups talk about when kids aren't around. So, it's *kind of* like we're on our own.

The sun has gone down, and the fluorescent glow of street-lights create eerie circles of light on the sidewalks, and we make a game of running from one to the next, so the Boogeyman won't get us. I don't believe in the Boogeyman, though. Not really.

We started in our neighborhood, and now we've moved on to the next street over. We stop at several houses, yell "Trick-or-Treat!" and get candy. Some of it's good, like full-sized Hershey bars, and some of it's not-so-good, like rock-hard pieces of cheap taffy. The farther down the street we go, the more nervous I become, until finally we reach *her* house.

The Clown Lady.

"Can we skip this one?" I ask.

Marcus and Lindsey exchange a look, then they smile.

"What's wrong?" Lindsey asks. "Scared?"

"Maybe . . . a little."

Marcus steps closer to me. He's taller than both his sister and me, and he likes to stand close to kids shorter than him so he can intimidate them.

"You don't believe the stories, do you?" he asks.

"I don't know."

"Have you ever seen the Clown Lady before?" Lindsey asks.

"No."

Marcus takes a step back then bends down until his face is close to mine. His breath smells like potato chips. It's gross.

"Then you don't really know *what* she looks like, do you?"

"I guess not."

I heard my mom and dad talk about her once. They said she's a dentist who works out of her home. The dentist I go to works with other dentists, and their office has lots of rooms with white walls. I wonder if the inside of the Clown Lady's house is white, too.

Marcus smiles. It's a mean smile, and I don't like it.

"Then there's no reason for you not to go ring her doorbell, is there?"

I glance at the house. The porch light is on, but there are no Halloween decorations.

"I dare you," Lindsey says.

"*We* dare you," Marcus adds.

I do *not* want to go up to the Clown Lady's house, but I also don't want Lindsey to think I'm a scaredy-cat. I don't really care what Marcus thinks. He's a jerk.

I look over my shoulder to check if our parents are nearby. They are, but they're talking and laughing, not looking in our direction. I face forward.

"Okay," I say, and – gripping the handle of my pumpkin-shaped candy bucket tight – I walk toward the house.

There's nothing scary about it. It's a ranch house, red brick, black roof, shutters, and garage door. It doesn't look much different from my house, really. I think of the stories kids tell about the Clown Lady – that she pulls all the teeth out of her patients and makes jewelry from them. Necklaces, earrings, bracelets . . . They also say that she saves the very best teeth to eat, that she puts them in a bowl, pours milk on them, and eats them like cereal. Her own teeth are hard as rock, so she doesn't hurt them when she chews. At this point, whoever's telling the story will make loud chewing sounds, and I imagine I can hear them now. Crack-crack-*cruuuuuuuunch* . . . I need to pee – *bad* – and I wish I'd gone one more time before we left my house.

I step up onto the porch, and I reach for the doorbell with a trembling hand. But before I can ring it, the door opens, and the Clown Lady is standing there. She's short, stout, and dressed in a blue suit jacket, skirt, and black heels. Her black hair is short, glossy, with severe edges, and it looks artificial, like a wig made of rubber. Her face is covered with some kind of thick white powder, and her small, pursed lips are a startling red. She looks at me, smiles, reveals teeth white as snow. I try to say "Trick-or-Treat," but I can't speak. Instead, I hold my bag out.

She's holding a large wooden bowl, and she reaches in, takes out a small chocolate bar, and drops it into my bag.

"There you go," she says. She takes something else from the bowl, a toothbrush, still in its box. "And this is for *after* you eat the chocolate." She drops it in my bag, too.

She's still smiling, but there's a strange coldness in her eyes. I'm shaking so hard now that my bag rattles, and suddenly I feel warmth spread across the crotch of my pink uniform, and I begin to cry.

AFTER KEITH'S BURIAL, I fall into a deep depression. I start drinking too much, contemplate suicide, and then one day, the idea comes to me that maybe I don't have to let Keith go. Maybe – just *maybe* – I can bring him back. Myths and legends are filled with stories of people returning from the dead. Those tales have to have some basis in fact, don't they?

I start researching on the Internet, tracking down and reading old books, meeting with people who claim to be experts in the supernatural, and six months later, I'm sitting at a small round table covered by a large crimson cloth, a woman on the other side who has no name that I'm aware of, but who's reputed to be a highly skilled medium, someone who communicates with the next world. She tells me of an old, abandoned cemetery, of an entity who guards the gate between worlds, one who takes the form of a figure you find most frightening and who only appears on Halloween night. And she tells me of the terrible price this guardian requires for its assistance. I don't care, though. I'll do anything to have Keith back.

Anything.

NIGHT FALLS while I hold Keith, and I keep holding him as it grows darker and the temperature drops. A light drizzle starts to fall, and his body becomes colder, until it feels as if I'm hugging a block of ice. I don't let go, though. I squeeze even harder. The Clown Lady – her feast finished – stands and watches us as she licks blood from her fingers. She says nothing, and I wonder what she's thinking. Is she darkly amused by my need to hold onto my dead husband? Does she pity me? Does she think I'm pathetic?

I don't care. I have Keith back, and that's all that matters to me.

After a time, my legs ache from standing still so long, and after more time, they become tingly, then numb. Keith has not moved since I wrapped my arms around him, hasn't so much as blinked. Tears of frustration merge with the rainwater on my face, and I shake Keith hard, yell at him to wake up, but he does nothing. Eventually, the rain ends, the clouds clear, and the sky in the east moves from black to dark blue to light blue. Halloween night is almost over. I don't know what will happen when the sun rises. Will Keith vanish like morning mist burned away by the day's first light? Is there any way I can possibly hold onto him hard enough to keep him with me?

The Guardian might know, but she'll likely demand a price for any additional help, a price even more terrible than the one I've already paid. But it doesn't matter. I'll do anything, *give* anything, to keep Keith in the world of the living. But before I can ask the Guardian, Keith speaks for the first time tonight. His voice is a raspy hiss, and blood dribbles from his mouth onto my shoulder as he talks.

"Sing . . . something . . . for me . . ."

Tears well in my eyes. I don't want to sing what I sang to him just before he died, that ballad of love and loss. But I can't think of anything else, so I begin. My voice is rough after a night of breathing cold, wet air, but I do my best. I only get the first few words out when the first light of dawn touches us. I'm still holding onto Keith, and I can feel him becoming . . . *less*, and I know that's he's going back to wherever the Clown Lady pulled him from – and there's nothing I can do about it.

The Clown Lady speaks for the first time in hours.

"You can't keep him here, but you *can* go with him – if you choose. You must decide quickly, though."

I barely feel Keith now, and I know I have only seconds left. I remember the first time we held hands, walking down the street after dinner at an Italian restaurant. Our first kiss was that night, too. Soft, warm, gentle . . . I remember how he always laughed too loud at people's jokes, even when they were bad, how he always looked directly into my eyes when I spoke to him, truly *listening*, how he'd lightly stroke my hair after we made love . . .

I look at the Clown Lady. "I'll go."

She smiles. "Nice doing business with you."

Shadows rush in from all directions then, and the world is gone.

NOTHING in the sky but darkness, air bitingly cold, a flat hard surface like marble beneath my feet. Off in the distance are large black spires, towers, or mountains, or maybe something else entirely. I'm still holding onto Keith, and I'm relieved that he feels solid once again. We're not alone, though. There are shadowy forms around us, so many that they're impossible to count, billions upon billions, stretching in every direction, all the way to the horizons and beyond.

I don't know what this place is, and I don't care. As long as I'm with Keith.

I open my mouth to continue singing, ready to pick up where I left off, but when I begin, no sound comes out. That's when I realize I've heard nothing since coming here. This is a place of silence, where there's never been so much as a hint of sound, and never will be.

The shadows drift closer to us, and I sense their anger and hatred. This is a realm of the dead, and I don't belong here. I'm *wrong*, and they can't tolerate my presence. I was a fool to think that Keith and I could be together again. He's dead, and I'm still alive.

Keith doesn't speak, but I hear his voice in my mind.

I can fix that.

He gently pulls away from me, wraps cold, stiff fingers around my neck, and begins to squeeze. I see bright sparks of light in my vision, then – sooner than I expect – darkness creeps in. My consciousness slips away as death comes for me.

It feels like love.

A Scavenger Hunt When the Veil is Thin

GWENDOLYN KISTE

I. Find the haunted house. You know the one. You've always known.

You're standing on a crack in the sidewalk, your gaze set on the decrepit abode at the end of the lane. It's a two-story Victorian, the paint peeling off in thick, pale clumps, the warped front door shimmering in the moonlight.

You recognize this house. Of course, you do. You grew up in this town beneath its shadow. This house has been waiting here all your life. Waiting for anyone brave enough to walk up those front steps and slip inside.

Maybe even waiting for you.

It's almost evening now, the clouds colluding in dark patches in the sky, and the crisp air whips around you, the smoky scents of dead leaves and dead promises filling your lungs. You stand frozen, even though you know exactly where you need to go next. Just keep going until you reach that front door.

In your left hand, you grip a small piece of paper, folded and refolded so many times the creases have almost worn through. It's a list for a Halloween scavenger hunt. An old tradition in this town.

Your friends are the ones who challenged you to this.

"It'll be fun," they said, and you pretended to believe them.

With your head down, you start walking. A row of jubilant trick-or-treaters shuffles past, witches and skeletons and superheroes with names you never did learn. You smile at them, and they smile back.

Growing up, this was always your favorite time of the year. The other kids preferred summertime with its endless days, their hair gone chlorine-green in backyard pools. Or they longed for Christmas with its mountains of gifts and chilly holiday vacation.

But not you. You wished every day could be October 31st. If you could, you'd disappear into this time of year and never come back again.

Only one place you never wanted to disappear into: this old Victorian house looming over you.

"Why don't they tear it down?" you always asked when you were young, but nobody could give you a reason.

You glance past the neighborhood, and waiting there in the distance is a vast forest brimming with birches and willows and hemlocks that grow wild, their skeletal branches reaching up to the sky. The forest seems so inviting, but that's not where you're headed. It's the haunted house that beckons you, and with your breath tight in your chest, you drift up the front steps, the porch boards shrieking beneath your feet.

You shouldn't be able to trespass like this. Someone should be watching out for this place. A concerned neighbor or even a whole concerned neighborhood. It's Halloween after all, the best night of the year for a bit of vandalism. But let's face it: the town knows about the scavenger hunt. They're an old rite of passage, even older than you. It's almost like the locals don't mind this ridiculous tradition.

Like maybe they want to appease the ghost, too.

2. **Look for the spiderweb in the doorway, glistening silver in the moonlight.**

You don't have to work very hard to find this one. Instead, it finds you, tangling itself in your long, dark hair. You roll your eyes, as you try your best to pick the flecks of gnat off you.

Your friends would get a kick out of this, the way you're making a fool of yourself before you've even crossed the threshold.

"Always the silly little klutz," they'd say. They're waiting for you, back at the local watering hole. A dive bar with sallow fluorescent lights and sallower beer. Until you showed up again in town this afternoon, you barely remembered that place. You barely remember any of your friends either. All you know is that you're back here, because you have to be.

Everybody in town knows the history of this house. They know about the woman who once owned it, the way she used to live, laughing so loudly her voice would ricochet off the rooftops. How easy it was for her to break the rules.

How easy it always is for women like her to die.

And then there are the ghosts. Everybody knows about them, too.

"Have fun," your friends said when they handed you the scavenger hunt list, the same one they've been using for years, even though no one ever finds all the items.

"Thanks," you muttered and started down the street. That was only a few minutes ago yet it feels like another lifetime.

You don't even know why you're here. You rarely talk to

your friends from high school these days, and you're not entirely sure why you picked up the phone when they called.

"It's finally your turn," they said, and you weren't even sure which of them it was on the other end of the line. One thing for sure: you knew they were right. You'd been avoiding this for years.

"So," the voice said, "are you coming home or what?"

You started to say no, started to hang up the phone, but then something happened. This house rose up in the back of your mind like smog, and you were suddenly speaking like a woman possessed.

"I'll be there," you whispered, and even though the words passed through your lips, you swore that it didn't even sound like your voice.

3. **Peek into the Wunderkammer in the foyer.**

You're barely through the door when you spot it. It's a breathtaking cabinet, made of stained redwood. Inside are too many treasures to count. Narwhal horns and butterflies stuck with pins. But you don't touch anything. You try not to look too closely. You're afraid something here might follow you home.

In a way, it feels like it's already following you. No matter which way you look, the past is everywhere. There are secrets in these walls, moldering in the horsehair plaster, trapped beneath the floorboards.

As you move down a long hall, the darkness enveloping you, you wonder about the woman who used to own this place. They say she was more beautiful than anybody had a right to be. You're curious if that's true. For what it's worth, you've never seen her, not in person, not even in a picture.

Shivering, you're afraid tonight might be the night that all changes.

This isn't a place you ever wanted to end up. You spent your whole adolescence avoiding the scavenger hunt. Your friends took their turn, one after another, their eyes wide and vacant beforehand, all of them trying to play it off like it was nothing afterwards.

"It's just an old house," they'd say, not looking at you, but you always doubted if that was really true. Because if it was simply a run-of-the-mill abandoned property, then why all the pomp and circumstance? Why does the whole town insist on leaving the front door unlocked, and why don't people come here any day of the year other than this one?

Because it's more than just an old house. Your friends know it, and you know it, and the ghosts know it, too.

That's why you keep walking, your footsteps quickening, desperate to outpace the shadows that seem eager to join you.

4. **Find her portrait, the woman arrayed in violet and lace.**

You make your way into the ballroom now. A crystal chandelier dangles sourly overhead, gray dust settled into every crevice.

She's peering out at you from the corner. You don't even notice her at first. That's because there are so many picture frames slung on the wall, a dizzying array of them. But here's the thing: most of them are empty. There's a canvas inside each frame, but no picture painted on it.

Except for hers.

They were right: she's so very beautiful, her red hair blazing like fire, her blue eyes wild and bright as the sea. But it's more than just her face that draws you in. There's an aura around her even now.

You know a little bit about her, the gossip that seeps out in a small town. The way she couldn't be bothered to be a bride, couldn't be bothered with anything so pedestrian. Instead, she opted for a different path, dancing to any music, singing without a choir, smiling at all the strangers she ever met. She was too silly, too fun, too free, and with their glaring eyes and their righteous tongues snapping, the locals never let her forget what they thought about it.

She did her best not to listen. That's because she wanted something bigger than this town could ever offer.

In that way, you're not so different from a ghost.

5. **Follow the black cat, her eyes burning gold.**

When you emerge from the ballroom, she's the first thing you see, perched at the bottom of the steps. Her whiskers twitching, she stares up at you like she knew you were coming. Like you're already late, and she doesn't feel like waiting all night.

"Hello," you say, as she twines between your feet, the two of you heading up the staircase and down the hallway, the darkness devouring you a little more with each step.

It feels strange to be back in this town, especially after you did your best to escape it. You left at eighteen and never looked back. Not until now.

You didn't want the things the other girls wanted. A quiet life, a quiet home. Instead, you were always looking to the horizon, to the sky, even to the forest beyond the city limits.

"What if there's another way to live?" you would ask, and everyone would eye you up like you were a heretic of yore.

That's why this town never liked you. A lot of towns are like that. You found that out when you went away. It turns out people are never too keen on the ones who don't fall in line.

But this house seems to understand. It seems to know what it's like to be discarded, to be maligned. You keep walking, your boots slipping into the crevices in the floorboards. There's a whisper around every corner, and you close your eyes because you already know they're speaking to you, the same way they always have.

Are you running from ghosts, or are they running from you?

6. **Sit before the fireplace, the flames set alight by a phantom hand.**

You see it up ahead. The glow inside a distant room. It's the last door on the left. With your shaking hands clasped in front of you, you walk toward it, slipping inside a small bedroom. There's no other light in the whole room, but that fireplace is more than enough.

The cat curls up in front of the hearth, trilling quietly.

You sit next to her, realizing suddenly how very tired you are. How comforting it would be to rest your head and fall asleep, melting into this place, into this moment.

But you don't fall asleep because you're afraid of what might happen. You shouldn't be here. You should have told your friends what you really think: that you're too old for games. Forty years and none the wiser for it.

And why are you here at all? You don't know what you're looking for, not really. Sure, you've got a list of items clutched in your hand, but part of you doesn't believe that's enough. You might find each thing scribbled on the paper, but at the end of the evening, you'll realize you found nothing at all.

You sit back, watching the flicker of firelight. It's nice to rest for a moment. You've been wandering a long time. Too long to count, shuffling in and out of dead-end jobs. The years bleed together after a while. That's the joke of getting older. How it feels at once like a hundred years yet not even a day.

Sometimes it feels like not even a day has passed in this town either. You come back, and everything and everyone is the same. Even the scavenger hunt. That's why this piece of paper in your hand is so withered—it's the same one you've all been using for decades, this whole town like a specter of itself.

Nobody's sure how the scavenger hunt got started. It's one of those urban legends, the sort of thing you hear about from a friend of a friend. If the rumors are to be believed, they say it began the year after she died, that woman in the portrait. On Halloween, no less, and in this very house. Naturally, right? Why else would you be visiting tonight? The official cause of death was listed as *Accident*, but there's nothing accidental about what this town did to her. The way they crept inside after dark. The way they made her pay for just being herself. After all, the world needs somebody to blame, and she was such an easy target: a woman who wouldn't do what they wanted.

But even once they buried her body, they couldn't stop her for good. She would still dance and sing and smile from the attic window. Even death couldn't tame her—if anything, it only seemed to make her more defiant. That's how the scavenger hunt began: as a way to appease her. To keep her wanton manners at bay.

That's, of course, if you believe the rumors.

7. Carve the pumpkin that's waiting in the attic.

You don't even know how it got there, but you find it in an instant. The gleaming orange pumpkin with a chef's knife glinting next to it, sitting in the middle of the attic floor. This place where they say she died.

Your hands still shaking, you pick up the knife. Though it's dark, you work quickly, as though from muscle memory. You don't want to be here. You want to go home, but you already know you need to finish this. So, you keep carving, yanking the guts out of your would-be jack-o'-lantern, carving out eyes and a mouth and a pert little nose.

Outside the attic window, the distant forest peers back at you, and you wish you could go to it, but you just keep cutting over and over again. Until at last, you look down, and your hands have gone red.

For a moment, you can't fathom what's happened. Part of you is certain you must have cut yourself, the knife slipping when you weren't paying attention, but somehow, beyond reason, you know this isn't your blood.

It belongs to her. The woman in the portrait. The woman the world is still punishing.

You won't glance down at the pumpkin on the floor. You don't want to see what it really is, what you were really carving into. The bone and the blood and the skin of someone who never deserved it.

You're part of this tradition now. The one that makes sure the world keeps punishing her, year after year after year.

From the corner, the black cat is watching you, her eyes a little mournful now. But you won't look back at her, not now. You need to leave here.

Before it's too late.

8. **Say farewell to the house on the way out.**

You're running now, through the dim hallways, the ancient carpets bunching up beneath your feet. The black cat tracks your every move, as if she knew it was only a matter of time before you'd flee. She's probably seen this dozens of times before. Maybe she's been around since the beginning.

You're back in the ballroom, but even though you've been here before, you're instantly turned around, the double doors slamming shut behind you.

You stumble from one wall to the other, trying to find the way out. That's when you see them. All the portraits are finished now, dozens of them surrounding you, their faces gaunt, their eyes following you no matter which way you run.

"Leave me alone," you say, and the others whisper their poison lies, calling you closer. They want to make you one of them. They want to make you disappear, the same way they did to her.

They keep murmuring, their voices like daggers in your gut, but as you gaze at her portrait in the corner, her eyes blink open, and she doesn't seem to be listening to them. She's only listening to you.

You stare back at her, and with your heart in your throat, you finally understand. This tradition isn't to appease her ghost. It's to keep the ghost in her place. Even now, this town doesn't want her to escape.

But that's exactly what you want, what you've always wanted.

Trembling, you put out your hand. It's such a small gesture, and at first, you're convinced she won't reach back. That she can't reach back. After all, she's been waiting a long time.

A long, agonizing moment passes, the other portraits still beckoning to you. Then all at once, the woman smiles at you, brighter than the July sun, and the rest of the voices in the room go silent. In a flash, she extends her hand, and you guide her out of the portrait. She's as ephemeral as a dream, but she's real now, not quite flesh and blood, but something else. Something stronger.

Together, you emerge from the house, and the cold night air rushes up to greet you. You feel brand-new, and when you turn to her, she beams at you, as if to say she feels brand-new, too.

Hand in hand, you start down the street. The last of the trick-or-treaters are still on the sidewalk, shambling home, their bags brimming with sweetness and promise. They watch the two of you pass by, and instantly, they know what she is. Something that doesn't belong out in the night. Something that's made its way into the world regardless.

"Such a pretty ghost," a few of them whisper, and at this, she can't help but blush.

There are so many places you could go. Follow the trick-or-treat route with all these eager kids or retreat back to the dive bar where your friends are waiting, each of them thinking this is just another evening, just another haunted Halloween.

But it's not just another Halloween. It's your last Halloween in this town. The whole world's shifted now, and you're finally free. As the list from the scavenger hunt turns to ash in your hands, you smile at the ghost, and she smiles back.

"Come on now," you say, and together, the two of you turn toward the waiting forest, where the promise of darkness swallows you whole.

When You See Millions of the Mouthless Dead Across Your Dreams in Pale Battalions Go

JONATHAN MABERRY

Alex had always been a ghost.

Long before he died.

Not before he went off to war. Alex was still fully alive then. Seventeen in the autumn of 1965. Dad signed the papers to allow him to enlist early. Mom screamed. Mom cried. We all cried. Except Dad and Alex.

He turned eighteen in basic training.

When he came home after that, he was still alive. Maybe there were some shadows in his eyes because by then, he'd heard the stories. The sergeants loved to tell those stories. They loved to make it real. Maybe they thought it would help, that it would toughen the kids they were training to be killers. Or maybe those sergeants were just malicious assholes. A case could be made either way.

Alex had enlisted in the Air Force rather than waiting to be drafted into the Army. Kids in our neighborhood always got drafted. Somehow poor kids in those parts of Philadelphia, where it was all crumbling homes in rows around factories, seemed to have numbers that always rose to the top. The sons of the factory owners must've had heavier numbers because they were never at the surface waiting to be scooped up. They stayed home, stayed safe, went to college, went to work for their parents. If they died, it was from wrapping their cars around the steel supports of the old El trains after nights of partying. That happened, and maybe it was sad. More ghosts. But none of the factory workers shed tears that I ever saw. Not with everyone's son, uncle, older brother, cousin, or friend getting shipped off to 'Nam.

Alex thought he was playing it cool. Being smart. Gaming the system.

"The Air Force is safe," he told everyone. "Soldiers are in the damn thick of it. Wading through swamps and mud and shit. Soldiers get their asses blown off or they step on punji sticks or toe-poppers or bouncing Betties. Soldiers are just meat for the grinder. But *Air Force*? Shit. They stay the hell out of the way."

He told that to the recruiting sergeant in that little shitty storefront place on Kensington Avenue. I remember standing outside with my buddy, Bob. We were seven. We saw Alex shake hands with the sergeant. We saw how that sergeant grinned and grinned. He never once stopped smiling. I think that's why I don't like people who smile too much.

Not after what happened.

Alex told us about it later.

"I *told* you it was the smart play," he said that afternoon. He was sitting on the top porch step, a sweating bottle of Coke dangling from a loop made from his index finger and thumb, a cigarette bobbing up and down as he talked. Alex in a white T-shirt, jeans with patches and scars, a pair of Chuck Taylor All-Stars that were stained and scuffed exactly the right way. He'd used a Magic Marker to draw music notes all over the white rubber toe caps. His buddies were on the steps, too, or standing around like a pack of lean jaguars. All of them with hair that was more 50s holdover greased-back Doo-Wop shit than the longer hair some of the other kids wore.

I was standing on the pavement with Bob and a couple of other kids. Listening to Alex talk about how he played his game with the recruiting sergeant.

"I told him straight up that I was no soldier," said Alex.

"You're a lover not a fighter," said Chick, right on cue. If Alex ever took to doing comedy movies, then Chick would be his straight man. Or side man. Not sure what you call it. The guy who feeds you lines and backs what you say. Not sure I ever heard Chick ever speak up first, but he was always there to back Alex's play.

"You damn right," agreed Alex. "And I told him that. I told him I was a mechanic, too."

"Yeah, you are," said Chick. "It's got a motor, you can fix it."

Alex pointed a finger at him. "You damn right. I told that sergeant that. I said my dad was a mechanic and my uncle and my cousin."

"It's in the blood," said Chick.

"Born to it," said Alex with a nod. "He said that the Air Force needed mechanics."

"Does that mean you'll be working on jet engines?" asked Bob.

Alex grinned but shook his head. "Naw. At least not yet. Going to start with trucks, Air Force has a lot of trucks."

"Cars, too," added Chick.

"Shit-load of cars," said Alex. "And get this…the sergeant says that there's such a big need for mechanics right now that he was willing to make me a deal."

"Deal?" I asked. "What kind of deal?"

"That's what I'm trying to tell you," said Alex. He took a long pull on his Coke. "Y'see, they need mechanics for bases right here in the States. Maybe over in Jersey. Close, you know? Well, he said that if I could get some of my buddies to enlist, then they'd guarantee us all a stateside gig working on trucks and cars."

"Really?" asked Bob, looking interested. His uncle Bill worked at the same garage where my dad worked. Where Alex hung out after school most days.

"Hand to God," said Alex. "So, I talked to the guys in the band, and they're all down."

The band was the Six Saints. One of the Philly a cappella groups. They'd cut a couple of sides on a promo album that featured ten groups. One of the sides, *"Sugar Sweet,"* even got airplay last fall. Local stations, but even so. How cool was it to turn on the transistor radio and hear Alex singing lead on a love song? The other guys singing harmony that would make you cry. You'd never think six tough cats like them could sing like angels.

"What'd the guys say when you told 'em?" I asked.

"What do you think they said?" my brother replied, looking me dead in the eyes. "They said hell yes."

"Hell yes," agreed Chick, nodding.

"So…you're really doing it?" asked Bob.

"Doing it? Shit, son, it's *done*."

That was on the last day of October 1965. Halloween, but in Philly that's not cold and blustery. The sun was nine inches above us. The blacktop on the streets was melting, and no matter how still you sat, the sweat just popped out. Boiled out. No one was out trick-or-treating yet. Hell no. Way too hot. We'd all wait for dark and then we monsters would be out in force.

Old Man Raynor down the street was fiddling with a wrench, trying to open the fire hydrant. The conversation kind of died then. We watched Mr. Raynor and maybe everyone was doing what I was doing. Thanking God for good-hearted sergeants at enlistment offices.

I WONDER SOMETIMES whatever happened to that sergeant.

That office closed in 1968. Well…not closed. Someone threw a brick through the window and then tossed in a Molotov cocktail. Happened on Mischief Night, October 30th. I saw the blackened shell of the place the next night when my friends and I were running around in costumes knocking on doors and taking candy from strangers. I was dressed as Sergeant Saunders from *Combat!* Bob went old-school cheap with his sheet and eyeholes. We stood there, fists knotted around the handles of bags heavy with Clark Bars, bags of M&Ms, boxes of Dots, sticks of Pez, and—God help us—apples. Me and Bob threw our apples into the burned-out building. Tricks, not treats. We ran away as if someone would chase us.

Police never found out who torched the place. Happened in the middle of the night, and the papers all said it was Mischief Night gone too far.

I never thought so. I think it was someone's dad. Or mom. Or brother. Someone who maybe had a folded flag at home, graveyard dirt on his hands, and a heart so filled with burning grief they just had to do something.

If I was older and bigger and braver, it *would* have been me.

I wanted to.

I needed to. We all did.

The ones who were too old or too young to go to 'Nam.

The ones who stayed home and watched it on TV. The ones who went to graveyards or vet's hospitals. The ones who visited rehab and brought books and candy and empty words.

Us.

THERE WAS a rumor it was Chick who did it.

He enlisted with Alex and the other Seven Saints, but he never made it past the medical. Perforated eardrum and feet flatter than snowshoes. I remember him sitting in the park under a sycamore, crying so hard that it made me feel like screaming. Crying because his friends went, and he didn't.

I remember him crying another time. When Alex wrote to say that he and the others were going straight from basic to a base out west, and then from there to Vietnam.

At funerals where we all stood looking stupidly at cheap coffins while airmen in uniforms folded flags in weird slow motion. Where officers handed those flags to mothers and saluted and turned away to hide their dead eyes.

We went to a lot of those. For the Army families. The infantry kids.

But we also went to funerals for the Angels.

Mickey.

Jimmy.

Ricky.

Big Greg.

Dan.

Five of them.

The ones who didn't come home alive.

And, no, the irony was lost on no one. In fact, it was a lot of fucking salt in everyone's wounds. Fucking angels.

Chick and Alex were there, but I saw how they couldn't

even look at the families of their friends. Chick because he couldn't go. Alex because he got them to go.

Everyone cried. Everyone was so fucking mad.

The fathers—the ones who fought in World War II—wore their medals and saluted the flag and sang the songs the loudest. Telling themselves it mattered. Adding worth to the coin their families spent. Trying to, anyway. Telling everyone their own war stories at the luncheons after each of the boxes were lowered into the ground and covered with cold dirt. They talked about their battles, their scars, their friends who never made it home. Trying to get everyone to feel proud, to sell the story that Vietnam was Anzio or the Bulge or Midway. Which it goddamn well was not.

The fact that they all had to lubricate their throats with Wild Turkey or Canadian Club in order to squeeze those words out was telling. Even to little kids like me.

Their wives drank, too. A lot. Quietly, in corners. Looking at one another but too destroyed to look at anyone else while their husbands told those stories over and over and over again. One funeral after another.

I lost count of how many people squeezed the hands of the parents and said, "If there's *anything* I can do..."

Maybe they meant it, but I doubt it. Not because people are unkind, but because, really, what *could* they do? The boys were dead. No kind words would bring them back. No actions they could take would seal the cracks in broken hearts. There was no way to rescue anyone from the images conjured at closed coffin funerals. I mean...most of Ricky wasn't even in the box. They brought home what they could find, and from I heard that wasn't much.

My folks went to the luncheons. Dad brought a bottle of whatever he could afford. Mom made a casserole. At Dan's funeral there were twenty-two casseroles on the dining room table. There had been twenty at Big Greg's. Seventeen at Rick's; sixteen at Jimmy's, and ten, I think, at Mickey's. I think people brought them as props because they'd already run out of things to say.

Once, years later, when I was drunk after someone else's funeral and I'd counted twenty-five casseroles, I wondered if they were some kind of charm, or talisman, or whatever the right word was. Bringing something, not just to feed the grieving family, but to appease the ghosts. To keep them from getting angry.

We all believed in ghosts.

We had to. For a lot of the families in my old neighborhood, ghosts were all we had left. Maybe that's why I stopped going out on Halloween even before I aged out of it. Some kids—the ones who didn't have anyone older who went to 'Nam—would wear mashup costumes. Zombie soldiers, vampire soldiers, werewolf soldiers. Like that. They scared the shit out of me.

Then.

And now.

ALEX AND I DRIFTED.

We were ten years apart, with four sisters between us. Well, three, now. One died of cancer a couple years back. Alex was haunted, and I think at times he resented the fact that I never served. Vietnam was in the rearview mirror by the time I got out of high school. And even if it was still on, I'd have skipped it because I got a full ride to Temple University. Journalism. I was going to be the reporter that broke the big story. Woodward or Bernstein. Maybe both.

Not really sure why he'd be mad at me for skipping war of any kind. It hadn't done him any damn good. It killed most of who he was. It turned him into a ghost—just one with a heart that still beat and blood that pumped. But the resentment was there. We both felt it. At times we saw the color of it in each other's eyes, but that wasn't a conversation we could ever have. Not then.

He stayed in Philly. He became a mechanic and worked that until it ground him down. Or at least contributed to that process. Every year, on the anniversary of his last day in country he'd go to Coney Island Joe's tattoo parlor and get more ink. He'd gotten his first—a tiger—in 'Nam. Back when it was cool, back before 'Nam *became* the tiger and his friends the meat. Now Alex was covered in tattoos. Full sleeves on his arms, nearly every inch of his torso. Most of his legs. I used to know each from the days when we were still family, still friends. Not anymore.

The ink was his scripture, but I was not a member of that church. Maybe Chick would have been if he hadn't skated sideways from whiskey to horse to a single-car accident while high. I wonder how many casseroles his mother got when they buried him. I'll never know. I'd moved away by then.

I live outside of L.A.

Never did become a reporter. Instead, I wrote scripts for crime dramas on ABC. Sometimes on CBS. My most recent stuff is on Hulu. Got some awards for it. One Emmy that the whole writers room shared for a TV movie spinoff of *CSI*. Plaques on the walls. Two ex-wives, and one giving that some real thought.

I hadn't seen Alex in the flesh for years. Like...fifteen years? Give or take. When people asked, I said it was because of politics. I've always been somewhere on the left, and he went hard right. These days you can float that explanation and people accept it without asking questions. No one wants to talk politics these days except when they feel the need to preach to their own choir.

So, yeah, I was really surprised when I got a call on a late Sunday afternoon. Another October 31st. Another hot Halloween. I was slouched on a loveseat on my porch, looking at the parents who *insisted* on dragging their kids around in costumes while the sun burned. I even had a bag of candy. First time in I don't how long. Full-sized 3 Musketeers because there is no real fun in 'fun-size' bars. Let's be real.

Then the phone rang. The caller ID said, "ALEX."

Alex didn't call me. Frankly, I couldn't remember even adding him to my contacts. But I guess I did. I answered after three rings, right before it would have gone to voicemail, and damn me if I nearly let it go there.

"Hello...?" I asked, surprise in my voice.

"Joey," said the voice. Pale and ghostly, like he was calling from another planet instead of three thousand miles east.

"Alex?"

"Yeah," he said. "It's been a minute, I guess."

"Really has." Neither of us wanted to do the math and say how long. That was one of those landmines you can see poking out of the dirt.

"You got some time?" he asked.

"Um...sure..." I said. "What's up? Is Joan okay?"

"Huh? Oh. Sure," he said. "She's good."

"Great."

"And...is it Cassie? How's she?"

"We got divorced seven years ago," I said. "I'm with Audrey."

With being a tricky word. Audrey was staying with her sister in Sacramento while we "figured things out."

"Oh," he said again. "Right. Audrey."

A bit of silence on the line. Cell phones don't have that soft white noise the old landlines used to have. There was nothing to listen to except silence.

"What can I do for you, Alex?" I said, trying to make it kindly. Trying to mean it.

"Can we get together? Maybe for coffee or a beer?"

"Next time I'm in town? Sure...but I don't know when that'll be."

"No," he said. "I mean now."

"Now?"

"I'm here."

"Here...*where*? In L.A.?"

"Down the block, actually," he said with a small laugh. "I'm in town."

"You're in L.A.? Why?"

"Funeral," he said.

I didn't ask. All of Alex's friends were vets. He was in a dozen veterans groups. They were all aging out, too. The war ended in 1975, close to fifty years ago. I was in my sixties, and Alex was in his seventies. Between Agent Orange, PTSD, and old injuries, they were prime candidates for hypertension, diabetes, suicide, cancer of every kind, strokes, and heart attacks. Funerals were a regular thing.

I haven't been to one since I moved away from home. Not even the funerals of my friends and work colleagues. Can't do it. Too many ghosts. Too much hurt hung like garlands. And even being a writer, I never know what to say. Maybe that makes me a coward. Could be. Better that than spending time with the dead.

"Wow," I said, meaning that. "Sure. I'm on the porch."

"I saw you when I drove by. Be right there."

. . .

HE LOOKED OLD. Not just older—*old*. His brown hair was snow white, his skin wrinkled in ways that distorted the shapes and meanings of a lot of his tattoos. His goatee was sparse, and he looked shrunken, somehow. We were both the same height—a bit over six feet—but while I still looked it, he did not.

He came to the foot of the porch steps and looked up at me. His smile was small and nervous. Maybe mine was, too.

"Come on up," I said, and he did.

We didn't shake hands.

He went and sat on a rattan chair in the corner of the porch, out of the direct California sun. I sat down on the wicker love seat. I opened the cooler next to my chair and lifted out a beer, cocking an eyebrow. He nodded, and I handed it to him. Alex twisted off the cap. There was a pause and then we clinked bottles and drank. I sipped mine and watched him gulp more than half of his. Adam's apple bobbing. Drinking like he'd just come out of the Sahara.

We sat and watched a pair of mothers herding a group of six-year-old Jedi and Sith. I saw Alex smile a little. Just a little, but it was there.

"What brings you to L.A.?" I asked.

He looked down the mouth of the beer bottle as if there was a script for him in there.

"It's been a long time," he said.

I waited.

"I guess I'm sorry for the way things went between us."

I sipped my beer. Said nothing.

"Life got weird, you know?" he asked, looking at me.

"Life's always been weird," I said.

He shook his head. "We never really had much of a chance to be brothers, Joey."

"Ten years difference in age," I said.

"Yeah. That was part of it," said Alex. We paused as the Star Warriors tromped up and held out their bags. I plunked candy into each. They looked down, assessed, and moved off. The mothers tried to get them to say thanks, but all we got were wordless grunts. Alex watched them go to the next house. "Was a time I'd have been royally pissed about that," he said, using his bottle to point to them. "Fuck, man, I don't even remember getting old, but I started doing the 'you kids get off my lawn' shit."

"I'm feeling it, too."

"What's that about, you think?" he asked, then before I could say anything he answered his own question. "Envy."

"Envy?"

"Sure. Those kids are alive. They got everything ahead of them. They got no scars, no ghosts haunting them. None of that shit. We see them running across the lawn or up and down the street and we get mad. We *say* it's because they should watch out, look both ways, respect property. All sorts of shit, but it's envy, 'cause *we* want to be running like them. Yelling like them."

I tapped my left knee with the bottom of my bottle. "Titanium," I said. "Had it replaced in '06."

He grinned and nodded and tapped his chest. "Pacemaker, five years ago. One of my buddies gave me a T-shirt that says 'Battery Operated.' It was funny for like two seconds."

"Surprised it was funny that long," I said.

We drank. We watched the kids. A couple of older teens—three boys and five girls in their late teens—were working the far side of the street. Costumes were bullshit. Whatever they could grab. Not really costumes at all. No theme. Just part of their grift.

"That's where it starts," said Alex. "When you're really too old for trick-or-treat, but you try to cling onto it."

I thought about that and nodded. When they came to us, I didn't bitch at them and let them each grab bars out of the bag. One girl took two and looked me right in the eyes when she did it. I smiled and nodded, and there was every chance she took it the wrong way because her face turned sour. But it was because of what Alex just said.

We finished our beers and opened two more.

Out of the left corner of nowhere, he said, "Been seeing a shrink."

I said something clever like, "Oh, yeah?" You can tell I write TV dialogue for a living.

"Yeah." He was using his thumbnail to peel the label off the bottle. Doing it carefully so as not to tear it. Years of practice. "You know how it is. PTSD and all that shit."

And all that shit.

I was not dumb enough or clueless enough to act surprised that he had *those* kinds of ghosts in his head.

I said, "Doing you any good?"

He looked up from his work, studying me with brown eyes under white eyebrows. "You ever see a shrink?"

"Up to and including yesterday," I said. "Been in and out of therapy most of my life. Out here, and in this business, it's kind of a requirement. Nobody I know's *not* in therapy."

He thought about that, nodded. "What for? I mean…you didn't…"

The rest hung there, but I didn't take offense. "Didn't serve? No. Didn't want to wear anyone's uniform."

There were old arguments hanging in the air between us. Military service makes a *man* out of you. Or, woman, if he was arguing with one of our sisters. Or, duty to the flag. Stopping the spread of—fill in the blank anything we Americans don't like, don't want, can't own, and doesn't look like us.

But he didn't go there. Not that day.

We gave out some more candy. Even had a kid with a really good Transformers costume that turned into a truck when he knelt down but must have been eight thousand degrees hot. Kid was maybe eight and he was pouring sweat. I gave him two bars.

"We all have our ghosts," I said, picking up the thread of the conversation.

"Yeah," he said. "I guess we do."

"Therapy doing *you* any good?"

He took a really long time to answer that one. He sat looking out at the kids, taking micro-sips, eyes unfocused.

"We covered some ground," he said at last. "He got me to a place."

"A place?" I asked. "What kind of place."

"Understanding the nature of my guilt," said Alex in the way people do when they are quoting or paraphrasing someone else's comment.

"Because you feel guilty about talking the guys in the band into enlisting?"

"Kind of," he said. "Mostly. Partly."

"How'd that get you to Los Angeles?"

He sipped. "Needed to close things out between us, Joey."

I leaned back and studied him. "This a twelve-step thing? What's the phrasing? '*Make direct amends to such people wherever possible, except when to do so would injure them or others*...? Something like that?"

He waggled his beer bottle. "I'm not in AA," he said, "but it amounts to the same."

"You don't need to make amends with me," I said. "And even if you felt you had to, they have these newfangled contraptions called cell phones."

I hated surprises. Especially when they felt like ambushes. Confrontation always felt that way to me. Our sisters always wanted some of kind of Hallmark Christmas movie thing where one of us would show up unexpectedly to surprise the other, bury the hatchet, make it all right as the music swells, and we hear Bing Crosby and David Bowie singing a holiday duet. The naivety of that always staggered me. As if a dramatic appearance could change anything. As if corny dialogue, familiar tears, and a shared belief that happy endings were part of the calculus of dysfunctional family dynamics.

If I thought that encounters like this *could* do some good, I'd have written a script for it and let some Lifetime Channel actors sort out the inflections for me. But this was the real world and people don't get happy endings just because they want them. I *knew* this, and it was one of the many, many reasons I loathed surprises. So, yeah. This was beginning to piss me off.

"Some things you got to do in person," he said. "I wanted to put things right between us."

"The thing is, Alex, you could have saved the airfare," I said coldly. "Why waste your time coming all the way out here. It's all fine. I don't hold grudges."

"Fuck that," he said. "Yes, you do. Everyone does. Maybe you're not aware of it, but you do. I did. I mean, let's face it, neither of us picked up a phone in years. Fuck, we never even sent an email."

Yup. That's a line of dialogue I knew one of us had to say. Cliché as balls.

"It wasn't about holding a grudge," I protested weakly. "We just lived different lives. Different—"

"Politics and shit," he interrupted. "Yeah, I know. But none of that really matters anymore, does it?"

"I haven't changed my political views," I said.

"I have," he said.

"You have?" I asked, greatly surprised.

"I left all of that behind," said Alex. "I shouldn't have carried that freight all these years anyway. And to be straight, little brother, I think it was deflection. Or maybe projection. Not sure which term applies. Point is, I got deep into my side of politics—or...one side of politics—because it was something to get mad about that had nothing to do with the Angels. I could get mad at borders and social security and who was in the White House and what color they were and feel like there was a *reason* for being mad. Good reasons, with ways to argue about it."

I said nothing.

"But it wasn't real," he said. "It was shadows and phantoms and all that."

He looked at me, and this time I could see miles deep.

"Joey," he said, "I was so mad at you for so long. Do you know that?"

My mouth went dry. I didn't even try to reply.

"You were a kid when 'Nam was happening. It was all around you, but you were bulletproof. Flame resistant. Invulnerable. You were too young to fight, too young to be drafted. And then there was no draft at all, and you skated. Fuck, man, I hated you for that."

I said nothing.

"Really hated you," he said. "Then you moved out here. Became a big time TV writer. Hollywood friends, all those hot actress chicks. All of that. And I was growing old in Philadelphia, dragging around all my shit."

"I'm sorry," I said.

"Sorry? Aren't you listening, Joey? You got nothing to be sorry about. I put that on you because I couldn't bear to carry it myself. I mean, you saw what happened to Chick. If he hadn't hit that El support, he'd have found another way out, and he hadn't even *gone*. I'm the last of the Angels, and every year it got harder to *be* that. So, I dished out the shit to everyone I could reach. You. My wife. Some friends from back then who went into the Army or Navy or whatever and, luck of the draw, never went to 'Nam. I went twice, and some of the guys from the neighborhood never got farther away than New fucking Jersey. They went home for Christmas and Thanksgiving while I was in the shit. And, hell, I was a combat engineer. They dropped Agent Orange, and before the smoke even cleared, they sent me and the guys in to build helicopter bases in forward areas. That's where we were when the Angels started dying. And you know what? It was a goddamn Halloween the night Mickey got killed. Took a round in the throat. Voice like he had, and a VC bullet blew his whole throat out."

I stared at him. How does one write dialogue to respond to that? Hell if I knew. My heart was hammering, and each beat felt like a separate punch.

"You know what we were doing when he got shot?" asked Alex, his voice still filled with surprise although the memory was decades old. "We were near a vil. Not VC, far as we knew. We had some time, and we were making benches and desks for a school. It was Halloween—they didn't know shit about that—but you remember how much Mickey was into it. He and Dan could speak the language. Not great, but well enough. They told the kids a bunch of ghost stories and made costumes and we all shared our chocolate bars and other shit. Trick-or-treat, but really just treats. Kids were laughing even though they had no real idea what the crazy Americans were doing. Everybody was having a good time. Then a sniper's bullet took Mickey in the throat. We all hit the deck, but the sniper got two kids, too. Punishment for them having fun with us, I guess."

He paused. There were tears in his eyes.

"There were a lot of things like that," he said. "Funny how it always seemed to be a holiday. New Year, Christmas, Good Friday. And fucking Halloween."

We sat for a very long time.

Alex said, "When I came back the last time...I mean came home for good... you were growing up. Going to junior high by then. Reading everything you could. Talking about writing books. Even talking about college in seventh grade. God...I was so *mad* at you. Want to know why? The real reason?"

The writer in me was already writing the script for this. Including all the self-recrimination about how I might have at least sent an email, left a voicemail, sent an emoji-heavy text message. It's not like I was unaware of PTSD. Shit, I'd written it into four or five TV scripts and one feature. Only on my denser days did I convince myself those insights came from watching the news. I grew up with everything anyone needs to know about what happens when the innocent go to war, and no one prepares them for coming home. Another cliché, but a real one. I knew this stuff. I knew it, and I never sent those messages. Never once picked up a phone. Fuck. I could *feel* my therapist getting richer by the moment. And here was my brother, having flown all the way across the country to do what I hadn't done with a couple of taps of thumbnails on cell keys.

"Sure, what reason is that?" I asked and braced myself for the kick to the nuts I knew was coming.

"Because you had a future and you knew it," said Alex, pawing tears from his eyes. "You shined brighter than me. As bright as I did when the Seven Angels recorded those sides. What's that old line? Future's so bright I gotta wear shades? Like that. When I came home, I was still in my twenties. Still young, but I felt so damned old. Too old. Older than you've ever felt, even with divorces and all that. You know it, too."

I felt my eyes burning.

"I hated you and everyone else," Alex continued. "Not our sisters, though. Women couldn't be combat soldiers then. Not in 'Nam. But when I looked at you, I saw what I wanted to be and never would be. I was broken. Dirty. Fucked up. And there were six ghosts haunting me."

"I…I'm sorry, Alex," I said.

"You don't have to be," he said. "I'm sorry for letting the war win. That's what we talked about in therapy. I wish I could go back and change things. I wish I could be the older brother you wanted, the brother I wanted to be. If I could fix it, I would. I'd give anything."

I wanted to run. I wanted to yell. I wanted to cry. I needed to pull him into my arms and hug him and tell my brother that it was *me* who was sorry. If this was a script I'd be all over it. Slick, polished, with the right words tumbling out so that some TV actor could start rehearsing his Emmy speech. Writing that kind of dialogue was easy—it was how I made my living.

Saying those words…? Even conjuring a reasonable reply to this…god damn. I was blank. I was scraped raw.

"Look, Alex," I began, fumbling for *any* useful words, "there's no--"

And my cell rang.

I glanced at the screen, then frowned. "You came out here alone?"

"Yeah. Why?"

"It's your wife," I said, waggling the phone.

He sighed and wiped the tears from his eyes. "Better take it."

"Why?" I asked. "Are you two breaking up or something?"

"More or less," said Alex. "There are some kids coming. I'll give out the candy. You take the call. It's cool. Better you know."

"Um…okay. Whatever."

I stood up and walked to the far end of the porch, turning away from him as I pressed the green button.

"Joan," I said, "good to hear from you."

Her answer was a sob. Not even my name. It was big and broken and ugly and filled with jagged glass.

"Whoa, whoa," I soothed, immediately imagining all kinds of very bad scenarios. Alex always had a temper. "Just take a breath and tell me what's wrong."

I could almost feel her gathering herself. It felt like a massive undertaking, and I wondered what kind of damage Alex had left behind. He'd been talking about rage and there was an icy chill in my stomach because I kind of knew what this was going to be. The polite phrasing is "domestic violence." Alex, even wasted as he was now, was big and strong and Joan was petite. I began bracing against the bruising violence of her explanation.

She said, "Oh, my god, Joey…it's so awful."

I lowered my voice and kept my back to Alex, not wanting to see the guilt on his face. Fighting the rise of my own rage.

"Tell me what happened," I said very slowly and carefully.

"I was downstairs making dinner," she said. "And I heard it."

"Heard what?"

She said, "The shot."

"The *what*?" I demanded.

"He did it in the shower…oh, my God, Joey. There was so much blood. I tried to help him, but…but…"

She said more. Probably. Certainly. But I wasn't listening.

I turned around.

The bag of candy sat on the top step next to an empty beer bottle.

Alex wasn't there.

Of course, he wasn't.

Some kids were walking away. I could see the 3 Musketeers bars in their hands. They were laughing, like kids do.

The step was empty. There was no car parked down the street.

I was alone there.

Joan was still talking. But I couldn't listen to her. I sat down on the loveseat and stared at the laughing kids in their Halloween costumes. The happy parents herding them along. The sun shining down.

"Alex," I said to the empty air.

I knew he could hear me.

I was certain of it.

Meet the Contributors

MAUREEN MANCINI AMATURO, NY-based fashion/beauty writer, has an MFA in Creative Writing, teaches writing, leads Sound Shore Writers Group, which she founded in 2007, and produces literary and gallery events. Her fiction, creative non-fiction, essays, poetry, and comedy are widely published appearing in: The Dark Sire, Flash Non-Fiction Food Anthology (Woodhall Press,) Things That Go Bump (Sez Publishing,), Points In Case, Little Old Lady Comedy, and many others. Maureen was nominated for the Bram Stoker Award and TDS Fiction Award in 2020 and 2021. A handwriting analyst diagnosed her with an overdeveloped imagination. She's working to live up to that.

Following a varied career in sales, advertising and career guidance, CATHERINE CAVENDISH is the author of paranormal, ghostly and Gothic horror novels, novellas and short stories, including: *Dark Observation, In Darkness, Shadows Breathe, The Garden of Bewitchment. The Haunting of Henderson Close, The Pendle Curse,* and many more. Her fiction collection – *The Malan Witch and Other Conjurings* is out in October. She lives in Southport,

England with her long-suffering husband, and a black cat called Serafina who has never forgotten that her species used to be worshipped in ancient Egypt. She sees no reason why that practice should not continue.

SCOTT COLE is a writer, artist, and graphic designer based in Philadelphia. He is the author of *Crazytimes*, *Triple Axe*, and *SuperGhost*, as well as the short fiction collection, *Slices*. Find him on social media, or at 13visions.com.

DENNIS K. CROSBY is a San Diego based indie author and speaker with an MFA in Creative Writing from National University. Originally from Oak Park, IL, he is the award-winning author of the Amazon bestselling urban fantasy novel, *Death's Legacy*, released November 2020, and its follow up *Death's Debt*, released November 2021. The bourbon loving Chicago Cubs fan and deep-dish pizza connoisseur is working on the third book in his Kassidy Simmons series and writing weird and creepy short stories in his spare time. To keep up with his journey, check out: https://denniskcrosby.com And on Twitter and Instagram: @denniskcrosby

DANA HAMMER is a playwright, screenwriter, short story writer, and novelist. Her screenplay, *Red Wings*, has been optioned by EMA Films, and she has signed a book deal with Cinnabar Moth for her novel, *The Cannibal's Guide to Fasting*, which will be released in

September, 2022. She has been granted a writing residency at Hypatia in the Woods, which will take place in summer of 2022. She has received over sixty awards and honors for her writing, few of which generated income, all of which were deeply appreciated.

LYNNE HANSEN is a horror artist who specializes in book covers. Her art has appeared on the cover of the legendary *Weird Tales Magazine*, and she was selected to create the cover for the 125th Anniversary Edition of *Dracula*. She has illustrated works by *New York Times* best-selling authors including Jonathan Maberry, Brian Keene, and Christopher Golden. Her art has been commissioned and collected throughout the United States and overseas. For more information, visit LynneHansenArt.com.

HENRY HERZ's speculative fiction short stories include "Out, Damned Virus" (Daily Science Fiction), "Bar Mitzvah on Planet Latke" (Coming of Age, Albert Whitman & Co.), "The Magic Backpack" (Metastellar), "Unbreakable" (Musing of the Muses, Brigid's Press), "A Vampire, an Astrophysicist, and a Mother Superior Walk Into a Basilica" (Three Time Travelers Walk Into..., Fantastic Books), "Cheating Death" (The Hitherto Secret Experiments of Marie Curie, Blackstone Publishing), "The Case of the Murderous Alien" (Spirit Machine, Air and Nothingness Press), "Maria & Maslow" (Highlights for Children), and "A Proper Party" (Ladybug Magazine). He's written twelve picture books, including the critically acclaimed I Am Smoke.

Henry has edited three anthologies, including Beyond the Pale -- adult dark fantasy stories from Saladin Ahmed, Peter S. Beagle, Heather (Zac) Brewer, Jim Butcher, Rachel Caine, Kami Garcia, Nancy Holder, Gillian Philip, and Jane Yolen. www.henryherz.com

GWENDOLYN KISTE is the three-time Bram Stoker Award-winning author of *The Rust Maidens, Reluctant Immortals, Boneset & Feathers, And Her Smile Will Untether the Universe, Pretty Marys All in a Row,* and *The Invention of Ghosts*. Her short fiction and nonfiction have appeared in Nightmare Magazine, Best American Science Fiction and Fantasy, Vastarien, Tor's Nightfire, Black Static, The Dark, Daily Science Fiction, Interzone, and LampLight, among others. Originally from Ohio, she now resides on an abandoned horse farm outside of Pittsburgh with her husband, two cats, and not nearly enough ghosts. Find her online at gwendolynkiste.com.

ALETHEA KONTIS is a princess, storm chaser, and bestselling author of over 20 books and 50 short stories. She has received the Jane Yolen Mid-List Author Grant, the Scribe Award, and is a two-time winner of the Gelett Burgess Children's Book Award. She was nominated twice for both the Dragon Award and the Andre Norton Nebula. In her spare time, Alethea narrates stories for a myriad of award-winning online magazines. Born in Vermont, Princess Alethea currently resides on the Space Coast of Florida with her teddy bear, Charlie.

JONATHAN MABERRY is a New York Times bestselling author, 5-time Bram Stoker Award-winner, 3-time Scribe Award winner, Inkpot Award winner, and comic book writer. His vampire apocalypse book series, V-WARS, was a Netflix original series. He writes in multiple genres including suspense, thriller, horror, science fiction, fantasy, and action; for adults, teens and middle grade. He's the president of the International Association of Media Tie-in Writers, and the editor of Weird Tales Magazine. He was a featured expert on the History Channel's *Zombies: A Living History* and *True Monsters*.

CATHERINE McCARTHY is a spinner of stories with macabre melodies. She is the author of the collections **Door and other twisted tales** and **Mists and Megaliths,** and the novella **Immortelle** (Off Limits Press). Her Gothic novel, **A Moonlit Path of Madness**, will be published by Nosetouch Press in 2023. Her short fiction has been published by Brigids Gate Press, Dark Matter Magazine, Dark Recesses Press and Black Spot Books.

JEREMY MEGARGEE has always loved dark fiction. He cut his teeth on R.L Stine's Goosebumps series as a child and a fascination with Stephen King, Jack London, Algernon Blackwood, and many others followed later in life. Jeremy weaves his tales of personal horror from Martinsburg, West Virginia with his cat Lazarus acting as his muse/familiar. He is an active member of the West Virginia chapter of the Horror Writer's Association and you can often find him peddling his dark words in various mountain hollers deep within the Appalachians.

Seth Ryan

LISA MORTON is a screenwriter, author of non-fiction books, and prose writer whose work was described by the American Library Association's *Readers' Advisory Guide to Horror* as "consistently dark, unsettling, and frightening." She is a six-time winner of the Bram Stoker Award®, the author of four novels and over 150 short stories, and a world-class Halloween and paranormal expert Her recent releases include *Haunted Tales: Classic Stories of Ghosts and the Supernatural* (co-edited with Leslie S. Klinger), and *Calling the Spirits: A History of Seances.* Lisa lives in Los Angeles and online at www.lisamorton.com.

LEE MURRAY is a multi-award-winning author-editor, screenwriter, and poet from Aotearoa-New Zealand, and a USA Today Bestselling author. Her titles include the Taine McKenna adventure series, supernatural crime-noir series The Path of Ra (with Dan Rabarts), fiction collection *Grotesque: Monster Stories,* and several books for children, and her short fiction appears in prestigious venues such as *Weird Tales, Space & Time* and *Grimdark Magazine.* A four-time Bram Stoker Award® winner and Shirley Jackson Award winner, Lee is an NZSA Honorary Literary

Fellow and a Grimshaw Sargeson Fellow. Read more at leemurray.info.

EVA ROSLIN is a disabled horror writer from Canada with a penchant for Southern Gothic themes. She received the Mary Wollstonecraft Shelley Scholarship from the Horror Writers Association in 2017, a Ladies of Horror Fiction Grant in 2021, and is a Supporting HWA member. Her work has appeared in such publications as Love Bites (Mischief Publishing), Dark Heroes (Pill Hill Press), Murky Depths, Ghostlight Magazine and others. She is a librarian, instructor, and researcher with a focus on 19th century American history. Website: https://roslineva.wordpress.com/ Twitter: @EvaRoslin

JEFF STRAND recently ended a rather impressive Bram Stoker Award-losing streak, so he now gets to put "Stoker Award winner" in bios like these. He's written over fifty books, including PRESSURE, DWELLER, and CLOWNS VS. SPIDERS. Several of his books are going through the slow and maddening process of being developed into motion pictures. He wouldn't go so far as to say that he's obsessed with candy, but he sure does love candy. He lives in Chattanooga, and you can visit his website at www.JeffStrand.com.

DAVID SURFACE lives and works in the Hudson River Valley of New York. He is the author of *Terrible Things,* a collection of

stories published by Black Shuck Books, and co-author with Julia Rust of *Angel Falls,* a YA novel forthcoming from Haverhill House Publications YAP imprint. His stories have been published in *Shadows & Tall Trees, Nightscript, Supernatural Tales,* and have been anthologized in *The Twisted Book of Shadows, Uncertainties III, Crooked Houses: Tales of Cursed and Haunted Dwellings,* and *Best Horror of the Year Volume 13.* You can learn more about David and his writing at davidsurface.net.

SARA TANTLINGER is the author of the Bram Stoker Award-winning *The Devil's Dreamland: Poetry Inspired by H.H. Holmes,* and the Stoker-nominated works *To Be Devoured, Cradleland of Parasites,* and *Not All Monsters.* She is a co-organizer for the HWA Pittsburgh Chapter. Find her on Twitter @SaraTantlinger and at saratantlinger.com.

Colorado writer STEVE RASNIC TEM is a past winner of the Bram Stoker, World Fantasy, and British Fantasy Awards. His novel *Ubo* (Solaris Books), a finalist for the 2017 Bram Stoker Award, is a dark science fictional tale about violence and its origins, featuring such historical viewpoint characters as Jack the Ripper, Stalin, and Heinrich Himmler. He has published almost 500 short stories in his 40+ year career. Some of his best are collected in *Thanatrauma* and *Figures Unseen* from Valancourt Books.

TIM WAGGONER has published over fifty novels and seven collections of short stories. He writes original dark fantasy and horror, as well as media tie-ins, and his articles on writing have appeared in numerous publications. He's a three-time winner of the Bram Stoker Award, has won the HWA's Mentor of the Year Award, and been a finalist for the Shirley Jackson Award, the Scribe Award, and the Splatterpunk Award. He's also a full-time tenured professor who teaches creative writing and composition at Sinclair College in Dayton, Ohio.

The Editors

JOHN PALISANO's nonfiction, short fiction, poetry and novels have appeared in literary anthologies and magazines such as Cemetery Dance, Fangoria, Weird Tales, Space & Time, Shmoop University and many more. He won the Bram Stoker Award© for excellence in short fiction in 2016, has served as President of the Horror Writers Association, and is the assistant editor of *LITERALLY DEAD: Tales of Halloween Hauntings*. Say hi at www.johnpalisano.com, www.amazon.-com/author/johnpalisano, www.facebook.com/johnpalisano, and www.twitter.com/johnpalisano.

GABY TRIANA is the author of 21 novels for adults and teens, including Moon Child, Island of Bones, River of Ghosts, City

of Spells, Wake the Hollow, Cakespell, and Summer of Yesterday. She's the co-author of YouTube ghosthunters Sam and Colby's novel, Paradise Island, and her short stories have appeared in Classic Monsters Unleashed, Don't Turn Out the Lights: A Tribute to Alvin Schwartz's Scary Stories to Tell in the Dark, and Weird Tales Magazine (Issue #365). She is also the editor of the bestselling horror anthology, Literally Dead: Tales of Halloween Hauntings and the upcoming Literally Dead: Tales of Holiday Hauntings.

The host of YouTube channel, The Witch Haunt, Gaby writes tales about witches, ghosts, and haunted, abandoned locations. She's ghostwritten over 50 novels for bestselling authors, and her books have won IRA Teen Choice, ALA Best Paperback, and Hispanic Magazine's Good Reads Awards. She also writes steamy romance under the pen name Havana Scott and para-normal women's fiction under Gabrielle Keyes. In her spare time, Gaby practices bass guitar, sewing, and doing nothing.

Acknowledgments

It took a village to get this project done, and I'd like to thank, not only all the contributors for their professional, high-quality, engaging stories, but also artist Marzy for their whimsical interior design ghosties, Lynne Hansen for the inspiring artwork that started it all, Lenore Sagaskie for helping me sort through submissions, John Palisano for helping me cull the last stories of the final round, and my husband Curtis Sponsler for supporting every ambitious endeavor I ever pull out of thin air ("Hey, babe…I'm going to make a dress!" Okay, do you know how to sew? "No! But I've never edited an anthology either, so…!"). Thank you for always believing in me and for being the Gomez to my Morticia. Happy Halloween!

- GABY TRIANA
September, 2022

Dear Reader

If you enjoyed this anthology, please:

Leave a rating/review on Amazon and Goodreads;

Post a book photo on social media. Tag one or more of the authors and Alienhead Press;

Join the Alienhead Press newsletter to receive updates, notices for open call submissions, and more.

Thank you for your support!

GABY TRIANA
Alienhead Press

Next in series

Available October 14, 2023!

Also by Alienhead Press

HORROR:

LITERALLY DEAD: Tales of Holiday Hauntings

MOON CHILD

ISLAND OF BONES

RIVER OF GHOSTS

CITY OF SPELLS

PARANORMAL WOMEN'S FICTION:

WITCH OF KEY LIME LANE

CRONE OF COCONUT COURT

MAGE OF MANGO ROAD

HEX OF PINEAPPLE PLACE

YOUNG ADULT:

KIMBO

UNRAVELED

CAKESPELL

ALIENHEAD
PRESS

Printed in Great Britain
by Amazon

29019462R00152